The *Alysé* Diaries

B. Danielle Watkins

Halo
PUBLISHING
INTERNATIONAL

ISBN: 978-1-63765-198-8
LCCN: 2022904320

Halo Publishing International, LLC
www.halopublishing.com

Printed and bound in the United States of America

To the little girl—in her room, in the corner, or in your heart—who is afraid of what being herself will do to the world. I want you to always remember to be true to yourself and stand in your truth. You are the best *you* you can be, and the only *you* you will ever be. They will either stand with you or stand behind you. Either way, you will STILL BE STANDING. You are enough, and we love you just as you are.

This one is for you…

To you: The truest quote that writers hold on to was spoken by author Mik Everett. "If a writer falls in love with you, you can never die."

The heart is odd. It evolves, revisits, and holds on to love in its purest form. To be able to capture that evolution is a writer's dream, and to be able to live that evolution is a woman's desire. I pray that, no matter where you are, you never forget this love…our love will always exist.

Contents

Prologue   9

Part 1   13

Curious

Part 2   166

Promiscuous

Part 3   285

Transcendent

Part 4   329

Relinquishable

Epilogue   357

Prologue

The following diary entries are those of the infamous Sentury Alysé. They were used to aid the Las Vegas Metropolitan Police Department, as they related to her case. Nothing regarding her story has been changed; these are her words, her life, as she saw it. Some names have been changed to protect those who did not want their stories told in this manner. The LVMPD reserves the rights to these diary entries, the diary's contents, and Sentury Alysé's possessions.

In a world and time when social media has taken over the world and caused such turmoil in sensationalizing suicide and glamourizing pain, the LVMPD decided that it was time to release this piece of evidence to tell a story, a tragic story. We ask that as you read these words, you take into consideration the depths of this woman's struggles. We put this out in hopes that it will save another girl from turning into a Sentury Alysé.

Sentury Alysé was a thirty-four-year-old woman lost in her own web of misfortune at the time of her death. Born and raised in Las Vegas, Nevada, disgustingly described as "Sin City," Sentury had a firsthand look at what sex and greed could lead to, but did not heed it as a tale of caution.

Born to Carlos and Amelia Alysé, Sentury learned early how to hide her pain and discomfort after the sudden loss of her father at age six. Tragedy is the gateway to self-destruction when not handled properly.

A psychologist, not related to this case, once said of Sentury, "A beauty so tragic it rivals the likes of Marilyn Monroe herself. Had Alysé received the grief counseling she needed as a child, the handling of pain as an adult would have been different. She didn't. So, what we see here is a classic case of childhood trauma coupled with the innate inability to accept pain. *Tragic* doesn't seem like the word to describe this; *lamentable* works better."

A natural athlete, Sentury dominated the Las Vegas high school scene with her amazing basketball skills and showstopping performances. Basketball was Sentury's outlet, as well as her way out of the trap Las Vegas could have set, and eventually did. All-time leading scorer four years in a row. All-time leading rebounder four years in a row. All-time leading assists four years in a row. Sentury's name was known all over the Las Vegas Valley, and she was one of the top recruits in the 1995–96 college-recruiting season.

It was no surprise when Montana State began courting Sentury to get her to come to their school. Sentury could have gone to any school in the country, but there was something about Montana State that caught her attention. She threw the Las Vegas sports community for a loop.

Coach Selina Francisco was Sentury's high school coach for all four years Sentury attended. At the time of Sentury's signing, Coach Francisco said this of her decision: "Sentury is a good ballplayer; there is no doubt about that. As a coach, you always want to see your players go off and do great things. Division One great things. With talks of a female professional league coming in some years, my hopes would have been that Sentury would go where she could be seen; however, she is a good enough player to get recognition at any school. I am proud of her and her decision."

On October 13, 2012, Sentury Alysé was found unresponsive in her Las Vegas apartment, the victim of an apparent suicide.

This is her story.

Part 1

Curious

Do not brood over your past mistakes and failures, as this will only fill your mind with grief, regret, and depression. Do not repeat them in the future.

—Sivananda

August 15, 1996

This diary belongs to Sentury K. Alysé. My mom gave me this when I left for college last week. I don't understand why; nobody wants to hear what I have to say anyways.

August 15, 1998

Let me start off by saying I DO NOT LIKE WOMEN. I don't understand what makes people think that I do! It is getting rather annoying. So what, I would rather wear basketball shorts than skirts and heels. Hell, I'm comfortable. Don't get me wrong, I am not hiding behind the baggy clothes. I know I'm fine—five foot eleven, 180 pounds, athletic build, Hershey-brown skin, and hair to my back. Doesn't mean I want to draw unnecessary attention to myself. Anyways, who cares that I would rather watch the game on television than go scout the clubs for men?! Hell, I'm chilling. I have been dealing with this my entire life.

Never have I ever been the girly-girly type of girl. When I was a child, I had a Barbie, and I had Matchbox cars. I climbed trees, skinned my knees, and made mud pies in the heat of the Nevada desert. That's what I did. By the time I was in sixth grade, I was already five foot eight, so basketball only seemed logically next on my agenda.

Playing youth basketball was the best time of my life (and how I got here, to boring-ass Montana State). The life of a female athlete in high school is demanding, and you spend a lot of time with your teammates before, during, and after the season. You eat, drink, and sleep ball. I was cool with that, I did that anyways. At a time when all the girls were going boy crazy, I was ball crazy. I kept my hair French-braided to the back, always had on sweats, and you never caught me without a ball. I noticed guys, or whatever, but that wasn't my focus. I had other shit on my mind.

The WNBA had just finished its inaugural season, and you couldn't tell me that I wouldn't be playing for the Los Angeles Sparks come summer 2000. That was and is my goal; there was no time to fall in love. My lack of drive towards the male species in high school started the initial "Sentury is a lesbo" rumor mill.

I would hear people whisper as I walked by, and I would see them point. That didn't matter to me. They didn't know me, nor did they know my life. I had a boyfriend; he went to a different school, and he loved basketball as much as I did. Every day after school, we would meet at the community center and practice; that was love to us. Nothing else was needed. We didn't think about sex; I think we may have only kissed twice.

My best friend, LaTrice Davis, has been playing ball with me since we were ten. They say watch the company you keep, and Trice is, in fact, gay. I never liked grouping people based on stupid shit. LaTrice and I have been friends since we were in middle school. Whom she is sleeping with makes me no never mind. We got to high school, and she got a girlfriend. That didn't bother me. What bothered me were other people's reactions to her and her inability to defend herself.

How many fights did I get in defending her before she finally came out of the illusionary closet everyone refers to? Countless, and I didn't give a damn; I tore up chicks all up and down those hallways. I love my friends, and I do anything for them.

I remember one time Trice got with a girl a little younger than we were, and far more established in the lesbian lifestyle than Trice, and I told her:

Hey, this is my friend, and she is now your girlfriend.

Yeah.

I just want you to know, if you hurt her,
I am going to fuck you up.

(Awkwardly) *Okay.*

About two weeks later, on a Friday evening, I believe, my boyfriend and I go to see Trice, and, lo and behold, she is heartbroken (two studs had no business being together in the first place!). The fool went and cheated on my friend, and didn't care about the repercussions that had been clearly defined prior to. I grabbed my brokenhearted friend, put my boyfriend in the back seat, and we took a ride. LaTrice knew that her girlfriend was at another girl's house, so we drove up to it and parked.

What are you going to do, Sent?

Beat her up.

You can't.

Watch me.

I got out of the car and nicely rang the doorbell. The girl's mom answered the door and let me in. I went straight to the girl's room and walked in.

I told you if you hurt her I would beat your ass.

(Silence)

Please come outside so I can beat your ass.
I got things to do.

Why outside?

Bitch, this has nothing to do with you (to the other
girl, who will remain nameless, in the room).
Bring your ass outside. I will not disrespect your
mother's house by tearing it up. I will meet you in
the driveway.

They followed me to the door. I smiled and bid the girl's mother a fond farewell; then I went to stand outside. They never come out of the door. I hear the screen door lock, and she begins talking shit from behind the door.

You ain't going to do shit! If I come out there, I am going to Mace your ugly ass!

MACE?

I was flabbergasted. The nerve of her to want to bring out biochemical warfare. I had a crowbar in my trunk, so I popped the trunk, got it out, and began knocking on the door with the crowbar.

Please come outside and Mace me. I want you to!

Sentury, get away from here, and go home!

I heard the girl's mother on the phone with the police, so I burned out, but I caught the bitch at school a few days later in the locker room after practice.

I said all of that to say I have been dealing with lesbians for a minute. I understood it and supported it, but I wasn't into it.

Most recently, I have been here in Montana for two solid years. I am now the captain of the women's basketball team, and I take that role seriously. I haven't had a boyfriend since I've been in college, and, frankly, that's fine with me. I did what I had to do for my team—I studied, and I practiced. Yesterday on campus, this rude-ass, random White dude walked up to me.

Aren't you Sentury Alice?

My last name is Alysé.

Oh, like Alizé the drink.

No, like Alysé my last name. What can
I help you with? I need to get to class.

> *I was wondering… Do you mind dyking with*
> *my girlfriend? I think it would be fucking hot!*

Excuse me?

> *You're a dyke, right?*

No.

> *You sure look like one; maybe*
> *you should look into it.*

And the motherfucker walked away from me. I was so mad I didn't know what to do. I wanted to beat his face in. There was nothing appealing about being with a woman, nothing at all. I am frankly tired of being accused of something I've never done.

This whole dressing-like-your-sex thing is beyond my mental capability. Every piece of clothing I purchase comes from the women's department of whatever store I am in, with the exception of my shorts. THAT'S IT. I don't understand why my comfortableness shouts out, "I WANT WOMEN." It doesn't. Half of my team is gay; we are ballplayers; that's about it, for the most part, with the exception of a few teammates who play while wearing a full face of makeup.

I don't even know why I am trying to explain this shit. It doesn't matter; people are just fucking ignorant. I don't like girls, and that's that.

September 1, 1998

Today on campus, I met a really interesting girl. Her name is Alana Willoughby, and she is a transfer student from South Dakota somewhere. She got late admission into my philosophy class.

Is anybody sitting here?

Nope, it's all yours.

Thank you, that's very kind of you.

It's not my chair, sweetie.

It's still kind of you.

Sure it is.

We were in the middle of a lecture discussing human nature and its roots as described by philosophy. Pretty deep stuff. I was into it.

Do you happen to have a pen?

I use pencils.

May I borrow one?

I hand her a pencil.

This is yours, so thank you; it's very kind of you.

Alana was smiling at me really weirdly. I got uncomfortable, so I turned to listen to the professor.

> *It was Socrates himself who turned philosophy into what it is today. Before Socrates, philosophy was the study of the heavens and the earth, not human beings. Human beings were nothing without the heavens and the earth. Socrates came along and said, "Wait a minute; there is more to being a human than being a product of the heaven and the earth." Human beings were rational creatures with minds of their own. With that came a totally different view.*

> *Socrates did not leave his own writings, but his students Plato and Xenophon did. By all accounts, Plato and*

Xenophon coined the term that Michael Jackson made famous: "If they ask why, tell them that it's human nature."

Come on, people, it's a joke! Ha ha.

White people kill me, trying to bring Michael Jackson up to relate to the Black people around them. When class was over I gathered my things as I usually do, and I made my way to the door.

Excuse me.

At this point, hearing her voice was irritating the shit out of me, but I'm such a nice person, so I turned around.

What's up?

You forgot your pencil.

Thank you.

What's your name?

Sentury.

That's an odd name. Like century or one hundred years?

Yes, but it is spelled with an S.

That's no longer odd. It's unique, and I like it.

Thank you.

My name is Alana Willoughby. I just transferred from a small school in South Dakota.

That's cool.

You're really tall.

I play basketball for the school.

I was wondering, because I saw your gym bag.

Okay, well, it was nice to meet you.

Are you busy later?

Depends on what time.

Here is a flyer. The Feminist Association is having a peace rally and Tolerance of All forums in the student union. I hope to see you there.

The flyer was rainbow colored and full of peace signs. I threw it in my bag, and I kept pushing. I went to basketball practice and back to my room to take a shower. I forgot all about the flyer, so when I went to pack my bag for tomorrow, I saw the flyer. I didn't have curfew for another hour or so, so I had time to check out what it was all about.

Sentury!

Hey, Alana.

You made it!

Alana reached in to hug me, and I wasn't prepared. Alana is about five four, a redhead with freckles. Not my usual company, but whatever. In Browning, Montana, you can't really expect to spend all of your time with people who look like you.

You didn't tell me you were a star!

What are you talking about?

Basketball, silly! Everybody knows you. You're very modest, aren't you?

Sure.

Cute.

The event was in full swing. It was a modern-day Wood-stock. Guitars, peace circles, political jargon, and posters promoting same-sex acceptance, peace, and rights for women.

*Don't leave. I have to go do
my speech. Be right back.*

*I have curfew in fifteen minutes.
I will be leaving soon.*

I will be right back.

I was ready to go, so I lied. My curfew was still thirty minutes away, but all of that was neither here nor there. I was stuck until she finished her part of the rally.

I stand here today as an out, proud lesbian woman. I have known I was attracted to women since I was young, but I was afraid to express it. I was afraid that my parents would hate me, my grandparents would disown me, and my friends would shun me. How do you function in fear? How do you stand up and be proud of who you are, if nobody else knows who you are? How do you change the world if you yourself are afraid of the change that you are asking for?

My fears of others' reactions were based on my own igno-rance to what I was feeling. I shouldn't have been ashamed of who I was; there was nothing wrong with me. I didn't elect to have these feelings for women, and anybody who thought that was just as foolish as I had once been. I was fourteen when I came out to my parents, and for them, I was going to hell immediately. I didn't care what they thought; I needed to get on with my life.

I was ridiculed at school for being a lesbian. They threw their lunches at me, teased me, and pulled practical jokes on every day but April Fools' Day. I still stood proud and humble. If I didn't, who would?

I believe that this rally is about teaching acceptance. It starts within; if you accept yourself, then the others around you will accept you.

By the time I was finished with my sophomore year in high school, no more lunches were being thrown; girls were coming to me and saying that they, too, liked girls and for so long had thought something was wrong with it. My parents sat me down and told me they loved me and wanted to learn who I was.

That's all it took—courage and patience. I charge you all to use some courage and take a stand. We will be accepted and treated equally here at Montana State!

Alana shocked the shit out of me! I didn't know she was gay!!! I wonder if she thinks I'm gay, and that's why she invited me. I wouldn't know. I was gone by the time she got off of the stage.

Alana got a standing ovation from the audience and was asked to speak more about her experience. Wow! Her speech was moving. She was so proud of who she was. So proud of what she had become. I bet she thought I would be able to relate. I can't.

September 17, 1998

Alana and I have been hanging out for a few weeks now, and she is supercool. I haven't gotten close to anyone on campus besides my teammates, so having a friend on the outside of that world is a breath of fresh air. Something about her is different.

After meeting her at the peace rally, I decided to go to many more of her events with the Feminist Association. It was a different feeling of acceptance when I was with them. I don't know how to explain what I'm feeling right now. Okay. It's as if you go your whole life just existing for what you know to exist for. And then something comes along, and you feel as though you are no longer existing; you are now living. Okay, maybe that was going too deep.

Let me think; let me think. Okay, got it. Being with the Feminist Association makes me feel as if no one is looking at me and wondering anything about me. I don't feel judged, I don't feel evaluated, and I just feel like Sentury.

The more and more I spend time with Alana, I am kind of starting to be into her—not like in a gay way, but we have a connection. I am totally fine with this connection.

> *Sentury, you are really pretty.*
> *You should show it off more often.*

Tonight, we went to a play down in the Arts Center, and I decided to dress for the occasion. My mother told me when I was young that, when you go to the theater, you should dress the part. Jeans and sneakers are not acceptable in such an environment. Dresses, heels, and jewelry, on the other hand, make you look as if you belong. I was raised right. What can I say? The fact that I actually owned all of that should prove that to be true. Needless to say, I outdressed half of Montana State's population (no need for me to say why), Alana included.

Thanks, Alana, I get dressed
when the occasion calls for it.

> *For things like dates?*

I don't date.

> *What do you mean, you "don't date"?*

Just what I said, I don't date.

> *I don't understand what that means.*

It means that I don't have a weekly roster of men
to take me out; I don't even have a monthly roster.

I wasn't asking about men.

Normally, when Alana brings up her lesbian references, I just ignore her and move on to another topic, but I decided to engage tonight.

In that case, yes, I have women beating down
my door, trying to take me out. But I don't
date them because if I go out with them,
they will find out I'm not gay.

As the play continued, I could feel Alana looking at me and smiling. I looked back, smiled, and kept paying attention. Finally, I got tired of her looking at me.

What are you looking at?

You.

I can see that, but why?

Trying to make a decision.

About what?

You.

I was officially weirded out by Alana's behavior, so I got up to go to the bathroom. My school is a little strange. The Arts Center does not have its own public restrooms, so in order for me to use a bathroom, I had to leave the center, walk a quarter of a mile to the nearest academic building, and use its bathroom. Considering I really didn't have to do anything, I took my time strolling there and took an even longer time on my walk back.

Where did you go?

I needed to use the restroom. Is that all
right with you, Ms. Nosy?

I was just wondering.

When the play was over, Alana reached down and grabbed my hand; we walked out of the theater, hand in hand. Hand in hand. Like hand in hand; as in, we were holding hands. Everybody saw us. I didn't let her hand go.

I felt as if I were having an out-of-body experience. I saw us walking through the crowd happily, hand in hand. I saw myself holding her hand as she held mine, and I saw it while I was doing it. It was like a dream.

Sentury!

(Distracted) Yeah, what's up?

Where are you right now?

Standing in front of my dorm room.
What kind of question is that?

Your body may be here, but your mind was some-
where else. Are we all here together now?

Yes.

By the time the *s* from the *yes* came off of my lips, it was as if time had slowed down completely. It was a true dream sequence from a low-budget Hollywood movie. Alana slowly let go of my hand and silently ran her hand through my hair. Her touch was so soft it sent chills through my body. She used her other hand to slowly caress my back. I just stood frozen in place. I think I even held my breath. I kept thinking to myself, *You have to stop her*, but I never did. I wanted to see what was next.

The more I wanted to know what was next, the slower the time went on. I think she took her finger and ran it from the root to the ends of my hair at least three times. She brought her hand around to the front of my jacket and slowly pulled me towards her. She smelled AMAZING. I couldn't place my finger on the smell, but it was something Victoria's Secret. I was sure of that. The closer she pulled me, the more I felt myself losing control. I started to have another out-of-body experience. I saw myself putting my arm around her small frame and leaning down close to her face.

I rubbed my nose against her skin, trying to smell her again, but this time engrave her smell into my brain. (I got it! It was Victoria's Secret Unforgettable, spring '97 line!!)

Okay, back to the story at hand. I saw myself grasping her as she reached up and placed her lips to mine. At that very moment, I was back into my body, and I was kissing Alana. I was sensually kissing Alana. I was kissing Alana as if she were my woman, no matter how much my mind screamed, *WHAT ARE YOU DOING????* I didn't stop; I didn't stop until she pulled away from me.

Are you okay?

Yes.

Sentury, you're trembling. Are you sure?

Yes.

That was it. I kissed Alana. I kissed a girl, and I think I liked it.

September 20, 1998

Man, I haven't seen Alana since Sunday. I don't know if I have been avoiding her, or if it is the other way around, but I know

I haven't seen her. I also know that, every time I walk outside, people are staring at me as if they know what I did with her. I go to get good food, and people are just staring at me. People always stare; you would think that I would be used to it by now, but I'm not.

I didn't go to class today. I'm sick. At least, I feel sick every time I think about walking into the classroom and seeing Alana in there. There it goes again. The thought sends my stomach into instant-upset, "I am going to hurl" mode. How am I supposed to act if and when I see Alana again? I am not used to this type of situation. I have never had a girl be so aggressive with me. She really was not even aggressive; I leaned in first.

I leaned in first! It was I who did it; I started this! I am the aggressive one. What the fuck? Who am I right now?

What have I gotten myself into? I have gone all this time being proud that I wasn't what they depicted me to be, and now I've gotten weak. I am still not "gay." Just because I kissed her, that doesn't make me gay. It's not as if I look at her and I'm turned on.

She does have a nice shape on her, not that I have ever looked, but I can see she isn't fat and has curves in the right places. Her eyes are a strikingly beautiful green color. Every time she talks, she makes it a point to look the person in the eyes. It's as if she were hypnotizing them. She has caught me in the eyes a few times, but I managed to pull away from her spell. Her haircut is funky, I have to admit. She reminds me of that comedian Ellen DeGeneres from the show *Ellen* (I think it just went off the air too!?!?). She has that same style as Ellen. She isn't necessarily masculine, but she sure has some testosterone. Damn!! Ellen just came out as a lesbian like last year, I think—probably why I can see such a striking resemblance.

Wait!! Stop it, Sentury, you sound as if you like this girl!

I do like her. I just don't like her like that. Whatever "that" is. All I know is I can't let things get out of control like that again. Ever. I can't. I won't.

September 21, 1998

Dammit! Don't you know, I have a test in class tomorrow, and I am not prepared. I should have taken my Black ass to class yesterday. Too busy hiding from the inevitable.

> *Aren't you going to say hello to me?*

Hey, Alana.

Just as soon as I walked out of the safety of my dorm, Alana, standing with her hair blowing in the crisp fall air that Montana is blessed with, was the first person I saw. I tried as hard as I possibly could to walk fast enough that it seemed as if I hadn't seen her—didn't work.

> *I have your study guide for tomorrow's oral exam.*

Oral exam!?! Oh shit!! Philosophy?

> *Yes, philosophy. The class you*
> *conveniently didn't make it to yesterday.*

Yeah, I wasn't feeling well.

> *I figured it was something like that.*

As hesitant as I was, I agreed to study tonight with Alana at her place, but I told myself I wasn't going to get suckered in again. As a matter of fact, I wasn't even going to get into that type of position with Alana.

I sat in a totally different room from Alana. When I needed help, I yelled to her from the kitchen, where it was safe. No need in making the whole house uncomfortable.

Why don't you just come in here and study, Sentury? You sound crazy, screaming every six minutes.

There is better lighting in the kitchen.

I will just come in there.

Not enough room. I study sloppy. I have books and papers everywhere; you won't be able to fit your things in here.

I was behaving erratically. I know I was. I was acting like a pure fool. I decided that I was going to man up and tell Alana things weren't going to go any further than they did the other night.

You kissed me, Sentury.

I know what happened, and all I am saying is that it can't happen again.

I can't make you any promises.

What do you mean, you can't make me any promises? I am telling you I am not gay; this is not what I want.

That's what your mouth is saying, but when I touch your hands, I can feel your pulse react to me. And that's not how straight women react to other women.

Alana was alluring and charismatic. As she reached down and touched my hand, I felt exactly what she claimed to have felt every time she touched me. I needed reasoning for my out-of-character behavior. It was the thrill. It had to be. Girl meets girl, girl connects with girl, girl exposes girl, and then girl gets girl.

Sounds as if girl likes girls. Sounds as if I like girls. I don't, so that couldn't be the reason.

I make you nervous, Sentury. You get into a state of confusion whenever I am around. That's fine, I understand that this is new to you; I am willing to help you through this.

That's what you do not understand. I am not interested in being helped through this. My confusion comes from this physically illogical reaction that I have towards you. I have been in the library reading; there is a name for this.

Yes, lesbian.

No, nausea.

It takes a lesbian to try to convince you that you are like them. I know what the hell I am into. And breasts do not fit the bill. I am a sucker for the bowlegged athlete with the Michael Jordan smile and personality of a much humbler man. Nope, breasts don't fit that equation.

Listen, Alana, whatever it is that you do to me, I can't continue to pursue it because it's not what I want.

How do you know it's not what you want if you have never tried it?

Because it doesn't fit the mold I am going for. So we have to stop this.

I can't just turn my feelings off for you, Sentury.

Where did you get feelings?
I thought this was physical.

So is that what you think about lesbians? You think that all we do is think with our pussies? That's the misconception that is keeping us oppressed in today's society. Are you attracted to every man that you see? Do you want to fuck every man that you see? There is the occasional man that comes across and you genuinely want to get to know him and develop an interest for him, right?

That's true.

Being a lesbian is still being a human being, Sentury. We aren't attracted to every woman we see, and we damn sure aren't trying to sleep with every pretty girl in the world. We are careful in our selection because we are lesbians, and we don't want to fall for the bitch playing gay.

Alana was making it hard for me to break things off with her. Ew, that sounds as if I were dating her. She was making it hard for me to create boundaries between us.

I don't want to play gay; that is why
I am trying to end this now.

Playing doesn't make you react the way you do.

Alana, stop it! I am not going to do this with you.

You're serious, aren't you?

Yes.

Then we should get back to studying;
you will have to be leaving soon.

She kicked me out! Now, this is my entire fault. I resisted temptation and got kicked out. I wasn't finished studying! I better not fail this exam tomorrow because I told her I don't want to deal with women!

September 27, 1998

I got my test back today! I passed! B+ is good enough for me any day. Alana didn't speak to or look at me in class today. Part of me was relieved, but the other part of me felt bad that she felt she needed to treat me that way because I said we couldn't be more than friends.

Do you have a pen?

(Silence)

Excuse me, do you have a pen?

You only use pencils.

I know, but I want to use your pen.

I took Alana's pen and began to draw a puppy's face surrounded by the words, "I apologize. Please forgive me," but before I could finish, Alana snatched the pen from my hands.

What are you doing?

Stop playing with my emotions, Sentury.

Nobody is playing with you. I am serious.

What should I forgive you for, dismissing my feelings? Or maybe I should forgive you for thinking that all lesbians want all women. That's it — I'll forgive you for being a closed-minded prick like everybody else around here.

Alana's face was so red with fury with me that her freckles began to blend in. She made me feel horrible about what I'd done to her. I like Alana, I know I like Alana, but Alana is a lesbian, and I am not. A relationship between us wouldn't work. I don't

B. Danielle Watkins

34

understand why she can't understand that. It was as if she had convinced herself that my reaction to her made me like her.

Let me take you to dinner.

What?

Let me take you out and make it up to you.

I decided I needed to make things up to her, one way or another, and at the same time get her to understand my side of things. I knew it wasn't going to be easy. As a matter of fact, I knew it was going to get as hard as trying to potty train a moose, but I was going to try anyways.

Why are you doing this, Sentury?

Because I care about you, Alana, and
I know that I hurt you. I'm sorry.

So are you done fighting this?

Excuse me?

I will take that as a no.

The question is, are you done trying to force this?

You can't force something that is already happening.

Alana was impossible to convince that the whole thing wasn't going to work in the long run. I figured I could show her better than I could tell her.

Are you sure you want to do this?

I decided that I was going to go back to Alana's place and allow her to work her "magic." I knew it would go nowhere. I was so sure that it wasn't going to go far that I wasn't even nervous as she began to instruct me.

Nervous?

Nope.

Good.

I am going to disconnect the telephone.
Do you mind drawing the blinds for me?

Why?

I don't want any disruptions, and no one
needs to see what it is we are about to do.

She was sounding kind of crazy; I was getting scared. She told me to check all of the locks on her doors, draw the blinds, and remain in the center of the room. I watched Alana as she danced around the room, well not literally danced, but she moved with a certain rhythm. She lit candles, arranged pillows, and set the mood using Bing Crosby's voice.

Kick off your shoes, and sit here next to me.

(Whispering) *Okay.*

Relax, baby.

I heard her tell me to relax, but I got tense, the direct opposite. I was grinding my teeth and everything. I had played myself. I thought I was going to get there and make her look crazy, but I was sitting in the middle of her living room floor and being slowly undressed. Her movements were so careful and so strategic that it seemed she had been practicing for this precise moment.

Kiss me.

(Kiss)

Now, take your hand and slowly move it across
my breast. Yes, just like that.

I found myself caressing her body, just as men in the past had done mine. As she kissed me, I imagined I was someone else. I took my brain to another place where what I was doing was normal. I found myself kissing Alana back and, with each kiss, becoming more and more exploratory with my hands. Everything she did to me I did to her.

As I moved my hand across her breast, I made sure I felt every curve that she had to offer. I made sure that I slowly and softly grazed her nipples, giving her sensations that I could feel in her kisses. I managed to remove the top half of her outfit very easily, to my surprise.

You seem like you've done this before.

I watch a lot of movies.

No more need for instruction; I decided to go for it. Alana had begun to sensually kiss my breast, neck, and face while managing to remove the bottom half of my clothes with one hand. Her kisses became more and more passionate as she rubbed my inner thigh in an up-and-down motion.

Each movement of her hand caused my legs to involuntarily separate; she was something like a snake charmer. She was using her touch to hypnotize my body into doing what it was she wanted it to do. Up and down, softly and slowly.

Don't resist me.

I'm trying not to.

Just relax, and lay back.
Let your inhibitions run wild.

The only time she removed her lips from mine, at this point, was to talk. Everything else was spoken through touch. I let my body relax, and I felt her grasp my inner thigh with such force I could feel it in my chest. It was so commanding and so sexy I let out a moan I'd never heard before. She made me moan, and she hadn't even done anything yet. Intensity was at an all-time high.

She looked up at me and smiled as I began to tremble with anticipation of how it would feel to be infiltrated by a woman, by this woman. She slowly kissed my face again, my neck, my left breast and then my right. Then my left breast and my right again, this time focusing more on my nipples and playing with them with her tongue, all while still grasping my thighs and ass slowly and strongly.

She made her way to my stomach, which jerked at every touch, causing her kisses to become uneven and less strategically placed. She never budged, never stopped on her path; she just continued down. My left leg is where she started. She used her tongue to trace my muscle definition, and then followed back over her tracks with elicit kisses and sucking motions. The same with my right thigh, she left no area untouched or unkissed.

Each time she moved from side to side, she would kiss the middle of my panties lightly, tug on them gently with her teeth, and then move on. Leaving me so unbelievably wet I was embarrassed.

I see you're ready for me.

Then it happened. She took my panties off, pulled me close to her, and dove right in. When I say dove right in, I mean dove right in. She was doing tricks with her mouth I couldn't even imagine trying to replicate. How could I? I damn sure couldn't see her, and at every new twist and turn of her tongue, I was yelping like a six-week-old puppy. No time to take notes. I needed to compose myself.

I tried reaching behind me to grab a pillow to cover my face. I could feel the pillow, but it was out of my reach. The more I moved to grab it, the closer she pulled me to her. I could hear her moaning between my legs. Her moaning, while sucking and blowing on me, did something strange to me. It sent me into a totally different realm of euphoria.

Fuck that pillow. I reached down and rubbed my hands through her hair. That brought her up to my level, and the shared passion was combustible, for lack of a better term.

Are you okay?

I'm cool.

Did you like it?

I did.

So do you still feel like there can never be an "us"?

Depends on what you want out of "us."

I want you to be my girlfriend. I want to take care of you. I want to be proud of you. I want to be the other half of you.

Yes.

Yes what?

I still feel the same way; there will never be an "us."

After all of that, I couldn't do it. I felt it, I experienced it, and even though I can't say what "it" is, I don't want it. Alana will probably never speak to me again, and at this point, I don't blame her.

September 28, 1998

I had sex with a woman, if that's what you can call it. A woman had sex with me. Unimaginably good sex. I couldn't sleep last night. Thinking about the line that I crossed with Alana, I kept

The Alysé Diaries

tossing and turning, wondering, "What happens now?" What if someone finds out? What if I want to do it again? I don't want to do it again, but what if I want to? What happens when Alana gets over the shock of my telling her we will never get together and she tries harder than she did before?

All of these questions swimming in my head, and none of them with readily available answers. I reverted to all that I have ever known. I was taught growing up that when you have something you cannot handle, you "let go and let God." That sent me into a totally different emotional issue.

How do I go to God about such a sin? It's not as if he doesn't know what I've done, but that's kind of odd, isn't it? What I'm saying is I have never gone to the Bible when it came to homosexuality; I never had a reason. I didn't care what my friends did, nor was it my place to judge them. It was almost like an unspoken unknown. They did what they did, and no one made mention of what the possible eternal consequences would consist of. It is no longer about them; it's about me.

I am the one engaging in an act that for all of my life has been taught to me as wrong, something that has been defined as an "abomination." Do you know what it means to be an abomination? The Webster dictionary describes *abomination* as "a vile, shameful, or detestable action or condition." Vile, shameful, and detestable sounds like the definition of *cannibalism*. All of my life I have been told that this one act is the equivalent of eating your best friend!

Now, not only do I have to think about the friendship I've ruined with Alana, but I need to add on the fact that I am an abomination and among the likes of Jeffrey Dahmer and Hannibal Lecter. Oh my word! And if that didn't keep me up all night, this sure did—I grabbed my Bible to research on my own what it said about such acts.

Thou shalt not lie with mankind, as with womankind: it is abomination.

—Leviticus 18:22

If a man lies with a man as one lies with a woman, both of them have done what is detestable. They must be put to death; their blood will be on their own heads.

—Leviticus 20:13

Wherefore God also gave them up to uncleanness through the lusts of their own hearts, to dishonor their own bodies between themselves: Who changed the truth of God into a lie, and worshipped and served the creature more than the Creator, who is blessed forever. Amen. For this cause God gave them up unto vile affections: for even their women did change the natural use into that which is against nature: And likewise also the men, leaving the natural use of the woman, burned in their lust one toward another; men with men working that which is unseemly, and receiving in themselves that recompense of their error which was meet.

—Romans 1:24-27

Even as Sodom and Gomorrah, and the cities about them in like manner, giving themselves over to fornication, and going after strange flesh, are set forth for an example, suffering the vengeance of eternal fire.

—Jude 1:7

Not that I wanted to look into the Bible and learn of my fate in hell, but you have to do what you know is right. And what I know is that God gives you answers—he must—and that is what faith is. What I also learned is that when you are already having mental issues, going to the Bible isn't always the best move, not when you are unstable in thought.

WHAT THE FUCK HAVE I GOTTEN MYSELF INTO? Panic mode has set in. I will be damned if I didn't just get so caught up in the moment that I have sent myself into eternal damnation. That is what reading the Bible did to me. I thought the Bible was a tool of comfort and relief—nope, not for this. I had really done a number this time. I sat there staring at the words, trying to make sense of what it all meant.

I cannot believe that this is what it truly means. I refuse to believe that this is the final say-so. The Bible is written from interpretation. There has got to be something in the Bible that will contradict what these Scriptures say. The whole damn book is nothing but contradictory statements written by and interpreted by man to make it sound as if God made it happen.

I searched and searched and searched throughout the Bible, and there are no Scripture verses that outright say that homosexuality is not a sin. But I thought that when Jesus came and the New Testament was written, the laws and ways of the old, wrathful God had been removed. I know somebody told me that in one of those Sunday school lessons I attended. I remember. It was something like, "As we all know, Jesus came to earth to reveal the complete character of God. Not only did he set out to accomplish this, but he did accomplish this." Jesus says this at the crucifixion scene, speaking directly to His Father as he dies on the cross:

I have finished the work you gave me to do.

—John 17:4

*Has in these last days spoken unto us by His son...
Who being the brightness of His glory, and the express
image of His person.*

—Hebrews 1:2,3

I and My Father are one.

—John 10:30

If you have seen me, you have seen the Father.

—John 14:9

For God…gives the light of the knowledge of the glory of God in the face of Jesus Christ.

—2 Corinthians 4:6

These Scriptures make it clear that when Jesus was on earth, He revealed the exact and complete character of God. We should not fear God, but love God as he has loved us.

Love the Lord your God with all your heart, all your soul, and all your mind, and love your neighbor as yourself.

—Luke 10:27

I knew I'd learned somewhere that God loves all of his people. Regardless of whom you are, if you love the Lord, the Lord loves you. That is the most simplistic idea of faith I have ever known. If this has been proven true, why do Christians teach hate of homosexuality as if it were the only sin in the world? I may not be a scholar of the Bible, but I do know that no one sin is greater than the next. It is a sin to steal, but people buy bootlegs from the man at the hair shop. Those same people go to church on Sunday, whooping and hollering about the sins of gays. That—judging—is a sin too. You cannot judge; it is not your place.

By the time the morning came, spiritually, I was in another place. I spent much of my childhood listening to what was being preached to me about the Bible—what it says and what God says—but I'd never taken the time to search for its meaning to me. To develop a relationship separate from that which had been pile-driven into my brain from infancy. In those six hours I was unable to sleep, I read the Bible, I cried in fear, and I learned from those tears.

I learned that God is an amazing God, and He created all of His people to love, and once you have conquered that one, a hard yet easy feat, and you rejoice in Him, all of your sins are forgiven. God made us the way we are. He didn't make us to fear Him. If this is what I am, if I am a lesbian, if my body yearns to be with another woman, it is okay because, before I took my first breath, God already knew. I feel so much better having gained my own understanding of what it means to have a spiritual connection.

Damn. That was scary. Doesn't help my situation. I was still raised to think a certain way. I was raised to believe that man and woman were made one for the other. Man and woman were made to become joined as one in marriage, with the sole purpose to procreate, to continue the human race.

I may not have been the most feminine of the bunch as I was growing up, but all girls dream about what they're going to be as grown-ups. I was no different. I saw myself with Bruce Leroy Green from *The Last Dragon* or a man that looked similar to him. We would have two children, a boy and a girl, and we would live in a middle-class area. We would drive two cars and go on family trips; he would drive and open doors for me. I dreamed of coming home from work (as a physical education teacher and a coach), my husband being already there with our children, and our evenings being something like *The Cosby Show*. That is what I wanted.

Yes, I love playing ball, but if I don't make it to the league, what is my fallback plan? Being a wife and mother has always been what I would revert to, especially when there was no such thing as the WNBA. Being a lesbian challenges all that I have ever known.

I don't even know if I am a lesbian. I don't know much of anything right now. I do know I liked it.

September 18, 1999

Damn! Basketball kicked my ass today. I don't know if I am just getting older, or if practice is just getting harder. Being one of the only seniors on the team has its advantages, but many disadvantages as well. Biggest disadvantage—AGE difference. These young girls are running us into the ground! HA! Coach brought in about six freshmen this year. That's all well and good; they are going to need six people to replace me when I graduate in May. They are not half bad either. We have this mentoring program for the freshmen on the team; I haven't decided which one I want to take under my wing yet. There is one girl that I helped out in workouts today.

You're Sentury?

Yes.

Wow. You're shorter in person.

I will take that as a compliment.
Do you need a spotter?

(Blushing)

What's your name, Fresh?

(Blushing)

Well, let's call you Dimples for now;
your smile is beautiful.

Dimples. She is beautiful. Not beautiful in like a beautiful way, but she is definitely easy on the eyes. She must be about six two, nothing but muscle, flawless body. She is an off shade of brown, but if I just had to give it a name, I would call her light sepia. Her dimples were the only things she couldn't hide; as soon as she opened her mouth to make sure I was, in fact, the infamous Sentury Alysé, her face dented in—gorgeous smile.

One more rep, Dimples; you got it.

(Exhale)

Good job, those guns will be
shining in no time.

So what are you doing tonight?

Oh, so you do speak.

(Blushing)

Just not that much.

She asked me to go with her to get some food after practice. I told her I needed to go back to my room and shower first, but I would meet her, and we could go. No big deal. Teammates chilling, getting to know each other outside of the court.

Dimples?

The problem when you are getting to know someone, off the court, is they are getting to know you off the court as well. Dimples came through the doors dressed so clean I almost didn't recognize her. Her hair was pulled back into a tight bun, and she wore a New York Yankees hat tilted just over her right eye. Her shoes looked as if they were fresh out of the box, Air Force Ones, all black. Jeans weren't too fitting, but they didn't hang off her ass like a regular street pharmacist either; they were placed just right to give off a boyish idea. I don't know why I noticed such detail, but I did. I didn't want to, but I did.

What's good, Sent?

Oh, so you put your Yankees cap on,
and now you can speak.

I always knew how to speak; just
wasn't the right time at the workout.

It isn't like I was asking you for
your Social Security number.

(Blushing)

You must use your smile to
get women where you're from.

Why would you ask me that?

Dimples, let's not play dumb here.

Do I make you uncomfortable? I don't want you
to think that I am trying to make a pass at you
just because I asked you to come eat. I just have
been following you since you got recruited here,
and I thought that it would be cool to be friends,
with the reason that I was here.

The reason why you're here?

Yes, I wasn't coming to school in Montana. Who
the hell willingly comes to Montana? Sentury, you
are fucking amazing as a ballplayer. Who wouldn't
want to play with you?

Shit, I got a few things you can play with!

Did I just say that? Let me review. Yup, I said it. I didn't mean it in the way it came out… I promise I didn't. Well hell, maybe I did. Dimples—that girl is something else.

So, Sent…

What's going on?

What do you use to get the women where you're from?

Nothing.

> *You just use your looks, and*
> *the bitches be all over you?*

I don't like women.

Damn right, that's what I told her. I didn't have time to sit there and play games with that girl. We weren't even going to pretend that I am willing to have another Alana situation pop off, especially not with one of my damn teammates.

September 22, 1999

I've decided to go ahead and mentor Dimples. She's not a half-bad kid. When we had our team meeting today, honestly, I was the only senior on the team who hadn't chosen one, and Dimples was the only freshman on the team who hadn't been picked.

> *SentA?*

Yeah, Coach?

> *What the hell is going on?*

I'm sorry, Coach. Are you sure you're looking for me?

> *Who's your mentee?*

(Silence)

> *SentA!*

Yeah, Coach?

> *Who's your mentee?*

(Silence)

> *There's only one left; you better figure it out!*

It's as if I really didn't have a choice, ya know. Then I look over at Dimples, and she is looking at me with the biggest smile in the world. What the hell was I supposed to do? I couldn't say no—to her or to Coach.

After the team meeting, and after Coach took me in his office to chew me another asshole about being captain and not the first person to have a mentee, blah, blah, blah, I was then forced to go get my mentee and take her to dinner with me to work on goals for the season.

So how does it feel to be a starting freshman?

                                        Did I take your place?

A dream is a wish your heart makes…

                                        When you're fast asleep.

I'm glad you knew where I was going with
that. No, you will not be replacing me.
Miller is out with a sprained knee; you
are going to be her fill-in for a while.

                So, are you telling me that not only am I playing next
                to you, but I will be starting next to you as well?

Me and three other people.

                                        But you.

Yeah, me.

See, people think I am a damn fool. Dimples was just staring at me while we were talking. I've seen those eyes before… I remember the White girl. How could I forget? Hell, I shake every time I think about her. Dimples had the same look in her eyes that Alana had in hers, and I am not about to even fall for that shit.

                So back to you not liking women.

*I don't even understand what that has
to do with your goals for the season.*

> *It has everything to do with them.*

What is that supposed to mean?

> *If what you say is true, then I have more than just
> basketball to focus on. And if you're just fronting, as
> I believe you are, then I can focus more of my time
> on basketball because the rest will fall into place.*

I don't like women.

> *Then why are you here, Sentury?*

Because you are my mentee.

> *Cut the shit!*

These aggressive-ass lesbians are getting on my damn nerves. I told her ass I don't want to deal with women, and she is sending out innuendos and shit as if I can't read in between the lines. Now, granted, I do think she is one sexy little… Well, no, I won't say that. I will say I think she is very attractive, but that means nothing. I think a lot of people are attractive. For example, Usher, he is funny looking about the nose, but overall he is attractive. Does that mean I want to jump his bones? No! Yeah, I check her out from time to time, but that doesn't mean I am trying to get with her.

> *I see you looking at me, Sentury.*

You don't see shit!

> *If it's not true, why are you so aggressive right now?*

(Silence)

> *Exactly.*

(Silence)

> *To answer your question, my goals for the season will be to be able to meet or surpass my senior-year scoring average. I would like to retain my starting position, and with that, I will work ten times as hard as the next person. I would like to improve at the wing to expand my range on the court, and, finally, I want to fuck you.*

(Silence)

September 29, 1999

Lord, help me. I'm sitting in my room right now, and I don't know what to do with myself. I don't know if I should cry, scream, punch a wall, or go to bed and crawl into a ball. I don't even know where to begin about this. Fuck me slow! That's the problem! I need to shower. I don't know what is happening to me. As much as I run around here playing and pretending that I am okay, I'm not! I'm not fucking okay! I keep getting caught up in shit, and I don't know how to get myself out of the fucking situation.

This is my fault. Had I not waited to pick a mentee, I wouldn't have been stuck with her. For some reason, I feel as if I did this shit on purpose! Did I purposely wait until the last minute, with hopes that Dimples would be the only one left? No. That doesn't make sense! How would I know that that girl wouldn't get picked? She is an excellent ballplayer. Why wouldn't someone want to mentor her? Match the best with the best! Fuck! This was a setup. I wanted to be left with her; I wanted it. And I wanted her to want me just as bad as I want her.

> *Why are you always smiling?*

> *Because I know you love to see me smile.*

> *Who told you that?*

You did.

Never did I ever.

You did.

Do you need help with that weight or what?

*Only if you come stand over me to get a
better view of what it is I am trying to do.*

Dimples and I went to the weight room late tonight. We didn't
have curfew, and there was really nothing else for us to do. So
I hit her up, told her to meet me at the gym. She walked her
ass in there in a wifebeater and some tight-ass shorts. I have
already said she is all muscle. The way those tights hugged
her ass…I almost dropped the damn barbell on my foot. I think
she noticed that shit too! Anyways, immediately we went into
a workout, nothing different than what we would do if the team
were with us. But this time it wasn't the team; it was just us.

So we going to hit the showers or what?

*Damn, girl, I haven't worked out this hard since
I was your age. I need a second to catch my breath.*

*Are you sure it was the workout
that got you losing your breath?*

*Don't you see me over here, red and glistening
in the face? This has nothing to do with you!*

Come on, let's head to the showers.

Man! When we got to the showers, I was walking slowly. Shit,
I'm sore now for more reasons than one. Dimples went into each
and every stall and turned on all of the showers. The water was
so hot that the entire place steamed up in seconds. I wasn't paying

attention really though. I was trying to find my soap in all the damn fog.

I think you are beautiful.

What the hell? Dimples? Is that you?
I can't see; it's so damn steamy in here.

You don't need to see this.

The next thing I knew, I was being pulled farther into the shower area. Water was running into the drains, and it was strangely sexy. She started tugging at my workout clothes as if they were rags on a doll, and I fell totally into her trance. Immediately, we both started sweating, and as each layer of clothing came off and our bodies touched and slid together, I got wetter and wetter, and not from the shower water.

I have been wanting to taste you since I first saw you.

There we are, ass naked on the weight-room shower floor, kissing and touching as if we had been doing this for years. Water was everywhere! On us, in between us, under us, and over us! The shit was so sexy I didn't even need the head. I could have come from the excitement and thrill of where we were.

If I taste you now, what will this make us?

What are you asking me?

Let me fuck you until you are ready
to admit that you are ready for this.

The first flick of her tongue made me quiver something fierce. She was a lot more aggressive than Alana. She was commanding, and she was rough! Alana was gentle, considering it was my first time. Dimples, she didn't care. She grabbed the back of my ass and slid me back and forth onto her tongue as if I were on a machine. In and out, in and out. With each penetrating vibration of her tongue, I fell more and more into her trance. The next thing I knew, we were turned around, and I was on my stomach with my face in the drain.

What the...?

Dimples cupped my breasts and arched my back with her hands. She slid under me so slyly I didn't even know what was happening. She kept one hand on my breast, and then she entered me with the other just as fast as her tongue touched me. The faster she licked, the harder she grabbed, and the longer she poked. And then it was over.

October 15, 1999

We got a hell of a win today! I am SO proud of the team and how we pulled together to win. Granted, traveling out to West Boondock Hell, Montana, and beating the hillbillies out here isn't our best feat, but it was still good to win. The coolest thing ever was the school had a party for our winning! What kind of backwards shit is that? They literally told us to stay after the game, set up the gym, and BOOM! "Congratulations, Montana State University, for your WIN."

So are we going to dance together?

Why would we do that?

Sentury, stop acting like you don't want me.

I don't have to act; it comes natural.

Fuck you.

Already did.

Of course, I had to deal with Dimples all in my grill, as she has been for the past three weeks. I didn't want to be bothered, to be completely honest. We had just won, we were thirty miles from boring-ass Browning, and I just wanted to chill.

Damn, SentA!

What?

You see that girl over there?

No.

Well, she sees you!

I've accepted the fact that there is something about me that turns more women's heads than men's. As a matter of fact, I will go so far as to say that I am okay with being attractive to them, him, her, and she. I am not a lesbian, so they can stare and gawk all they want. Those little affairs I've had with Alana and Dimples were just that—little affairs. Being out in the streets and getting the attention of a woman doesn't move me or sway me to do anything different than what I've been doing—chilling.

You're Sentury Alysé?

And you are?

(Music too loud)

Okay…

I think you are an amazing ballplayer…

Okay…

I just wanted to tell you that.

As the night went on, the girl that my teammate had so graciously pointed out decided to make her way over in my direction. She was cute, whatever the definition of cute is. About five two, petite, and very fair skinned—NOT Alana fair skinned—like a

Faith Evans complexion. As I said, she was cute. Never did catch her name.

Do you like this song?

(Silence)

Next is a good group.

Is there something else that you wanted to say?

Let's dance.

It's not that I had anything against dancing with Dimples, but this girl was standing too close to me at the same time, ironically, that the Next's new song, "Too Close," came on. So I said, "What the hell!" and I got on the dance floor with her. What I didn't expect was for her to start backing it up on me as if I were some man or something. She was bumping and grinding to the song, singing to me and shit. MY ENTIRE TEAM was watching us. You would think I would have stopped.

As she did her routine to the lyrics, I looked around and met Dimples in the eyes. I could see something in her eyes; I am unsure if it was rage or hurt, but, whatever it was, it made me nervous as hell.

Are you trying to make a fool out of me, Sentury?

What are you talking about, woman?

Dancing with that bitch!

Who? Too Close?

SO SHE HAS A NICKNAME NOW TOO!?!? I thought I was special! I thought I was the one whose nickname meant something to you.

Are you on your period?

You're a bitch!

That was rude.

The whole ride back to Browning, I had to listen to Dimples bitch and complain about how I treated her at the party. I don't know what the fuck she expected out of me. I am not her woman, and we are not dating. We had sex. Once. That's it. Once. Now I owe her something?! She better get the hell on with that bullshit. I was just sitting on the bus, listening to music; every now and then, I would hear this vicious-ass whisper come from behind me.

You ain't shit!

I just shook my head and kept on listening to my New Edition CD. No one has time for an overemotional bitch. Let me rephrase that—no one has time for an overemotional bitch that ain't mine.

SentA.

What's going on, Chris?

(Hands me a note)

What's this?

That girl told me to give it to you.

The note said:

Call me when she isn't around…

Too Close

October 17, 1999

I called her! I am not quite sure why I called her, but I did. I had walked by the damn paper for the past two days and hadn't paid it any attention. Then something made me look down at the paper after practice today.

Can't ever have enough friends, I guess.

The crazy thing is, I didn't even know her name. That took another twenty minutes because I didn't know who the hell I was asking for.

Hello?

Hey.

Hey. Who is this?

Sentury.

Who is it that you are looking for, Sentury?

(Silence)

I got it, Jess. It's for me.

(Silence)

Saved by the damn bell, or other phone. I really need to ask the girl what her name is before it is all over and done with. I hoped that whoever Jess was would have said her name before she hung up the line, but no such luck! Ha! Nevertheless, she is a pretty cool chick, a senior at the community college, majoring in nursing, and an avid basketball fan.

Your last triple double could have been a triple, but the damn refs acted like they had sand in their asses and called an over-the-back on you, which took your board back.

Her knowledge of the game was cool, but her knowledge of my career was pretty impressive. We talked for thirty minutes about basketball, the idea of going to the WNBA, and my chances of being in the draft—nothing major.

So who was that girl?

I should have known it was coming. The conversation was going too well for something not to ruin it. That damn Dimples really made her damn presence known to Too Close. Standing right by us while we were dancing, watching us as we were talking—well, while she was talking and I was struggling to hear—giving me the evil eye every time she had a chance. Dimples's ass has got to go! She is fucking up my groove! Not that I have any particular groove to be messed up, but what I am saying is… Well, you know what I am saying.

Is she your ex or something?

Ex what?

Ex-girlfriend.

(Laughing)

What's so funny?

Do you think I like women?

(Silence)

Hello?

Oh my God!

What?

I am so sorry, Sentury!

(Laughing)

I promise I didn't know you were straight. I am so embarrassed! That's what I get for listening to people.

I'm sorry, what do you mean, "listening to people"?

> *The rumor was that you were gay, and then I saw your teammate and how she was acting, and I thought she was something like a jealous ex...*

Wow.

> *Sentury, please don't be offended. I am truly sorry.*

It's cool.

What I don't understand is why people can't mind their own fucking business. With whom I am sleeping or have slept is none of anyone's concern. Why do they feel the need to go around discussing all that they think I am doing? Who gives a fuck that I've had sex with women before? That's no one else's business but mine! And the nerve of these people to then take their assumptions and spread them around the world as if it were a flattering compliment. Going around calling me a lesbian puts out the wrong idea about me. I am a woman who likes men, who happened to have come across a few women with whom, in the comforts of their own homes, I had some sort of sexual contact. NO ONE ELSE KNOWS THAT, except for me, the White girl, and the whiner! I've been hearing this shit all my life! I am so tired of it!

> *Sentury?*

What's up?

> *I will understand if you are offended and you never want to speak with me again.*

It's cool. You aren't the first and won't be the last. You're cool, Too Close.

> *I like that nickname.*

(Silence)

Sentury?

What's up?

*Do you mind if we hang out
sometime, maybe this weekend?*

That's cool with me. What do you want to do?

Leave the plans to me.

October 20, 1999

What is it about me that makes the bitches swoon? Whatever it is, can I get it surgically removed? This shit is bananas, and I keep walking right into the trap! I can't stop pacing my room right now. I don't know what to do. I don't know if I should just stop talking to people in general, or if I should make sure that, if they don't have a penis, I do not hang out with them! These chicks just don't take no for an answer! It must be something in the Montana water, and if that's the case, I am glad my ass drinks Gatorade! I thought I was going to see Too Close, and we would just kick it. She was a cool chick, much like me, different from these Mon State chicks. And, most importantly, she said she respected my sexuality, so our hanging out shouldn't have been a problem.

Hey, beautiful!

What's up, Too Close?

*For a straight girl, you sure give
off some strong stud vibes, ma!*

WHAT THE FUCK IS A STRONG STUD VIBE?! How does one achieve the honor of not being a stud but yet giving off a stud-like vibe? Do I walk with a slight manly gait? Yes, I do; I am a ballplayer! I am not graceful unless I am on the court! Do I talk with a charismatic tone that could be confused with trying to mack someone? Yes, I do, dammit. I'm charismatic; that's who the hell I am! That doesn't make me a stud! What does it make me? A damn jock in the wrong fucking sport!

So what are we about to do?

We are going to go to the roof.

The roof?

Yes, the roof.

Why would we do that?

The roof of my building is very serene; trust me.

I must admit, I've never been on the roof before, especially in thirty-nine-degree weather, but it was very cool up there. It was almost as if I were no longer in Montana. From the roof, we could see at least one hundred miles each way. Every mountain peak, valley road, and country wind was easily seen from our view. It was peaceful.

This is where I come to clear my head.

I can understand why.

The night I told my parents I was a lesbian,
I spent the entire night up here.

You slept up here?

Yes, it was better than sleeping
in a house full of ignorance.

How do your parents feel about it now?

They are dead.

Why do I get the muthafuckas with the deep-rooted issues and causes? Alana was an activist, and now Too Close is in mourning. Have you ever had a moment when you wished you could reach down on the VCR of life and press Rewind, and then record over what just happened and watch it all over again? Yes? No? Either way, I felt that way!

I'm sorry to hear you have lost both of your parents. My father passed when I was young; it's just me and my mom now.

> *Yeah, it's cool. It's just me and my sister, Jess, now. It's been a year; I've dealt with it.*

It's cold up here. Don't you want to go inside?

There was a fireplace on the damn roof. Now, for all intents and purposes, I would like to state that the idea of burning wood on the roof of an apartment building is not safe. I would not suggest it to anybody, and I wouldn't even tell anybody else that I participated in such an unsafe act. But on the flip side of that, the shit was funky! We were on the roof, with a fireplace, enjoying the Montana air and, most importantly, each other.

> *You know, it's a shame that you aren't a lesbian.*

There goes the neighborhood. I thought I was going to make it through our friendship session without having to deal with some pushy-ass lesbian shit.

Why is it a shame?

> *Because you would make an excellent partner.*

You don't know me well enough to make such a judgment.

> *I am sitting here with you, and I know enough.*

Sure you do.

What happens to me is my fault. I challenge these women. I tell them something they want to hear, and they think that I want for them to pursue me more than I let on. That's not the case. When I say no, I really mean no. I'm okay; I don't need it. I don't want it.

> *You can't look me in the eye and tell me you've*
> *never thought about being with a woman.*

(Silence)

> *I knew it.*

You knew what?

> *You like pussy.*

Please don't make me vomit; I'm scared
to lean over the top of this ledge.

> *You like pussy.*

She pounced on me! I felt as if I were a poor little gazelle at the hands of some overly strong lioness. This girl hopped on me so fast I didn't even know what was going on.

What are you doing?

> *Whatever happens, you are going to like it.*

Let me paint this picture for you. It's sunset; we're on a rooftop overlooking the countryside; there's a crisp October breeze, and we're in front of a fireplace. That is what I was faced with. What is a girl supposed to do? This is one of those once-in-a-lifetime experiences. I had choices. Either I could overpower her and leave her on the roof by herself, or I could play along and see how far she is really going to take it. It wasn't as if I had curfew or anything like that.

You're a really good kisser.

Everything about my rooftop experience was just as romantic as it was confusing. Her kisses were so passionate and soft. She ran her hands through my hair as we kissed, and she never moved from her position, firmly on top of me. It's not as if we were sitting on any chairs or anything, just blankets and the roof.

Lay back.

No.

Lay back.

No.

While I was sitting straight up, she managed to swindle me out of my pants, and she was still kissing me. Fairly skilled, I must say. Once my pants were off and the damn air hit me, I let out a whimper. I did; I bitched up. Too Close laughed and moved on down, much as the two before her had done.

It's a lot warmer down here than you think.

Her tongue was so cold! It felt as if there were nothing but ice in between my legs. She latched on to my thighs so tight I started to lose feeling in my feet. To be honest, I don't know if it came from the actual tightness or what was happening between my thighs. This girl was a professional. Not once did she use her hands on me. Everything she did was with her tongue. She fucked me with her tongue! I could feel her taking deeper and deeper breaths as she mover lower and lower and finally got to my hole.

Whoa! What are you doing?

That was it; everything thereafter was a blur. It was like a pulsating snake, in and out! She was breathing so damn hard the cold air blowing out of her nose was hitting my clit with vengeance. Each breath sent me into an orgasmic scream, all while she was still sucking every ounce of juice out of me and fucking me with her tongue.

(Panting)

I felt her let go of my right thigh, and then I heard her panting harder and harder. SHE WAS PLAYING WITH HERSELF! Still holding on to me and using her tongue for something I'm sure hers was made for. Before I had time to comprehend all that happened, my body exploded from the inside out. Too Close sat up and licked her lips.

Yeah, you like pussy.

November 25, 1999

Thanksgiving. What is there for me to be thankful for? I spent the entire day in my room, doing nothing. I haven't even eaten today. What for? You know, I really haven't been in the best of moods lately. This whole sleeping-with-women thing is starting to get the best of me. I don't know if I am coming or going. I've got Dimples in my face every chance she can get, trying to see when she can get another taste, and then I've got Too Close calling my damn room every hour on the hour, trying to get me to come see her again. WHY ME?! I needed someone to talk to, and you would think that calling my best friend, who is a fucking professional LESBIAN, would have done me some good.

I don't know what you want me to say, Sentury.

LaTrice seriously put me deeper into the depression I was trying to avoid. I understand that you call someone your best friend because you think that they will tell you the truth whether it is sunny and bright, or dark and gloomy. The problem with that is sometimes you just don't want to hear that shit.

> *You are sleeping with women! You can't get mad that people are going around saying that shit, and you are really doing it.*

But I am not attracted to women.

> *You must be.*

I'm not!

> *So you are telling me that out of the three chicks you've let in between your legs, with two of them being damn near within thirty days of each other, you never thought to yourself, "Hey, I am engaging in lesbian-like activity, and if I am not a lesbian, maybe I should stop."*

Trice gets on my damn nerves! Of course, every time I had one of my women—not *my* women, but my women—I thought about it and continued to think about it. I am still thinking about it, which is why I thought calling her was a good idea. I can't stand for someone to tell me something that is obvious. What the hell did I look like to Trice? Only an idiot wouldn't know that kissing and touching a woman is lesbian-like behavior. I knew that. She didn't have to ask me what I realized and what I didn't. I needed some guidance to kick this habit; I didn't need an instant replay.

> *Sentury, all jokes aside, you have allowed yourself to sleep with not one, not two, but three women; you can't expect me to tell you that you aren't gay. Your actions are speaking a lot louder than your words.*

But, Trice…

> *But what, Sent? There is no but. The reality is you are attracted to women, and if you weren't, Alana wouldn't have happened, which wouldn't have opened the door for Dimples, and ultimately Too Close.*

All jokes aside, Trice was absolutely right. There is something in me that wants to know what it is a woman can do for me that a man can't. I have been curious about the lifestyle since I was first introduced to it. There was something mysterious about the fact that a woman could look at a woman and have the same feelings that another woman could look at a man and have. It drew me in. It was as if I were around movie stars.

When I say movie stars, I mean the Hollywood lifestyle, which is something totally different from what we live day to day. There is a different culture in Hollywood, a different level of acceptance, expectation, and, most importantly, a certain level of exclusivity. The gay culture has all the same attributes; it was an escape to be a part of that club. So do I think that what I am doing is about being attracted to women? No, I don't.

> *You're kidding, right?*

It's a fascination with the lifestyle. The idea that for that moment, I can be given an inside track to their world, and not have to compromise my own existence, excited me. These women gave me a way into the world I had been wondering about for years. That's what I liked about it; I thrived off the invite to be a part of it.

> *So you are one of those bitches who play gay for the shits and giggles of it?*

No, I am not playing.

> *Then what do you call it?*

I don't call it anything. I am not doing anything;
it's not like I am going down on them or anything.

> *That means nothing; all it means to us is that you*
> *are a pillow princess. That isn't convincing to me.*
> *Either you're gay, or you are a bitch playing gay.*
> *And I really hope you wouldn't be playing gay, espe-*
> *cially being someone so close to me, knowing what*
> *I go through.*

I am just chilling.

> *Sentury, be serious. You know that being a lesbian*
> *isn't easy. You watched what I went through with*
> *my family when I came out. Hell, when I got kicked*
> *out of my grandmother's house, I came to live with*
> *you. All because I was a lesbian. You were there*
> *when I was talked about and outed to our class-*
> *mates in high school. You saw what that did to me.*

But you made it, Trice.

> *I made it because I had to, Sent. I am a lesbian*
> *woman. Period. There is no turning back for me. I*
> *have known this since I was like ten. If I had it to*
> *do over, I would have come out earlier so I could*
> *save myself some heartache that came along with*
> *coming out as a teenager. Why would you will-*
> *ingly put yourself through something like that?*

Who said anything about coming out?

> *Sentury! You cannot continue to sleep with women*
> *and ignore it. If this isn't what you really want,*
> *stop. Stop before you hurt someone or, most impor-*
> *tantly, before you hurt yourself.*

That was my Thanksgiving—sitting on the phone while staring into the mirror. Everything Trice was saying was right. I knew what it meant to be put on blast for living the life that you wanted to live. I saw the pain she went through to be able to be who she was. I saw when she had to hide who she was from the ones she loved the most because she knew she wouldn't be accepted. That wasn't me though. I didn't have to hide because there was nothing to hide. What I'd done was behind closed doors, with women who were already in the lifestyle.

All I am doing is exploring. I don't want to be in the lifestyle. I don't want to be considered someone who is playing games either. I am not playing.

Trice made me feel bad. The idea of playing gay is bothering me. It's similar to (I'm about to go deep) White people wearing blackface in the early part of the twentieth century. I don't know what made them think it was okay to make a mockery of our everyday lives, but they did. It was entertainment for them; it was something to pass the time until going back to their nicely made homes and forgetting about the little niggers they offended. That's what I picture when the words "playing gay" are used. That is derogatory! Why would someone purposely imitate a life they have no intention of trying to live?

Lesbians and gays who are out have gone through the fire and back to be able to proudly represent themselves, and I would never make a joke of that. I am not a lesbian, but I understand the struggle, and I never want to take that from them. I just have a different struggle…with myself.

December 9, 1999

Home sweet home! There is nothing like Nevada in the winter. Dusty and cold, my type of town. This will be my last Christmas at home, and to be honest with you, I am perfectly okay with that. Not that coming back to the place where I was born is a bad thing, but coming home to a household of dysfunction is not something I am into.

My father passed when I was six. My mother hasn't been right since, and when something like that happens, it really can destroy the foundation of the home. When I get to Las Vegas, there is never a warm greeting, a "good to see you," not even so much as a "welcome home."

> *I see you are still looking like a boy. I don't know how you expect to find a husband like that.*

I'm doing well in school, thank you for asking.

Home sweet home. So not only do I have to defend myself from the world, but my mother won't let up either. The months following my father's death, I used to sneak into the closet and dress in his clothes. I would put on his suit and tie, his shoes and hat, and I would go into my room and play; it made me feel as if I were playing with him. My mother would get PISSED off at me. She would come into my room and scream at the top of her lungs.

> *SENTURY! What are you doing?! Why have you been in my room?! I told you to stop going into my closet! These things do not belong to you!*

After a while, I didn't even cry anymore. I would just get up and go back into the closet, remove the items, and retire to my room for the remainder of the night or day, depending on what time she caught me. You would think she shouldn't have been surprised when, as I got older, it was an innate reaction to stay in my room, out of her way.

> *So you come home to be locked up in that room all day?*

No, Mom. I came home to get away from the demands of being in school all day, every day.

It's not like you are going to be here long;
you get here late, and you leave early!
What is the point of coming home?

I don't know.

Needless to say, after she jumped down my throat for doing what I've always done, then came the million-dollar question.

Sentury, are you gay!?

What are you talking about?

You know what I am talking about? Are you gay?

Yes, Mom, I sleep with women all of the time. I can
actually still taste the last one before I got on the plane.

I'll slap you where you stand for standing in my
face lying to me like that! If your father knew how
you turned out, he would just get up out of his
grave and hide! You are not gay, so look like it, and
stop hanging around with all of those lesbians! Find
some straight friends, and find a husband!

I got in my car, and I left. I wanted to go see Trice, but, as usual, when I'm home, she isn't here. She's somewhere with one of her many women, I'm assuming. Heifer didn't even tell me she was leaving; wait until I catch her ass when she gets back!

December 11, 1999

I finally got a chance to catch up with Trice today via telephone. I don't know what it is about life these days, but everyone is on this "get on Sentury's nerves" kick.

You talked to any of your girlfriends
since you been home?

No.

Why not?

I don't have any girlfriends.

*Oh, I do apologize. I meant to
say your female fuck buddies.*

Something about the term *fuck buddy* really irritates me. I don't have fuck buddies; that sounds as if I am going around collecting bitches to screw. Not the case.

Sentury, I love you, but you are delusional.

(Silence)

*I know you are still there, and
you did not hang up on me.*

(Silence)

Anyways, like I was saying, you are fucking delusional if you think that what you're doing makes sense. Okay, so you're not quote-unquote gay. Your ass is bisexual for sure. No straight woman is going around sleeping with multiple women for the joy of it; that's not straight-woman behavior. It's actually lesbian behavior, but you're not a lesbian, so I will say its bisexual behavior.

It's neither!

That's what I'm talking about, Sent! You are fucking delusional. You like women! What the hell is wrong with you? And furthermore, what the hell is wrong with that? Who cares? Be who you are—nothing more, nothing less!

Bisexual: the romantic attraction or sexual attraction towards both males and females. Okay, I can take that. I can say that I have come to a point in my life where I notice women just as easily as I notice men. That is not something that I want to outwardly admit, but I can admit it to myself. Let's say your mom does crack. You know your mom does crack; hell, the world knows your mom does crack. The people on the street call her a crackhead, but you will never call her a crackhead. When you go home at night and you close the door, you know she is a crackhead. Saving face, that's how I see it. I will never admit to anyone that I am what they call bisexual because I have yet to get home and close that door. My door is still open, and it is not going to close anytime soon.

December 15, 1999

I met the coolest girl EVER in the mall today! Since staying in the house is not an option, I find myself making up things to do; today, it was walking around the mall and people watching. Something to do—nothing major, if you ask me. Anyways, I saw one of my old teammates from high school, Dawn, and we decided to walk through the mall together.

> *Damn, SentA! It sure is good to see you.*

> *I know! It's been a long time!*

> *What you got going on these days?*

> *Girl, you wouldn't even believe me if I told you!*

Dawn and I walked through the mall, laughing and talking about things that happened during our four seasons together.

> *Remember when coach was running with us,*
> *and fell into the bleachers and got stuck!*

I love when I can just hang and reminisce about things; it passes the time, and it also takes my mind off of the real situations at hand. Just when I think everything is going away, I get reminded I have shit on my mind.

Let's go in Lids.

Okay, cool.

There she was. She. There SHE was. We walked into Lids, and Dawn started looking at the fitted caps on the wall. I just lagged behind, wasn't really looking for anything in particular.

Excuse me.

I turn around, and the most beautiful woman I've ever seen, in boy's clothes, was standing behind me. She is much shorter than I am; I will give her five five, maybe, on a good day. She has a short haircut, something like a pageboy haircut from the early seventies. Her skin, flawless! There was not a blemish on her face. Her eyes, the shape of almonds and the color of honey. Honey.

Aw, man, what's up, (Name Omitted)?

Hey, Dawn, what's good?

As I am drooling over Little Miss Honey, Dawn walks up and introduces me.

Sentury, this is (Name Omitted), but we all call her Honey because of her sexy-ass eyes.

Yeah, I noticed.

When she smiled at me, I saw her perfect teeth, and at that moment, I knew I was smitten. Luckily for me, Dawn was about to leave the mall, and she left Honey and me in Lids together, alone.

Sentury, I've heard a lot about you over the years.
I'm glad I finally get to meet you.

Really? I'm sorry I cannot say the same, but I would
really like to hear what all you've heard about me.
I'm not sure if I should be excited or scared.

Nah, not like that. There is no need to be scared.
All good, Mama. All good.

Honey went on to tell me that she'd heard that I was one of
the best basketball players to come out of Wolders High School,
and also one of the prettiest.

I always wondered how someone so beautiful was
such an aggressive and athletic ballplayer. It's sexy
though, I must admit.

(Blushing)

Yes, very sexy.

So, we exchanged numbers, and then I ran home so I could
be there when she called. Not that we were about to talk about
anything major, but there was a chance that we could hang out
while I was in town. I still had another twelve days there; that's
long enough to build on a friendship, I think.

She called, and I didn't answer at first. I didn't want to seem
anxious, so what I did was watch the phone ring, and then I turned
around and called right back!

Hey, Honey!

What's going on with you, Sent? I just called you.

Yeah, I was walking in the door as the phone was
ringing, had to run a few errands after I left the mall.

That's cool.

Yeah.

(Silence)

So…

Yeah.

Tell me about yourself.

It was so cool to be able to sit on the phone and not have to talk about myself, or have to try to digress from a conversation brought on by a fan of my basketball career. Honey talked about life, her life, and all that came along with it. I learned that she has two brothers, lives with her mother and younger brother. She has a dog and a cat, and she is currently in school at the community college. She is actually a few months to the day older than I am. I was born on June 6, 1978, and she was born on April 6, 1978. We both like scary movies, as well as children's movies, we both like eating our Quarter Pounders with cheese, no pickles, and we put French fries in between the meat and the bread!

> *Damn! I'm mad I'm just meeting you; we could have definitely hung out while you were in town.*

Who said we can't?

> *No one, but I am sure you have family and friends that want to spend time with you. Montana is far, and it's rare that you come home.*

Believe me, they will manage.

December 16, 1999

I like Honey. There, I said it. I have not known her for twenty-four hours, but I like her. I have never felt so liberated in my life. To say it, to admit it—yes, I like the woman, and I am okay with it. Man, it is a breath of fresh air.

So what do you want to do today?

I don't know. What do you do for fun?

I know what we can do.

She took me to the park today, not to ball, but to relax. It was about sixty-five outside today, a beautiful day, and I spent it with a beautiful woman. This girl made a picnic basket, had a blanket and a portable boom box, and had it all set up when I pulled up.

What is all of this?

This is our afternoon.

(Blushing)

I may be a lot of things, but a fool I am not. Honey was genuinely trying to impress me, and she didn't even know if I was gay or not. She never asked me if I liked women; she never mentioned that she liked women; there was never any mention of anything. Granted, I can look at her and tell that she is into women, but if she looks at me, I look like her. I have the same domineering presence she has. She didn't care about that; she just cared about who I was.

This is so weird.

How so?

You, me...here, this. This is weird.

No, that sentence was weird!

What?

"You, me...here, this." What the hell was that?!

Forget you, man!

The you is me, and the here is this; that is
what this is. If that makes it weird, then
it's weird, but, to me, I think it's nice.

Just as charismatic as she is beautiful! Her eyes are hypnotizing. Anyways, while we were there, the fact that she hadn't brought up sexuality was baffling! We talked about everything from sports to politics, and even if we believed in extraterrestrial existence, but she wouldn't bring up whether or not I liked women.

Why haven't you asked me if I was gay yet?

                           Why did I have to?

Don't you want to know?

                           I already know.

Do you really?

                           Yes.

So do I?

                           Probably not, but you like me.

(Silence)

             Exactly, why state the obvious? I didn't bring you
             here to figure out your sexual orientation. I brought
             you here to enjoy you while I have you here, because
             I knew that soon I wouldn't have this opportunity,
             and you would move on in life without me.

(Silence)

             We are here because this is an experience we both
             deserve, and even if you leave Las Vegas next week
             and you spend the rest of your life dating me, you
             will never forget how I made you feel.

My God! Why can't I take Honey with me to Montana? Fuck Alana, Dimples, and Too Close; those bitches were just trying to invade and conquer! Honey, on the other hand, is a woman about her business and about handling that first. Do you know she wants to be a firefighter and is studying to take the test? She is in school full-time, and she works full-time. Ironically, while we were on the blanket "enjoying the experience," K-Ci and JoJo came on the radio.

I love this song!

                              What does this song mean to you?

What do you mean?

                              You said you love the song, Sentury. Why do you love it?

Have you heard it before?

                                                          Yes.

That's why I love it!

                              You can't tell me, can you?

Tell you what?

                              Why you like the song.

(Silence)

                              Don't get quiet now.

I'm thinking.

                    You need to hurry; the song is only four minutes long.

You hear the verse that's playing now?

                                                          Yes.

The expression of love in that verse is something I've never felt, but when they sing it, I feel it.

You've never been in love?

With basketball.

With a person, Sentury. You have never been in love with a person?

No.

(Silence)

That is why I love this song so much, because it makes me believe in something I have otherwise not seen, felt, or known. You want to talk about faith; it gives me faith in the possibility that there is someone in the world who will look at me and think I am beautiful, fall in love with me for me, and I will do the same for them.

(Silence)

These people write these songs on purpose. They know that there are people in the world, like me, who need to have faith in something other than nothing, and they pour their souls into the music and draw us in. That is the conclusion I have come to. There is no other reason for them to write such fucking amazing songs! They make money off of us. Just think about it. Think about your favorite song. I don't care if it is a Destiny's Child song, Patti LaBelle, New Edition, or Bon Jovi! Think about how you feel when you hear that song and what the song does to your spirit. You see how much money they have made off of you, off of a feeling! The music industry is full of geniuses, and they have got all of us because, damn it, they've got me. And, hell, it had Honey sitting there thinking too!

Wow.

What?

Never?

No.

That's crazy.

Have you ever been in love before?

I don't know.

What do you mean you don't know?

I'm unsure now.

*Honey, how do you not know if you
have been in love before?*

*The passion you just had about not having
been in love, I've never felt that way before.*

(Silence)

*What was said in that verse, the simplicity of it, I've
never experienced. I don't know what it means to feel
that way for someone. I thought that I was in love with
my ex, but now I don't know. Thank you, Sentury.*

Thank me? For what?

Being here.

Help me out; I don't get it.

*Sentury, I have been struggling with getting over
my ex because I thought I was in love with her.
I am sure you are going to think this is strange, but
you and I being here is not an accident. This conversation is not an accident. That song coming on the
radio was not an accident. You are here with me for
a reason, and that reason was to help me realize she
wasn't the one for me. You are.*

Yeah, Ms. Honey, I like her.

December 18, 1999

I FUCKED UP! I fucked up in a major way! Oh my goodness, I fucked up! Just when I thought I was doing something great, I wasn't! I freaked out! I fucked up! I fucked up! Today, Honey and I had a movie date to see *Sleepy Hollow* (the new Johnny Depp movie), and, needless to say, it was the date from hell! I don't even know if it was a date! Well, okay…yes, I do; I know it was a date.

Hey, beautiful!

What's up, Honey?

You got plans tomorrow?

No.

Well, now you do. I'll pick you up around noon.

I knew what that meant. We were going on a date in the daylight, in my hometown! The first place we went was out to eat at Jason's Deli over on the southwest side of the city, where all of my father's old friends hang out.

Sentury? Sentury Alysé? Is that you?

Rex Hopkins, my father's old boss, the first damn face I see when I walk in the door! And to make matters worse, his wife, Trisha Hopkins, yeah, she led the walking team my mom joined this past summer to get her out of the house.

Hey, Mr. Hopkins.

How have you been? Come here; give me a hug.

I'm well, Mr. Hopkins. How are you and Mrs. Hopkins doing?

Well, you know us, still kicking pretty tough for some old fogies! Your mom tells us that you are scoring big over in Montana, and you have the guys chasing you for more than just autographs.

Okay, seriously? As if the situation wasn't already awkward, did my mom really tell them some bullshit like that?! She really knows how to jazz up a story, doesn't she? So as he is talking my ear off about all the men my mother had lied to and told that my beauty was being hidden by my talent, Honey is standing in the shadows and is being completely ignored. I didn't make it any better—I didn't make her presence known, nor did I make it a factor.

Okay, Mr. Hopkins. It was nice to see you! Please give my love to Mrs. Hopkins. You ready, Honey?

(Silence)

I may not be the brightest light on the Christmas tree, but I do know that that silence wasn't because she had nothing to say. The whole interaction with Mr. Hopkins made her uncomfortable, and I can't say that I blame her; shit, it made me uncomfortable.

Then, to make matters worse, we get to the cash register, and we see Isaac Washington. Who is that, you ask? Isaac Washington is the son of Zackary and Christine Washington. Who are they? The Washington family used to be our next-door neighbors for about fifteen years.

Sent! Man! What are you doing in town?

Isaac and I were in the same class from kindergarten until freshman year in high school, and his parents and my parents would do shit such as go on vacation and allow us to stay at our respective house for the duration. Do I consider him a childhood friend? No. He always got on my nerves because of his infatuation, nothing I was interested in entertaining.

You are still just as beautiful as you have always been! Did you come home finally to be with me?

AWKWARD! Honey was standing right next to me as Isaac did what he considered his version of flirting.

Boy, you are something else. Can we order?

We?

Yes, Honey and I.

(Silence)

Honey, what are you getting?

Hold on; real fast, there is something I need to do in the back.

That son of a bitch left us and never came back. We were standing there looking stupid for more reasons than one. Not only was it awkward, but I was embarrassed the fool acted like that after I said I was with Honey. It sent me into panic mode. Is that going to happen every time I walk into an establishment with her and someone knows me? Will they accept me until they see her, and then not accept either of us, regardless of what the relationship may be? Will every person I see who is associated with my family dismiss her presence as if she were nonexistent? Is this what I will have to face if I make the decision to pursue something with her—banishment, lack of acknowledgment, and embarrassment every time we step out of the door?

I'm not hungry anymore.

Yeah, me neither.

The car ride to the movie theater was freaking silent as hell! She didn't turn the radio on, she didn't say shit, and I don't even know if she was even breathing. Considering the ride from

Jason's Deli to the movie theater was no longer than five minutes, and we were super early for the show, we pulled into the parking lot and just waited.

Hey, beautiful.

(Silence)

Honey?

(Silence)

HONEY!

Yes?

Hey, girl!

What, Sentury? Matter of fact, I don't know if this was such a good idea.

Why do you say that?

Did you forget what just happened back there?

No, we left Jason's Deli.

You don't get it.

Help me get it.

I am a lesbian, Sentury. I don't know if you realize it, but you are living in a world where my lifestyle is not accepted fully.

(Silence)

When we walk into a restaurant, whether or not we are in a relationship, we are automatically seen as a couple, and your people didn't give a fuck about that. The problem with that is you didn't make them want to know who I was.

(Silence)

I get it. You are not gay, but I am, and I am not okay with being out with someone who is ashamed of who I am when we get in public.

That's not it, Honey.

Yes, it is, Sentury. If that wasn't it, then why wasn't I introduced to either of the people we just encountered?

I told Isaac about you.

No, you mentioned to Isaac that I needed to order my food. You did not introduce me, not even as a friend.

I understand, but please know it is nothing like that, seriously. Let's go watch the movie and finish this wonderful day. I apologize.

(Smile)

As I smooth that over and we get out of the car, Honey seemed to believe what I was saying to her. But what I couldn't understand was, when I was at school and I was frolicking around with Alana, I didn't give a damn who saw us and what we were doing. I was holding her hand; hell, I even kissed her in front of the dorm after a major campus event, and there were a million people out and about who could see us. Then I get to Las Vegas, a place that I've known all of my life, and I am unable to function with a person I am truly interested in.

Something about Las Vegas put my guard up. Made me think about LaTrice's ass and the whole "playing gay" thing, and then I got sick to my stomach. I wasn't playing gay; I truly liked Honey and the time we spent together.

Do you want some popcorn?

So we get inside of the damn movie theater, and everything is well and good; Honey is smiling and laughing, and I am enjoying myself; everything is gravy-train smooth. When the muthafucking movie was over, shit shot to hell in a handbasket, and there was nothing I could do about it. Walking out of the movie, laughing and recalling what'd happened on the screen, Honey reached down and grabbed my hand. Nothing major, interlocked fingers, something you would do if you may, in fact, be dating someone. I was cool when it happened; I didn't snatch my hand away or anything. We walked on, talking and holding hands.

SENTURY ALYSE!

I turned around so fast I thought I would rip Honey's arm off, and when I saw who was calling my name, I snatched my hand away from her. So cold. It happened before I even knew it was happening.

Coach?

> *SentA! What the hell are you doing in town; you are supposed to be working on your post game.*

As Coach Francisco began to imitate posting me up in the paint, she boxed Honey out, and Honey got lost in the crowd. As I tried not to be rude and discussed season plays and my likelihood of an after-college career, I desperately searched the crowds for a sign that Honey was still in the area. Nothing. Coach F talked my head off for about fifteen minutes and then noticed her party had also left her at the theater.

> *SentA, don't forget to come by the school before you leave to go back to Montana. I have a lot of ball-players that would love to see you in their practice.*

Okay, Coach.

When I got outside, I ran over to where I thought Honey's car was parked. There was a totally different car there. I looked around the parking lot for an hour. Nothing. She was gone. Yeah, I fucked that up bad!

January 11, 2000

I don't know what it is with Montana State that they cannot get classes straight at least one damn time in their lives! I have been in school four years—that is a total of eight semesters, including this current and final semester—and, don't you know, they have NEVER gotten my schedule right! It just doesn't make a bit of sense that I always have to spend the first week of classes running back and forth, between professors' offices and the registrar's office, trying to get some shit done! The only good thing about today's run-in with the school was a new face in the registrar's office.

Hello. How may I help you?

Yes, my name is Sentury Alysé, and I am here to see someone—I don't care who—about this fucked-up schedule they have managed to give me yet again!

When you are on the basketball court, I would never think you had a mouth like that.

Listen, dude, I'm tired of this shit, and until they fix it, I am going to talk like this. Now, can you help me or not?

Are you just upset, or is this how you are?

What is that supposed to mean?

It means I've heard you were an arrogant bitch, and I was wondering if the rumors were true, or if people were just misunderstanding who you are.

In the middle of my rage, I was stopped in my tracks by what seemed to be the secretary from hell. Who the hell did he think he was? I was there to talk about my classes, and he wanted to talk about the rumors in the streets! Out of all the rumors out there about me, he wanted to discuss some old irrelevant shit!

Camden, is it?

Yes, that's what my name tag says.

Whatever, dude! I am not here to discuss what you may or may not believe about me. I am here to see someone about my classes, so I will ask you again. Can you help me, or is there someone with whom I can speak that can?

"With whom" you can speak? Well, at least I know you're an educated arrogant bitch.

Camden?

Yes.

Don't make me fuck you up. Do what I need you to do, and then get the hell out of my face. This is not the time to get on my nerves; I got shit on my mind.

I thought he was cute before he opened his damn mouth! He was about six two and had a caramel complexion. Different than the men on campus, in more ways than one, he was clean-cut and very handsome. I was so irate with the school that his inter-action just elevated me to another level, and when I finally got my business handled, I had ripped everyone in my path a new asshole.

I see you have calmed down.

And I see you are still talking.

Dinnertime on campus can be touch and go sometimes. On some days, the cafeteria can be packed, and they are almost to the point of running out of food. And then on other days, you can go in there, and they are practically giving away doggie bags, trying to get the food out of there. Nevertheless, today was one of the light days. Not many people, so it was easy to see who was there and who wasn't, and just as my luck would have it, Camden was the first and only person I seemed to come in contact with.

Sentury, I've been watching you interact—well, if that is what you call interacting—with the campus for the past four years. When are you going to stop acting like you don't see anything but the basketball and enjoy college?

WHO IS THIS MUTHAFUCKA? He was far too comfortable with his mouth and talking to me. We had never met, and he was talking about he had been watching me for four years.

Does that make you a stalker?

No, a fan.

I'm sure that's not the case.

Why do you think that?

You don't behave like a fan.

Oh, I'm sorry. Do you expect me to drool over you and follow you around, begging for your attention?

(Silence)

Seems to me I've gained your attention without doing either.

And now you have lost it.

I went on to my table and had a seat watching *Sports Center*. There was no reason for me to look around and see where that boy went; there was no reason for me to care.

Is anyone sitting here?

Yes.

No, there isn't.

So why did you ask?

Because you wouldn't have let me sit down any other way.

I'm not going to let you sit down now.

Sentury, I'm interested in getting to know you. Let me.

Why?

Because you want to.

Who is the arrogant one, you or me?

Neither.

Then what kind of comment was that?

It was just a comment, Sentury. So you mean to tell me that behavior you displayed earlier is something you want to be remembered by?

(Silence)

Let's start over. Hello, Sentury Alysé, my name is Camden Brooks, and I am your biggest fan.

January 13, 2000

This Camden fellow is a lot more interesting than what meets the eye. Well, actually, he is overwhelmingly interesting. I know I was hard on him when we first met; I guess, if we had to bond over initial experiences, we would be worse off than what we are right now.

You aren't a bitch after all.

Since we met two days ago, I've spent each and every waking moment with him. Before and after class, before and after practice, before and after his work-study, before and after the before and after. I like Camden. He is such a sweetie. He has a smart-ass mouth, but what is a little sugar without the spice? Was that corny? If it was, I don't really care too much, as long as I get my point across—I like Camden.

So you've spent four years here, and you mean to tell me you have never been on a date.

I have spent four years here at Montana State University, and I have lived to tell the tale that I have never been on a date.

You're lying!

What do I have to lie about?

Alana.

ALANA??? When he brought the White girl up, I almost shit on myself! There was no way in hell he should have known anything about Alana. Why would he? No one did; there was nothing for him to know. But he knows. Camden knows about Alana. You would think that at such a pivotal point in the conversation, I would have known something to say or do. I just sat there looking guilty as O.J. White women will get you every time.

Am I wrong?

About what?

Alana.

What about her?

Did you date her?

No.

So you still lying?

I did not know what Camden knew, I didn't know how to approach the conversation, and I had never been in such a sticky situation. I became genuinely scared by our conversation. I began to think of all its possible outcomes. What happens if I tell the truth—that I slept with Alana—and he decides he is no longer interested in getting to know me? What happens if I tell him some of the truth, and he already knows all of the truth? Then, will he think I am a liar for the remainder of whatever it is that we call ourselves doing? What if he finds what I did with Alana repulsive? What if I am just tripping and all he knows is that he saw us together a few times? Mix that with the rumors about me, and—boom!—we have a relationship. What if the what-if is all that I have?

I don't have a reason to lie.

Then tell me what was up with you two.

I need more than that Camden; I need you to tell me what you are asking me.

Let me start with this. Are you attracted to me?

Yes.

Okay, were you attracted to her?

(Silence)

You have no reason to lie, remember?

Something like that.

Did your "something like that" turn into something you liked, or something you could have done without?

I was at a point of no return; there was no coming back from this conversation. Once I answered the question, that was it.

Whatever was going to happen was going to happen with or without me.

Alana was something that
should have never happened.

                                   You shouldn't be ashamed of it.

What?

                     You shouldn't be ashamed of what happened between
                     you and Alana. I don't look at you any different for it.

(Silence)

                     You can totally close your mouth right now; I am
                     not saying anything that deep. All I am saying is
                     only God can judge decisions made by man. The
                     decision you made when you were with Alana was
                     something that at the time needed to happen. I do
                     not know all of what occurred, but I am sure that it
                     was something that needed to happen to get you to
                     the place you are at now in your life. I don't think
                     that that isolated incident defined who you are as a
                     woman or as a person in general. It made you human.

(Silence)

    Holy shit, this man, this man, this man! Camden told me that that isolated incident (Lord knows, I wish that my run-ins with these broads were just a collective one-time incident) made me human. He did not condemn me for what happened between me and another woman. He told me not to be ashamed of who I was then and who I've become now. The Lord did not bring me this far to leave me hanging. I've spent so much time hiding from what I was doing; I never took the time to accept it as something that needed to happen. I am not a lesbian. I am a woman who made a few left turns until she came to a fork in the road, and when she went to the right, she saw Camden.

> *I want to take you on the date you feel you never had.*

(Silence)

> *Give me that chance to show you something other than what you think you know. If you don't want to, I understand. But if I can read those eyes, then I think it is a yes.*

Yes.

I like Camden.

January 15, 2000

I'm singing in the rain! Just singing in the rain! La-da-da-da, da-da-da! Tonight was fucking amazing. My first date. I am twenty-one years old, and tonight I had my first real date. I am walking on clouds right now. My God, this man is nothing short of amazing. It is pouring down sleet and rain, a million degrees below zero. (Well, it feels like it. I know it can't be raining and below zero; just vibe with me for a second.) This man was still able to show me the time of my life.

It was the type of date that you only see in the movies. He came to the dorm dressed oh-so handsomely, and he had flowers in his hands; they were for me. I was completely dressed out of the norm for who Sentury is supposed to be.

> *You look amazing.*

I took three fucking hours after practice to take my ponytail down and flat-iron my entire head of hair. I went into my room-mate's stash of makeup and made my face look like that of Tyra

Banks in the early runway days, and I even had on heels. I put on heels for this man. I can't even walk in heels, and then the ground is wet and shit. All trying to impress Camden. Camden, he's worth the struggle. Anyways, so he knocks on my door, I open it, he hands me the flowers, I grab my things, and we walk out.

Watch your step.

He has an umbrella, and he covers my head so that I don't mess my hair up. He walks to the car, and opens the passenger side for me. Waits for me to get in, and then he closes the door. He hurries and gets in the driver's seat, smiling from ear to ear. I was so impressed and, most importantly, intrigued with how the night was progressing I didn't even care to ask where we were going. We drove for about twenty minutes, and then I looked out of the window.

Trampoline World?

(Smile)

I have on some tight-ass jeans and heels, a fresh flat iron, and face make up, and we are at damn Trampoline World. It was so random that it became cute, and I couldn't even be upset about the hours of preparation that came with trying to be "beautiful" for him.

So, I've never been here.

Never?

Never.

Why not?

I don't know. I guess, with basketball and everything, anything else that is physically exhausting I tend to shy away from.

Can you at least flip?

Do you see this head? I am not flipping anywhere!

Yes, you are!

I haven't laughed so hard in so long! It has been a long time since I was able to let loose. I didn't have to worry about who was watching me, whom I was mentoring, or whom I needed to impress. It was just Camden and I being big-ass kids in the trampoline park. We jumped, flipped, fell, got up, and fell again, and laughed until there was nothing left to laugh about, and then we laughed about nothing. It was great. We spent like two hours in that place. My calves hurt so damn much right now, but I don't even care (I will tomorrow in practice though). After we left Trampoline World, we stopped off to get some pizza and rest our bodies.

I told you, you were going to flip.

Yeah, and now you got me in the pizza parlor looking like a troll about the head!

At least you are a cute troll.

(Blushing)

And she blushes; she must like me.

Who the hell is she?

Sentury.

Why are you referring to me like you aren't talking to me? That shit is weird!

You like it.

You have a cockiness to you. I don't know if I should just curse you out, or if I should take it as a compliment.

*You should take it as I have taken an interest
in getting to know Sentury Alysé, and
all that comes with her.*

Are you sure that's what you want?

Why wouldn't I be?

I don't have time for a relationship, Camden.

I didn't ask to marry you.

(Silence)

*I told you I wanted to get to know you. That means
nothing more and nothing less. If at the end of the get-
ting-to-know-you period we remain friends, I am fine
with that because I have had the chance to spend time
with and develop a friendship with a woman such as
yourself. That's reward enough.*

*With basketball and meetings and curfew, it's so
hard for me to be able to get out and do things,
especially now; we are in full swing of the season.*

You're here now, aren't you?

Yes.

It's not that hard.

I must admit I was making up excuses to not have to continue this feeling with him. There was no real reason that Camden couldn't get to know me. Yes, my schedule is demanding during the season, but you make time for what you want to make time for. I want to make time for him. But what happens when we make time, and then it doesn't work? What are we even working towards? I don't want to waste my time or his on something that has the potential to not even work. I've never been in a real relationship before. What does that even look like? What does it mean to be a "girlfriend"? How do I successfully complete a task I've never tried? How do I go into something so blind? He said he wasn't asking to marry me, but we know what getting to know someone means. It means that at the end of this incubation period, he wants something to be born! Is that such a bad thing? Why shouldn't I be wanted by this man who wants to want me? Why don't I want this? What is it about me that has become suddenly fearful of the unknown?

What happens if at the end of getting to know me, you don't want to do this anymore?

What is "this"?

Whatever this is.

You sound silly.

What the fuck does that mean?

It means you sound fucking silly. I'm sure you know the definition of silly, and if not, I can get a dictionary for you.

I am being serious.

And so am I, Sentury. Do you think I would be wasting my time with you right now if I wanted this to end badly? You don't have to answer that because I am going to answer it for you. Hell no, I wouldn't.

Okay.

But I do understand that you are scared, and I will be patient with that. But for now, we are just dating; there is no commitment.

January 16, 2000

Date number two was AWESOME! Okay, so I am totally stoked right now, and I don't know why. It's as if Camden takes me there, you know? Anyways, so tomorrow is Martin Luther King

Jr. Day, and Camden is on the Black Student Council (ain't but about four people on the whole damn council, but I digress). The BSC decided they were going to put together a parade and social in the name and observance of Dr. King. Brilliant idea, wrong damn school. They had an entire hall to decorate, and about ten people showed up to do so.

Ms. Alysé?

Mr. Brooks?

What are you up to?

*'Bout to get in this cocktail of rubbing
alcohol, Epsom salt, and hot water.*

One of those days?

One of those days.

*What if I needed a favor; would that
stop you from helping me?*

*If it includes any heavy lifting, count
me out; the kid is in pain.*

*What if I promise to rub you
down good when we get done?*

*If I didn't know any better, I would think you
were trying to sweet-talk me, Mr. Brooks.*

Is it working?

Maybe, keep talking.

I soaked for about thirty minutes in my concoction, threw on some sweats, and went down to the student union to see what all the fuss was about. It was such a sad, sad, pitiful sight. There wasn't a person in the building with a decorating bone in their body, including Camden's ass. They had streamers up all wrong, wasn't no type of theme going on, just shit put up any old kind of way.

This is horrible.

What?

Camden, like for real, you guys have to start over.

Why?!

Because this shit makes us look bad as a collective unit. There is no reason Harriet Tubman should be sitting in a bus! Who did that shit? And they got poor Rosa in the chair getting her hair done by Madam C.J. Walker. Come on, people!

I spent almost six hours in the student union directing Black people on how to be Black for one damn day. They were hopeless. They had Martin Luther King quoted as saying "by any means necessary," and Eldridge Cleaver had a dream. Everyone in there ought to have been ashamed. At the end of it all, it looked pretty damn spiffy in there when I got done with them. What I won't be doing is going to that sorry-ass parade tomorrow; this was enough embarrassment for the year for me.

Thank you, honey.

I'm honey now?

After all that work you just put in for us, yes, you are honey now.

I can deal with that, so where is that rubdown happening? My room or yours?

Camden and I stopped by the cafeteria, grabbed some dinner to go, and headed back to his dorm room. Now, I am usually not all too keen about going into some boy's dorm room to spend quality time, but after all the trouble I went through with his ass and the White-Black student union fiasco, I felt it was only right to relax in his space and not mine. His roommates were stunned to see me walk through the door with him.

Sentury Alysé? Is that really you?

Last time I checked.

What are you doing here?

Really, Greg?

Camden, you aren't cool enough to know her. How did you get her here?

Camden and I are dating.

Dating? Aren't you gay?

Fuck, man! We are going into the room!

Wait, Sentury, can you sign my poster of you?

Oh, the joys of being an on-campus celebrity. Camden was so embarrassed when we went into his room I think he was almost burgundy. I wasn't offended; though, I think he went into the living room and cursed those boys out something fierce. I was used to it; it came with the territory. People became starstruck when they saw me actually being a student on campus. And they thought I was gay—nothing new, no need for Camden to get his boxers in a bunch.

I'm sorry.

Don't be.

That was wrong.

Camden, that's the life I lead. You wanted to get to know who Sentury is; that's it right there. Live and in living color. A superstar dyke.

That's not who you are.

But that's how I am perceived.

I don't see you that way.

Camden looked me deep in my eyes. I was paralyzed, and then I had to quickly turn away. I felt myself becoming emotional about absolutely nothing. When he looked into my eyes, I saw more than what I was looking for, and I wasn't even looking to see anything. Camden's deep-brown eyes were sincere, caring, and loving. I saw in his eyes the last memory I have of my father's eyes, of a man's eyes. That of someone strong yet vulnerable, someone loving yet stern, someone transparent yet inhibited—the eyes of a man. Camden gave me a sense of completion, and we had only known each other for five days. I am unsure about this whole dating-men thing, but isn't that a little fast to be looking all deep into his eyes and shit, seeing my dead daddy? Too fast for me.

What's wrong? I felt you tense up.

The body rubdown was getting so good I began to feel it in other places. That freaked me the fuck out; no way in hell I should be getting hot and bothered this soon in the game. I know with some of my chick friends I didn't have this Mother Teresa timeline, but with this young man, I needed to protect my virtue. Doesn't mean I don't want to one day maybe, if we make it to that point of dating, but not tonight!

Curfew!

I thought you said you didn't have curfew?

I lied.

I left. I had an amazing time. I know I sound crazy. Bear with me...I'm sure it will get worse!

January 30, 2000

Tonight was the night. I knew it was coming. I knew it; I knew it; I knew it! He kissed me! That damn Camden has been plotting on me, and tonight…was the night! Mon State decided to bring some diversity to campus by having a music festival with Sisqó headlining. You know someone Black had to be on that committee because half of these damn people don't even know who Dru Hill is, let alone Sisqó as a solo act.

> *Are you going to the festival?*

Do I have a choice?

> *If you did, what would it be?*

No.

> *Then you don't have a choice.*

Camden practically dragged me out of my room to the festival. I just wasn't interested in what was happening. The majority of the acts were from school. BORING! And I don't even like Sisqó like that, so why would I waste my time and energy trying to see him? That is neither here nor there because I was there, and I wasn't into it.

> *Damn, a smile wouldn't kill you.*

(Dry smile)

> *Oh, so we are funny today.*

I did what you asked.

> *Can you at least act like you want to be here when Sisqó comes on? We are dead center. You know that, right?*

I don't give a damn about Sisqó! Where is Nokio?

About nine thirty, Sisqó graced the stage, and I have to admit he was a lot better than I anticipated him to be. I found myself moving and dancing to his renditions of his hits with Dru Hill, and I even found myself doing a two-step to his new music.

So you do like Sisqó?

Sisqó took a small break so that the band could adjust the sound, and I felt Camden walking behind me.

What are you doing?

The next thing I knew, Camden was behind me with his arms around my waist. I am sure that if I could have looked at my own face, I would have laughed at myself right there in front of the world. I could have screamed. It felt so comfortable, but I was so uptight I couldn't enjoy it.

Sisqó turns around, walks to the mic, and happens to notice Camden and me.

Hey, man, is that your girl?
Yeah, it is.
I need you guys for this song. Come on stage.

WHAT THE FUCK!?!? I did not agree to be his girlfriend, and I definitely didn't agree to be put on stage in front of the whole campus. I was cursing Camden out in my head the entire time it took for us to get on the stage. Sisqó pulled a chair out and handed Camden a rose.

Have a seat, and when I finish this song, I want you to show her how much you appreciate her by your side.

Within seconds, the stage was filled with the sounds of Sisqó's latest hit, "Incomplete." Life changed for me at that moment.

I didn't care that the world could see me anymore. I turned towards Camden, and once again I was in a movie.

The stage lights were bright, and all I could see of Camden was his outline. And what an outline it was! Lord knows. Sisqó was singing his little ass off, Camden was smiling his ass off, and I was just in a state of love. A state of love. I am unsure what a state of love is, but I am assuming that if there is such thing, that is what I was in. I even found myself singing, "I just can't help loving you, but I've loved you much too late."

I must have been loud because Sisqó turned around.

Sing it with me.

I looked up at Camden and back over at Sisqó, and, all of a sudden, I must have thought I had a nice singing voice because I took the man's microphone and began to sing, "Even though it seems I have everything, I don't want to be a lonely fool!"

When it was all said and done, I had an autographed shirt from Sisqó, a picture, and a rose from Camden. It turned out to be a totally nice event. Not because of the event itself, but because of whom I chose to spend my time with.

I didn't know you could sing.

Hell, neither did I!

You lie so much!

What am I lying about?

How do you not know you can sing?

I sing around the house, but I ain't never thought nothing of it. I knew I could hold a tune, but I ain't never tried to get on the mic and rock it.

Well, you did that tonight.

I had a reason.

What was that?

The music was talking to me.

What was it saying?

(Silence)

What was the music saying to me? The song was about completion. As I said the other day, Camden made me feel the closest to completion since the last time I looked into my father's eyes, but how do I tell him that? How do I tell a man that I've known not even a month that he has given me the only secure feeling I've had since my father? How do I tell a man that I've known not even a month that his presence completes me? It was too soon. There were too many underlying factors to be considered before I made the decision to allow Camden to know that emotional side of me.

Like what would be next? If I confessed that I was falling for Camden, what would that mean; would I then have to be his girlfriend? And what the hell does a girlfriend do? Too many questions and not enough time to figure them out. He wanted an answer right then, and Camden isn't the kind of man to wait.

Hello?

Yes?

What was the music saying to you?

That I waited too long.

For what?

This.

And what is this?

Completion.

And he kissed me. That was the most passionate kiss I have ever experienced. It was as if he reacted to my words with his lips. Camden kissed me from his soul.

So are you my girl now?

Do I have a choice?

If you did, what would it be?

Yes.

Then you have a choice.

Not only did he kiss me, but I'm his girlfriend now. Sentury has a boyfriend!

February 14, 2000

What I don't understand is how I am speechless and I am still attempting to write. I am sitting in my room in the dark, and my mind is blown. I don't know what I am supposed to feel. I don't know what I am supposed to do. I don't know anything right now. All I know is I am a different person than who I once thought I was.

Valentine's Day. The one day of the year when lovers attempt to outdo other people with tokens of affection and cards written by people who get paid to write them. Valentine's Day. The one day when women get dressed up in their best attire and step out to show how proud they are of the plans that their men put together in probably less than twenty-four hours, but it looks as if they had been planning for weeks. Valentine's Day. The day my father took his last breath.

About a week ago, Camden asked me about Valentine's Day, and I gave him my usual spiel.

I usually have a game, so I don't think too much about it.

The difference this year—I didn't have a game. Camden knew I didn't have a game. Of course, he knew that. Why wouldn't he know that? I never want to talk about Valentine's Day. My memory of Valentine's Day isn't pleasant; it is one of the most painful days of my life.

I remember walking into the hospital, looking around at the nurses, and wondering why none of them would look at me. I had been coming to the hospital for weeks, and they would play with me and give me candy, but this day was different.

I went with my mom into the room where we had to put on gowns to protect us from the radiation and to protect Daddy from our germs. My usual routine—nothing more, nothing less. We walked into Daddy's room, and there weren't any lights on.

Why is it so dark?

Be quiet, Sentury!

I just wanted to know why it was so dark. I wanted to be able to see Daddy; that's why I was there in the first place. My grandparents were standing at Daddy's bedside, and I can vividly remember the way my grandmother was stroking his head. It was vicious and deliberate. It scared me. It sent me into panic mode.

What's wrong with Grandma?

Be quiet, Sentury!

At this point, being told be quiet was getting old. I snatched away from my mother's grasp and ran to the opposite side of Daddy's bed.

Daddy?

I attempted to climb up the side of the bed to look into Daddy's eyes. I've never seen such a cold glare in my life. His skin was a greenish color, and I didn't understand it because brown can't be green. Something had to be wrong. It couldn't be my daddy.

Daddy!

My mother pulled me down off of the bed as the doctors came in.

I'm sorry…

Valentine's Day. The day my father took his last breath and took a part of me with him.

> *I want to do something for you, since*
> *you are my girl and everything.*

Camden, I'm not sure if I can handle celebrating.

> *Sentury, I will never take your father's death*
> *from you. All I am trying to do is show you*
> *how to celebrate life, rather than mourn it.*

He showed up here today at seven on the dot. All he had in his hand was a piece of paper.

What is this?

> *Read it.*

I opened it up to find a printed picture of my father and me when I was a child.

How did you…?

> (Kiss)

As Camden and I walked out of the door, every few feet there were pictures of my father and me for the first six years of my life. On the trees, in the grass. He even had one hanging on the door to the student union. I laughed, smiled, and cried all at the same time. I didn't know how to react. I'd spent so long hiding from the reality that this day brought to me, and everywhere I turned, it was staring me in my face. My father's face. Daddy.

You did this for me?

Yes, I told you I wanted to do something for you.

The trip down memory lane led me to a secluded corner of the campus, where Camden had placed a table with candles and two place settings.

Want to sit down?

IT IS FEBRUARY IN MONTANA! Hell no, I did not want to sit down outside and eat. It was cold as hell, but I was so overwhelmed with emotion I needed a moment. As I sat down, I heard my father's voice coming from a speaker. I turned around to see a tape recorder playing a tape that Daddy and I recorded one day while being silly and singing "Let's Hear It for the Boy" by Deniece Williams. That was it; I fell into a full-crying fit. Camden's roommates, dressed in full winter gear, brought out our food as I cried into my plate, my cup, and my mittens that happened to be preventing me from eating anyways. Camden just smiled.

Thank you.

For what?

Tonight.

Once I got myself together, we went back to Camden's room. I was almost frozen at this point, so I snuggled close to Camden as we lay on his bed and watched television.

You don't have to thank me, you know.

*You must have gone through a lot to
get all of that from Vegas to here.*

(Silence)

How did you manage to get all
of that from Vegas to here?

(Silence)

Secrets don't make friends!

Your mom helped me out.

WHOA! My mom? My mom doesn't even know about Camden, and if she does, it isn't because I told her.

My mom?

Yes, you know the woman you live with in Las Vegas.

Yeah, I know her.

She helped me out.

As the night went on, Camden and I began to get a little more comfortable than usual. Loud kissing sounds started to fill the room as he and I rolled around on the bed as if it were bigger than a twin.

Camden, this is just a little much for me right now.

What?

This.

What is this?

Dude, look at us. We are three kisses away from fucking.

And?

And, I don't know if I am ready.

Did I mention I never had sex with a man before? I am sure it was assumed, or maybe it wasn't. If I am supposed to be gay,

The Alysé Diaries

why would I have had sex with a man? Regardless, I am twenty-one years old, and I have never even been in a position in which I thought sex was the next step with man.

Yes, I know that I am in a relationship with Camden, and in mature relationships, that is what goes on, but I had to make sure that I was doing it for the right reasons. It's not as if I were super religious and had planned on waiting until I was married, but I did just meet this dude like a month ago. I knew we were moving fast, but not this damn fast! Plus, was I just doing it because he had made me an emotional wreck about my dad? Did I really want to lose my *V* on my dad's death anniversary? I just don't think he would approve.

I am not pressuring you.

*Fucking cunt! He is so sweet
and nice he makes me sick.*

I know, it's just...

Just what?

(Silence)

Sentury, talk to me. It's just what?

I've never done this before.

Camden's smile was the prettiest thing I'd seen thus far, and that was it. He leaned in to kiss me, and he began to whisper to me.

I won't hurt you.

The longer he kissed me, the more comfortable I got. Camden didn't look as if he really knew what he was doing, but I had him pegged wrong. He was so seductive and sensual, all at the same time; it was as if he were giving a tutorial. Each move he made, he gave me instructions.

Scoot up a little. Right there.

Within minutes, we were both ass naked with our bodies pressed up against each other. Let me paint that picture a little better for you. It is midnight, and the window is slightly open; a crisp Montana breeze is seeping in. There is no light on in the room, but the streetlight outside is so bright the room is illuminated with a glow, as opposed to a direct light. Our bodies are outlined as shadows in the room. And then he said:

I need you to relax. I am going to begin.

Camden took his hand and with one motion put the condom on. I had never even seen a condom before. The next thirty seconds felt physically as if someone were ripping my skin apart. The pain was excruciating. I wanted him to stop.

Are you okay?

Mm-hmm.

I couldn't tell him to stop. While I was lying there in pain, all I could wonder about was what could be the right reason why I was in this position. I thought back to looking into his eyes and seeing the love my father had for me. I realized that he wasn't Daddy, but if Daddy were here, he would approve of the man I'd chosen to share this part of me with.

I closed my eyes tight and fought back the tears that the pain brought, and then I felt Camden's hand grabbing mine. I quickly interlocked our fingers and took a deep breath. With every pump, I could feel Camden pulsate, or maybe I was pulsating… Something was happening, and it was something that I never experienced before. The pain subsided eventually, and then there was a burning sensation.

I think you will like this.

In one quick movement, Camden's head was in between my legs. The cold of his tongue was soothing and calming. The more his tongue played with my nether region, the more I began to get flashbacks of my past encounters with Alana, Dimples, and Too Close. The memories began to overlap, and the feelings began to come back. I felt myself bucking and moaning loudly. Camden locked down on my thighs and began to press harder, and I just couldn't take it anymore.

I figured you would like that.

What he figured was right, but what he didn't know...he wasn't what I liked. It was the memory of what a woman can do to me that I reacted to. Now...I'm speechless. Emotional day, I'd say. Yeah...really.

February 16, 2000

I am such a weirdo! Ever since I lost my *V*, my mind just hasn't been right in any sense of the word. I have been rigid and short with Camden for no reason at all.

Want to go get dinner?

Why the hell would I want to do that?

Yes, why the hell would you want to eat something with your man?

I don't know what the hell my problem is! And on the basketball court, I don't know if I am coming or going, and that damn Dimples will not evaporate, as I continue to pray she will.

SentA!

Yeah, Coach?

You got sand in your ass, don't you?
Nah, she is getting dicked down these days!

(Silence)

Needless to say, we lost yesterday, and I got called into Coach's office promptly after the game ended.

Anything you want to say?

Not really.

You sure you want me to go first?

Go for it.

Who is this guy you are running around campus with? Your so-called boyfriend?

What does this have to do with anything?

Answer the damn question.

Camden Brooks.

Is that what your problem is?

What problem?

You played liked shit today, Sentury! I've been coaching you for four years; today is the first day I have ever seen you play below your potential! Your head was not in the game; hell, your body was barely in the game! What are you going through? And I swear to God, if it has anything to do with this Camden Brooks, I will be so deep in your ass you will wish you never met the bastard!

(Silence)

Now get the hell out of my office!

My mind just can't get it together. There are so many things happening to me emotionally right now; I do not know how to handle it. It's like this—who the fuck am I? Simple and complex at the same damn time.

Camden is everything I should want, right? I shouldn't regret having sex with him and making the decision that he's my boy-friend, right? He is handsome, he is smart, he has a relationship with God, and he is respectful, for all intents and purposes. He makes me smile, he holds me, he consoles me, and he sees a future with me.

Isn't that what I am supposed to want in a mate? Yes. Then why, when we were having sex for the very first time, were the WOMEN who came before him all I saw in my mind? I felt my body yearning for the touch of a woman. I felt myself wishing that the head between my legs was Honey and wondering if she thinks about me as often as I think about her. Or if I should have given Dimples's sexy ass more of a chance than what I did. What am I doing?

All I ever wanted was a normal relationship. Remember the childhood dream? I saw myself with Bruce Leroy Green from *The Last Dragon* or a man that looked similar to him. We would have two children, a boy and a girl, and we would live in a middle-class area. We would have two cars and go on family trips; he would drive and open doors for me.

I dreamed of coming home from work as a physical education teacher and a coach, and my husband would be home already with our children. Our evenings were something like *The Cosby Show*. That is what I wanted. Yes, I loved playing ball, but if I don't make it to the league, what is my fallback plan? Being a wife and mother had always been what I would revert to, espe-cially when there was no such thing as a WNBA. Being a lesbian challenges all that I have ever known.

Remember all of that. I know what I want. I have always known what I wanted; I have it in its purest form right now, and I am about to fuck it up 'cause I can't get my mind right. GET IT TOGETHER, SENTURY! This man sees you for who you are, inside and out, and he accepts it. He does not want to change you; he does not want to change your past. All he wants to do is be the man in your life, and you cannot accept that.

Yes, I am talking to myself as if I am not talking to myself; someone needs to get some sense into my head. I would call LaTrice, but right now is not the time for her to tell me how confused I am—shit, I know I am confused!

There is really no need for me to be confused though. I see it as black-and-white; there is no gray area in this. Camden is the one. Camden is the one. I want a husband. I want a family, and Camden can give it to me. There is no confusion.

February 17, 2000

Ever had to explain your life to a man? Fucking frustrating! All I was trying to do was give Camden a clear understanding of what I have been going through the past few days, and all he could think about:

> So we ain't fucking?

WHAT THE HELL? I didn't go to his room for sex. I am still sore from the original encounter. I tried to have as much patience with him as possible, but he really wanted me to hand him his ass on a silver platter.

> You know things have been going through
> my mind the past couple of days.

> Oh yeah?

Yeah.

                                Like what?

Things with us and the direction we are going in.

                         What does that mean?

*Camden, my whole life, it has just been me. I never
had to consider anybody else in my plans. Now
I have a relationship, and I am having a hard time
wrapping my mind around what that means.*

The way he looked at me, you would have thought I told that
damn fool that he had three heads and smelled like a garbage pail.

                     So you want to break up?

That is not what I am saying, Camden.

               Then what are you saying, Sentury?

*I am saying that this is all new to me, and rather
than you rushing me and making me do shit on
your time, you should take into consideration this
is my first relationship ever, and I need more time
to process what it is that you are asking of me.*

          *Seems to me you're saying that you aren't ready
for the kind of relationship I am asking for.*

You made that shit up.

                      You just said it.

You aren't listening!

              You aren't listening to yourself!

*Goddamn, Camden, do I have
to spell this shit out for you?*

                             (Silence)

I am Sentury Alysé, top basketball player in the state of Montana. I have dreams of going to the WNBA draft in April, and the likelihood of my getting picked in the first round is into the ninetieth percentile. That is all that has ever mattered to me, and then I met you. I have fallen for you, and that challenges everything I've ever thought about, even how I viewed myself. I have to consider you in my plans. I have to consider you in the life I wanted for myself before I became committed to basketball.

And what was that?

Every little girl's dream—a husband, kids, and a white picket fence.

You think I could give you that?

If you had a choice, what would it be?

Yes.

Then you have a choice.

Why did that conversation have to be so fucking difficult? Oh, I know why.

Want to go lay down?

Because he was still worried about sex! SEX! Ugh! I am disgusted.

February 21, 2000

Pray for me as I pray for myself. Sometimes I get myself into things, and I seriously do not understand how I got there. I am a straight woman, right? Don't answer that. I am. So…tell me why I cannot get this woman out of my head.

Hello?

Honey?

If I would have known then what I know now, I would have saved my little thirty cents a minute that Sprint just got me for.

Here is the thing—I just need to be the best woman I can be for Camden. Nothing more, nothing less. And if that means that I needed to go through the devil's lair with Honey, then so be it.

What do you want, Sentury? I haven't heard from you since I left your ass.

Yeah, about that.

What about it?

What was that about?

Is that what you called me for?

Part of the reason.

Get to the important part.

It is all important.

(Silence)

Honey, a beautiful woman inside and out, I hurt her with my behavior; I know I did. I hurt them all with my behavior, but she was different. I still feel for her, and to think that she hurts because of me has been weighing on my chest.

You don't have that much power over me, Sentury.

I must have something; you're still angry as hell.

I am not.

Then why are you so aggressive right now?

Because you are wasting my time!

No, because you are mad. Just tell me.

I'm hanging up.

No, you're not.

(Silence)

Hello?

Hello.

I figured as much. So tell me.
What was all of that about?

So finally, after I broke down her wall, she began to tell me how she felt about my treating her as if she were invisible while we were on our day date back when I was home for Christmas. Everything she said made perfect sense, and I didn't expect anything less from her.

> *I told you I am a lesbian, Sentury, and you were fine*
> *with that when we were alone, but as soon as you had*
> *to face the public with me, it turned into something*
> *like a disease. I live this life every day, and I cannot*
> *afford to have friends who are ashamed of someone*
> *that I am proud to be.*

Okay, I get it. I fucked up, and if I had to do it all over again, I wouldn't have even begun being friends with her so that she wouldn't be feeling that sort of pain now. I never intended to hurt her when we saw all of Las Vegas out on the town that day. I had never been in that situation before, but as I am learning, there is a lot of shit I have never experienced that this last year has brought to the forefront. When I was walking about holding hands with Alana, it was different. I don't give a damn about what these people in Montana think about me. I couldn't care less. As a matter of fact, if I had to look around, I wouldn't find one fuck to give about them, but being home is different.

My father's memory is home. My mother's friends are home. My friends are home. Thinking of all that, I cared about how I was viewed by those people. I am not trying to be something I'm not, so my initial reaction was to ignore the situation at hand and pretend things were the same as they had been time and time before. I was wrong for that.

I apologize, Honey. I never meant to hurt you.

(Silence)

To be honest with you, I do not know why I called
you. I know that I haven't stopped thinking about
you since I left, and I know that calling you was a
risk, but it was a risk I was willing to take.

Why is that?

What?

Why were you willing to
take that risk and call me?

Because you are too beautiful a
person not to take that type of risk.

The bottom line of it all is Honey gave me something no one else had ever given me, and she was still giving it to me—butterflies in my stomach. Honey's voice is so soothing that it makes me relax. I felt as if I were cheating. SERIOUSLY, am I? Honey does something for me that Camden doesn't.

It's not his fault, of course. He is a good man, handsome and sweet, but, Honey, she's got that vibe that is undeniable. If I were a lesbian, I would definitely make her my woman, hands down…IF I were a lesbian.

So what's his name?

Camden.

Yeah?

Yeah.

Does he treat you good?

Yeah.

Yeah?

Yeah.

That's cool, Sent. I am happy for you, and I wish you luck.

(Silence)

Hello?

Yeah.

Is that not what you wanted to hear from me?

(Silence)

I will take that as a no.

(Silence)

Is there something else you want to say?

(Silence)

I will take that as a yes.

In order for me to move on and be happy with Camden, I needed to get my feelings about Honey out in the open, and I wasn't quite sure how to do that, considering that I had no idea how to articulate my feelings. I wanted to tell her, "You made me feel alive, and you made me feel beautiful, and you made me want to love you," but, hell no, I am not telling a chick that! No way in hell I am going to say all of that…can't pay me to do it.

It's nothing really.

(Silence)

You know Erykah Badu's song "Next Lifetime"?

Yeah, I kinda remember it.

I never really understood it until I met you.

(Silence)

One day if you ever happen to hear it,
can you do me a favor?

Sure.

Smile for me. Your smile is so beautiful, and when
I hear this song, I will think of your smile and this
last time I heard your voice.

I couldn't tell you why I called her if it were worth a million dollars. I was yearning for something, and she couldn't give it to me. To be honest, she shouldn't have had to. I am in a relationship. Honey shouldn't have been the one I went to for validation, if that was even what I was looking for. Confusing, isn't it? How the hell do you think I feel?

After I hung up with Honey, I spent a lot of time staring at myself in the mirror and wondering who I really am. I toyed with the idea that inside of me was a woman who would one day be okay with dating women. I only toyed with it; I couldn't take myself seriously. What does that even look like? A woman who dates women? Give me a fucking break! That is not a look; it is a lifestyle that I personally am not interested in exploring, but I have to take into consideration my encounters with women as I have matriculated through this last year in school. I have given myself to those women in so many different capacities, and I have allowed them in. Honey has a piece of my heart, regardless if nothing ever happened or I allowed her to fuck my brains out. Honey was the woman, the one who—if I ever had to admit it—got away.

But in reality, Camden isn't a bad catch at all. He isn't fully aware—but he isn't a fool either—of my indecencies with women, and he accepts me anyways. Camden looks into my eyes, and he sees a different woman than I see.

I looked into the mirror hard and tried to see the woman he sees. All I saw was a fake.

Pray for me…

February 27, 2000

I love my best friend—I swear I do—but she is not the one I need in my corner during these trying times in my life.

> *So you are enjoying the sex, eh?*

There are times when she can be the best, best friend ever, and then there are times when she can be a pain in my ass!

> *Who would have thought you like dick?*

Since I've been with Camden, things have moved so fast that I have hardly had time to even discuss life with her, let alone my relationship. I should have been prepared for the conversation before I even called her.

I miss you too, Trice.

> *No, you miss Camden, oh, Camden!*

Stop it. I am being serious.

> *So are you done playing gay now?*

"Playing gay" is a constant theme in our conversations lately. I have said it before, and I will say it time and time again—ain't nobody trying to fucking play gay. I was just exploring an alternative lifestyle before I settled into my own future.

I cared about Honey!

> *With your gay ass, of course, you did,*
> *and you hurt my friend too!*

She told you about it?

> *Was she not supposed to? What were you thinking,*
> *Sentury? That's why I tell you that you are playing*
> *gay. These straight girls, you included, find it*
> *intriguing until they have to face the world, and then*
> *all bets are off.*

That's not true, Trice; that wasn't my plan.

> *It didn't have to be planned, fool; it happened! Now*
> *you swear to be caring for this lesbian woman two*
> *thousand miles away, but you have a boyfriend.*
> *Yes. That makes perfect sense.*

I do care for her.

> *So which one is it: are you playing*
> *gay or playing straight?*

Neither.

> *It is one of them! I think you are playing straight*
> *personally, but I will keep my professional opinion*
> *to myself.*

I won't say that my best friend is judgmental because that is not godlike. But what I will say is she has the tendency to speak strongly against things she doesn't understand. Yeah, that's it.

Tell me about him.

Who, Camden?

Fucking any other men?

I was just making sure.

Yeah, me too.

So I spent the next hour explaining how Camden and I met, how we began dating, and how our first time in the bedroom went. The more I talked, the more comfortable I got with the idea of what our relationship actually stood for. Those are the times when I appreciate Trice and our friendship. You have to hear the passion in your own voice for something or someone sometimes before you can actually appreciate their value in your life.

I gave myself butterflies discussing our relationship with Trice, and it made me stop talking.

Hello?

Yeah.

What happened; did your phone cut out?

No.

Why did you stop talking?

It happened.

What did?

The feeling I was waiting for.

Stop doing those drugs, Sentury.
What the hell are you talking about?

I'd been wondering if I was doing the right thing with Camden because I didn't feel the butterflies in my stomach with him, but I felt them with Honey.

        What changed?

When I was just explaining us to you, I realized that he does give them to me. It may be in a different realm, but he does, and I love it!

        I'm glad you came to that conclusion. I guess this means I am supposed to be happy for you now.

I would think so.

        To be quite honest with you, the only way I can be happy for you is if you can say that you have gotten Honey and all these other women out of your system and that you will focus on what it is you really want.

Then you should be happy for me.

I am so excited right now I can hardly even see straight! I see Camden and his purpose in my life right now, and it just excites me to no end. I think I am going to go see him, like right now…

March 1, 2000

Can't teach an old dog new tricks, or should I say you can't teach an old girl new habits? I simply amaze myself sometimes. Let me explain.

Today was my usual dinner date with Camden, and we decided to go to Red Lobster. Nothing major, nothing fancy, but it is honestly the only place in Montana where we can get actual crab legs that aren't thoroughly disgusting. Nothing was different; we walked in, we sat down, and we began discussing the article entitled "Russians Declare Chechens Defeated," which we'd both read earlier in the day in the *Washington Post*.

> *It took them six months to finally end this war.*

> *It was a Russian war, not American, so I do not understand the amount of interest you have in it.*

> *It is world news.*

> *Yeah, I know that, but no need to be up in arms about it.*

> *Sentury, do you not know the effect it has on the global economy with Russia at war with itself.*

> *No, I don't.*

Camden began to go on and on and on as the waitress walked up. A new waitress. We go there once a week, sit in the same seat, and see the same old-ass woman every week, but we had a new waitress today.

> *Hello, my name is Lindsay, and I will be your server for today. Can I start you off with some drinks?*

CAN WE SAY BEAUTIFUL?!?! Camden was on his rant, so he paid her no mind—and didn't notice me drooling over her, for that matter. I wasn't really drooling; I was just taken aback by her appearance.

> *What happened to Alma? Is she off today?*

> *No, I'm sorry; she passed on.*

Our usual waitress was old as dirt. Sorry to hear about her passing, but I was ultra-satisfied with her replacement. This woman gave me something to look at. She had a short haircut that was slightly modern. I'm thinking Monica when she first came out—that type of style, short and sassy. Her face was highlighted with beauty marks, and her lips were upside down. I am laughing at myself right now. When I say upside down, I mean she had a pouty demeanor, but her features came together to present something very pleasing to the eyes, and that was something I could deal with.

What happened to our usual old bat?

She died.

Damn, for real? How you know?

Didn't you just hear Lindsay tell us that?

Who is Lindsay?

Our new waitress, Camden. Damn,
Russia's got you all messed up.

I guess so, but Lindsay needs to hurry
up and come back so I can order.

Camden's obliviousness was all I needed. I sound sneaky, huh? Listen, I am not trying to be sneaky, but I cannot deny how I responded to Lindsay's presence. The rest of the dinner went quite well. We talked, Lindsay checked on us quite frequently, and everything proceeded nicely.

Excuse me, I don't mean to be unprofessional,
but aren't you Sentury Alysé?

All I needed was a reason to start talking.

Not unprofessional at all. Are you a basketball fan?

For the next twenty minutes, it was *Sports Center Live*! We talked about stats of the NBA, WNBA, NCAA, and even the local high school teams. Camden just looked back and forth between the two of us. I was unsure of what he was thinking, and I really wasn't interested in knowing either. I was interested in knowing what Lindsay knew, how she knew it, and why.

It came out that Lindsay was an ex-basketball player, but after a torn ACL, she decided to hang it up.

It just wasn't fun anymore after I got hurt.

I can't imagine ball not being fun anymore.

Ever been hurt?

Outside of a sprained ankle here and a pulled muscle there, no, I haven't. I have been blessed in that area, I guess.

Keep playing.

Damn, don't jinx me. The draft is in a month; I have to keep playing until then.

(Smile)

Once dinner was over, Camden and I pooled our money together and began to walk out. I could feel the tension when we got in the car, but I was so high on Lindsay I didn't even think about addressing it. We rode all the way to campus in silence, and I had a smile on my face the entire time.

So you are just going to throw that shit in my face like that?

I'm sorry, are you talking to me?

Who else am I talking to?

You couldn't be talking to me because I don't know what the hell you are talking about.

How you just flirted with our waitress.

Camden, please.

No, Sentury, don't disregard me like I'm some fucking crazy-ass dude on the street. I know what you were doing, and you do too, so be real about it.

I was engaging with someone who was obviously a fan. You are being paranoid. I don't even like chicks.

So being real is something you are choosing not to do?

If that is what you call it.

I'm only going to tell you this once, I don't give a fuck if you consider yourself bisexual, or a lesbian, or whatever. I will not be made a fool of with you romping around with women while we are together. I am not going to tolerate it. You are my woman, and this shit will end today.

I don't know if Camden scared me or not, but he sure did put me in my place—if there was a place for me to be in. If it had been any other day, I would have asked, "So if I go romping around with another man, will that be acceptable? But because it is a woman, I can't do it?" I knew that this wasn't the time though.

Now I am sitting in my room and thinking about it all over again. I am frankly tired of getting into positions which could potentially debunk the idea that I am truly happy with Camden. I am going to sleep on this. Lindsay was only a waitress at a restaurant that we go to every week—nothing more, nothing less.

I don't understand the issue when it comes to men and their views on women possibly cheating with other women. It seems to me that, if anything, cheating is cheating, no matter whom it is with. So why make a bigger deal if your girl cheats with a girl?

Pride is probably a big factor in all of that. What will your boys think when they find out that your woman stepped out on you with a woman? You weren't man enough to take care of her? You couldn't handle your business in the bedroom? All the same damn questions that normal people ask when anybody cheats.

Not that I plan on cheating or anything, but I am just saying that relationships, nine times out of ten, go through some sort of cheating situation. If it so happens to be with a woman on my end, why should it be a bigger deal than if it were with a man? If Camden cheated on me with a man, I would react the same way as I would if it were a woman; I would be mad as hell. The issue isn't with the person you cheated with; the issue is with the person who did the cheating. That's how I would approach it, but I am new to this relationship thing.

People need to check their egos at the door.

March 2, 2000

I lied to you yesterday. Maybe I didn't exactly lie, but I mistook my own actions and gauged them way wrong. I went back to Red Lobster today. I couldn't stop myself. No matter what I said to deter myself from starting the car and driving across town, I just had to see her again. And I did.

Back again?

I pulled up to the Red Lobster and tried to gain my composure before walking in and acting as if I weren't there to see her, and as I got out of the car, she was walking up. I didn't even have time to pretend that I was there for any other reason.

I'm glad I ran into you, Lindsay.
Are you working today?

> *Yes, I was just running to my*
> *car to get something really fast.*

I will be waiting in your section.

> (Smile)

I found myself fiddling in my seat as I sat down, trying to figure out what the hell I was really doing there, and wondering if there was an escape route should Camden come walking through the door. I was a wreck!

I knew damn well I had no business there, but at the same time, there was a certain draw and excitement that came with showing up there again, the very next day. I knew realistically Camden wouldn't walk through the door, but the idea that, if the planets aligned correctly and the universe opened up a vortex in the parking lot, he could show up sent adrenaline up and through my body something fierce.

> *I have a moment to sit down. Mind if I join you?*

As a matter of a fact, I do not mind. I would
actually love if you joined me.

> (Blushing)

You have a beautiful smile. Did you know that?

> *I don't know what to say right now.*

Just say thank you; that's a start.

I don't even know who the hell I was, sitting in there. It was as if I had turned my mack game on high drive, and I was going for her. And the craziest thing was, she was super receptive to me. I did not plan to go there and make a love connection; at least, I don't think I did. My plan was to go there and see her again, maintain a schoolgirl crush from a distance and then go on about my life, but it didn't happen that way.

I am not making you uncomfortable, am I?

     No, why would you ask that?

I am being rather forward, and I just met you yesterday.

    Speaking of yesterday, was that your boyfriend?

No, what would make you think that?

I said it. That is number one in the cheaters' manual—deny the liability. It came out so fast I didn't even know what I'd said until she was responding.

    I'm glad because I was thinking to myself, "Damn
     she is too damn fine to be with a square like him."

(Smile)

    You have a beautiful smile. Did YOU know that?

I don't know what to say right now.

     Just say thank you; that's a start.

I think that this would be a good time to interject again that my plan was not to go to that spot and pick up a mistress or anything like that. Lindsay Maine (I learned her last name tonight also), a twenty-three-year old lesbian pursuing a career in the arts. Acting, to be exact. Her plan is to attend Mon State in the fall, get into the theater department, and earn a degree in drama. A woman with goals.

I've never met an actress before. Should I be nervous?

     Why would you be nervous?

You may just be acting like you are interested me,
and when I leave, you will call, "Scene."

I was acting yesterday like I wasn't interested.
When I saw you today, I called, "Scene."

I left out of there feeling like a new woman. And I am not sure if it was just my being happy because she was into me, or my being childlike and excited that I got a new toy to play with, but overall today was a good day for me.

I don't know what to say about Camden.

March 5, 2000

It is clear that I don't know what I am doing—or why I am doing it—and that I am just doing shit to do it! I have seen Lindsay every day since Monday, and I have to admit I am smitten by her. I don't want to do this to Camden, so I am in a really fucked-up place right now. I did this to myself because I allowed myself to have feelings for another person, knowing that I was in a relationship, but you can't, like, control feelings, ya know?

Why should I be held accountable for the feelings that developed for Lindsay? It is not as if I went into my body and said, "Hey, heart, you see that girl over there. I need you to think she is pretty hot and want her in your life." So I shouldn't feel bad about the ways of the universe, right?

Then why do I feel like shit? Oh, maybe because Camden called this shit as if he were a psychic or some shit, and I still went and did it anyways; on top of that, I lied to Lindsay and told her he wasn't my boyfriend. Now she is interested in dating a SINGLE Sentury, and that Sentury doesn't exist. That's why I feel like shit.

This is the classic conflict between what you want to do and what you need to do, and in case no one has already learned this, I am not the best in conflict resolution. I know the difference between right and wrong. The dictionary lists *right* as "being in accordance with what is good or proper," and *wrong* is listed as "not in accordance with what is morally right or good."

I want to take a good look at what's right when it comes to my current situation. Good and proper is my wholesome relationship with Camden. Camden is an educated Black man who is caring and willing to do what he needs to do to work towards a future with me. Who am I? I am an educated Black woman in a relationship with a man who would be considered to be equally yoked. That puts me one step above the rest. I could graduate in May and work towards our lives together. Camden is the first man I've trusted since I was six years old, and he is the man to whom I lost the big *V*; Camden is what is right with this situation.

Lindsay is the wrong in this situation. The very definition of *wrong* says, "not in accordance with what is morally right." And guess what? Ain't shit morally right about my digging Lindsay. Let's start with the least obvious of all the issues involved—she is a woman. When you think of what it means to be morally right, lesbian isn't the first thing that pops into your head, right? Right. So how in the hell could I possibly consider what I am trying to do with Lindsay morally right? The second major "wrong" issue with her is I am in a relationship with Camden. HELLO, SENTURY!

She may not know I am in a relationship, but I know. I have always known what was happening was wrong, and I continued to pursue it. Like Eve in the Garden of Eden. Eve knew damn well God told her not to eat from the trees in the garden, but that little snake came up talking that shit, and she reached her ass up on that tree and bit into the delicious, succulent, juicy, and inviting apple. Whoa, was I describing an apple? Shit, I made that apple sexy, didn't I? Ha! Nevertheless, Eve knew she was wrong, but it didn't matter; she was so drawn to her…I mean, *it*…she was so drawn to *it* that she couldn't do anything but bite into it.

I'm drawn to the wrong. I do not have a snake in my ear telling me to take a bite, but I have a snake in my shorts wanting her to take a bite! That sounded so raunchy, oh my goodness, but I mean that shit! That girl is something sexy, but it is wrong, and I know better. I don't know what to do.

What I am failing to understand in all of this is why I am so prone to being drawn to something I do not want. It is almost as if Trice was right. Am I playing straight, or am I truly just a victim of circumstance? The circumstance being curiosity about what these women can do to me and what my reaction will be. It is like a drug. I do not want to do this, but there is some innate thing that keeps pulling and pulling and pulling, and then when it finally gets my attention, it's as if I am fixated until I get what I want, whatever that is.

When it happened with Alana, I was attempting to disprove her theory that we had a connection, and I failed miserably. The other three? I was testing out theories and coming up with my own in the meantime. Honey and Lindsay have both done something to me that neither Alana, Dimples, nor Too Close did; they gave me the sensation that told me I had the capability to love them.

I have the capacity to love Camden too, and I honestly think that I already do love him to some degree. If I didn't, I don't think I would be toying back and forth so hard about what I am doing or thinking about doing with Lindsay. I know that this would not only hurt him, but it would piss him off so tough he wouldn't know what to do with himself or me. He deserves more than what I am giving him right now. The crazy thing is, we have only been together like a month. When did life get so fucking intense that a month into a relationship you have these types of issues? What happened to dating, testing the waters, and just plain having fun?

I think I am making excuses so I can do what I want to do. As a matter of fact, I know I am. I know the difference between right and wrong. I can outline it 12,000 different ways, and it will still say the same thing—if I even talk to Lindsay again, I am wrong.

There isn't much of a conflict if I just do the right thing. I just want to do right.

March 7, 2000

Tonight was a disaster, and all I can say is it was my fault. There is something wrong with me, and if I don't figure it out, I will be single as hell!

Camden and I went to the Black Student Council awards banquet this evening, and we were the "it" thing to be watched.

Is that Sentury?
Damn, she knows how to walk in heels?

Everywhere we turned, someone had something to say about our being at the event together. It was pissing Camden off.

I don't understand what the fuck the issue is!

Why are you acting surprised?

Why aren't you?

Because, Camden, this has been my life. I would be surprised if they weren't shocked to see me walking around in a gown with a man.

There was nothing for me to be surprised about; all of the glitz and glamour that came with being a campus celebrity brought the ugly as well. I didn't think anything of it, and my boyfriend needed to develop some thick skin if he wanted to keep this thing going.

Stop it, Camden!

Man, fuck these people!

I understand that, but there is no reason for you to go around turning your nose up at every person you think may be saying something about me. It is not worth it.

Maybe you aren't worth it.

I will attribute that to the fact that you might be somewhat stressed out by your current environment.

The awards ceremony went on as usual, boring as hell. Awards were given, people gave speeches, and the five Black people in the room (okay, maybe fifty) were made a mockery of as the White students prepared for their own campus-wide awards gala, at which none of us ever won anything anyways.

When it was announced that I'd won Female Athlete of the Year, I was shocked. To be completely honest with you, I wasn't even paying attention. I had been daydreaming about Lindsay the majority of the time I was sitting there, so I didn't even hear them say I was a nominee.

(Smiling and clapping)

What's going on?

You won.

Won what?

(Silence)

I quickly got up and accepted my award. I looked out into the crowd, and Camden had a cold glare directed towards me. I took a deep breath and began my acceptance speech:

> *I am blown away by this; I would like to thank the BSC for this honor. It isn't easy to use your body day in and day out as your sole means of functioning, but it feels good to know that my hard work and my efforts do not go unnoticed. I would like to give a special thank-you to my boyfriend, BSC member Camden Brooks. You have definitely been more than a blessing in my life, and I am humbled to receive this award from your organization with you on my arm. Thank you and I love you. Thank you all again.*

I threw that L-word in there because I thought that he would soften up. It didn't work.

> *What were you thinking about?*

When?

> *When we were at the awards—hell, all night! You have been distant all fucking night!*

I don't know about all night, but I had been rather distracted. I couldn't help it. With Camden isn't where I wanted to be, and since I'd made the decision that Lindsay was what was wrong in my equation, I hadn't spoken with her. I missed her.

> *Sentury!*

What, Camden?

> *You were doing it again!*

Doing what?

> *Being distant.*

I think you are being paranoid once again. No one is being distant; maybe you are the one being distant. Have you ever considered that?

Camden was staring at me, and all I could do was laugh. I knew what was wrong with me. I wasn't going to tell him that shit, but I knew what it was. I was fighting myself, and it was going down like the Civil War. Camden reached out to hug me.

What's wrong now?

That hug wasn't right.

What the hell does that mean?

You aren't even here. Where are you?

You sound like a lunatic. Do you know that?

Sentury, I have been intimate with you. I have been inside of you, and that means we are now connected. When I touch you, I know what you feel like. What I just felt wasn't you.

Who was it?

I wish I knew.

I spent the rest of the night sitting and looking stupid in a gown on his bed while he went to sleep. The pain in his eyes when he pulled back from me was undeniable. He felt that my feelings had gone elsewhere, and I didn't have to say a word.

That is deep to me. The idea of after being intimate with someone you can feel that person's soul and whether or not you are connected to it; that is scary. I wonder if I go touch Dimples what I would feel. Lord knows, I don't want to touch that girl. I wonder if it is the same with a woman though? Sex with a woman is obviously different, and if you never go inside and you never exchange juices and fluids and press the bodies together and connect as one, I wonder if you get the same connection. I would like to find out. No, I wouldn't. Yes, I would. No, I wouldn't. I just want to know what he means.

I didn't do it on purpose. I didn't disconnect from him; I want him. I just want to make sure this won't be a mistake. I've already let one "her" get away.

March 10, 2000

Ever done something so wrong it must be right? Ever done something so fucked up that when you got done there was nothing to say but "damn"? Me either, but I think I was close to it today. Camden had to leave with the Black Students of America to go to some retreat in the woods yesterday, so when I got out of practice I took some time to myself. I bathed in my cocktail of alcohol, Epsom salt, and ice. I pulled out a few books and called it an early evening.

Hello?

Sentury?

Yes?

This is Lindsay.

I sat right up in the bed when I heard her voice. I didn't remember giving her my direct line to my room, but I wasn't going to complain that she was using it. After a few moments of awkward silence on the phone, I decided that she must have called for a reason.

What's going on?

Are you busy?

I don't have to be.

Can you meet me?

Where are you?

My job.

I threw on some clothes, and I made the decision to speed over to Red Lobster. When I got out of my car, Lindsay was standing by the front door with a slight smile on her face. Her smile was so fucking beautiful I couldn't help but smile my damn self.

Nice of you to come.

I didn't come to be nice.

Then why are you here?

To be nosy.

Lindsay thought that my witty answer was cute, so I went with the witty character for the evening. She told me that she wanted to take me to see something, but she wouldn't tell me where we were going.

*So let me get this straight. You call me over here to
pick you up, to take you somewhere, and you aren't
going to tell me where, but I am the driver?*

Yes.

That's strike number one.

*Can't wait to see the punishment
for making it all the way to three.*

(Silence)

While we were driving aimlessly around Browning, I asked the usual questions—where are you from, why are you here, what is your favorite color, etc. The normal "I am trying to get to know you" bullshit. Interestingly enough, she moved to Browning from Los Angeles to attended Montana State. After a bad breakup, she ended up flunking out, and she had just been hanging around the town, trying to get back on her feet since '97.

Her story was something different than I'd heard from anyone else I'd dealt with while I was in Montana. Nothing of what she had to say was about favor and fortune, no luck, no blessings. She grew up hard; she came to college to get away and then still had to struggle. Something about that was sexy to me. I don't know if it was her realness or her ability to continue pushing through homelessness, domestic violence, and a few stints of depression, but, whatever it was, it had me hooked.

Where are we?

You've never been here?

No.

Come on; my friend is having a showing here tonight. I think you will like it.

We were sitting in front of an old, dusty building in the roughest part of town. I can't lie; I was a little bit nervous, but I couldn't show it.

What's wrong?

Nothing. Why do you ask that?

Because you are walking like a cardboard box.

I'm good, just sore from practice.

As we walked into the building, I felt like a jackass! It was an art gallery, and the works inside were amazing. The farther into the building we walked, the more and more exclusive the pieces began to get. We came to an opening where a few guys were standing and looking very artsy, compared to my basketball shorts and tee shirt.

Lin? Is that you? I am so happy you could make it.

*Thank you, Alex. I hope you don't mind; I brought
my friend Sentury with me.*

*Sentury Alysé? Wow! I am honored;
thank you for bringing her.*

I guess being a household name in Montana could be a good thing. Anyways, when we walked into the room, there were about ten paintings dedicated to African-American sports figures. I was amazed and in love at the same time. They even had Dawn Staley. That was all I needed to see; I could have gone back to the door after that.

Sentury, we have one more painting to see.

But wait, she is my all-time favorite; this is amazing.

*If you want to come back after I show
you this, then I won't fight it.*

Okay.

We walked over to where a crowd of people were gawking, and then one turned around and looked at me.

It's her!

Me?

On the damn wall was a painting of one of the stills hanging up on campus of me doing a layup. I was in shock. I didn't know what to do or say. My eyes immediately filled with tears. I could feel Lindsay reaching down to grab my hand, and all I could do was cry.

The artist walks up as I am having this bitch moment and begins to speak:

About a week ago, one of my best friends, Lindsay, called me and told me she'd met the woman of her dreams. If you know anything about Lindsay lately, dreams have been nothing but fairy tales in her life, so I got excited when I heard her rave and rave and rave about this new woman she was into. I continued to ask her who she was and who she was, but she never would tell me. Finally, I said, "Well, girl, I got to go. I have to figure out who this final painting will be of for my showing. I don't have time for the games." Lindsay was quiet for a minute; then she told me she had an idea, and she would make me a deal. She would tell me if I painted the woman who was making her heart skip all these beats. I agreed because I just knew that whoever it was wasn't going to be good enough of an athlete to be featured, and I would be able to shut her down. When she said Sentury Alysé, I could have shit bricks. One of the best female athletes to come from Montana State University ever, I jumped at the chance, and here she is tonight to see it unveiled in her likeness. Thank you, Lindsay and Sentury. This was divine intervention, and I am glad you both were a part of it.

Listen, let me tell you. Hanging up in a gallery, I have a painting that looks like me because Lindsay told her best friend that I was the woman of her dreams. The crazy thing about it all is she never asked me if I was a lesbian. After she figured out that Camden wasn't my boyfriend, even though he really is, she just assumed. I am not mad about it at all, but I ain't a shit either for not coming clean, but no harm, no foul. I won't hurt her.

After I got done crying and we took several pictures, I told Lindsay I had curfew.

Do you need me to drop you off somewhere?

> *No, I will ride back to my car with*
> *Alex; you go ahead and get back.*

Will I hear from you tonight?

> *No, but I will see you same time
> and same place tomorrow.*

She leaned in and kissed me on the cheek, and I went on about my way. I am going to go to bed right now and see what tomorrow brings.

March 11, 2000

Jesus, Mary, and Joseph, I need all of you right now! I don't know what the hell is on my mind, but I am not right in the head, and if I don't stop this shit sometime soon, life is going to get super bad for me on so many levels that it is not even funny. I don't know where to begin or nothing. It is just, like, what the fuck, Sentury? Didn't you learn your lesson before? Haven't you been continually shown the right way to go? Why the fuck do you keep deviating from the plan? The Lord keeps showing me the right way. He does; I know He does, but that devil, that son of a Christmas tree… Yeah, his ass knows temptation, doesn't he? I know you don't know what I am talking about right now. Why should you? As usual, this is my ramble about my fucked-up decisions.

So remember yesterday, the whole painting and story and shit? Yeah well, I went back to Red Lobster today.

> *Glad you came.*

> *I already told you I was nosy, and with all this
> mystery that you exude, I think I will continue to
> come and see what you have for me.*

> (Smile)

The restaurant was closed when I got there, and the only two cars in the parking lot were mine and hers.

Come in, I have to finish closing up.

Okay.

We walk in, and it is eerie inside. There are live lobsters crawling in the tank, they have this oldies station playing in the background, and there is no one there to enjoy it. I continued to follow Lindsay as she led me to the back of the restaurant, told me to have a seat, and said she would be right back. The music cut off, and I thought nothing about it. All I was thinking about was what I was going to eat for dinner at the café tomorrow. I wasn't focused.

Luther Vandross begins to blare through the speakers. Scared the shit out of me. As I looked around, Lindsay comes walking up with two glasses of wine and a huge smile on her face.

What is this?

To us.

To us?

Yes, to us.

I don't drink, so I placed my glass back on the table, and then I began to recognize the setup. I knew what it was, and I was already too damn deep in to get out. Lindsay went and quickly locked the doors and turned all the lights out, with the exception of the candles on the tables, which weren't actually flames, but small lights.

I know you can fuck.

Excuse me?

Don't play with me, Sentury. I can see it in your eyes, and I want it.

(Silence)

Before I knew it, she started kissing me while trying to take my clothes off, and we were in the damn booth. It was awkward and confusing. I was trying to keep up, but little did she know this wasn't my forte. She was about to find out.

You go first.

Go where?

Down.

Fuck me.

I want to.

I wasn't talking in that way.

I had said, "Fuck me," as in "Fuck me, shit, I can't do this," but this chick thought I was talking dirty. I don't even know how to talk dirty. It was a hot-ass mess.

Lindsay took all of her clothes off and then crawled out of the booth and got on the floor. She was already so turned on that she was touching herself and moaning and shit, and I was sitting there looking like a fucking idiot. Scared out of my mind because I knew damn well I was in far above my head, but I could not let her know that I didn't know what I was doing, so I slowly got on the ground next to her.

Don't make me wait, Sentury.

The more she talked to me, the worse I began to feel. I thought back to Alana, and I remembered I had to suck on the breast for a little while, and my hands needed to explore her body. So that's what I did. I went back and forth between the two, and I used my finger to play with her nether regions for as long as I could. Then she grabbed my hand and screamed.

I want to feel your tongue.

YOU HAVE GOT TO BE KIDDING ME. I did not want to go down on her; that is kind of gross, but I couldn't not do it. She thought that was something that I did, ya know? Well no, you don't, but I was stuck between a rock and a hard place, and all I could do was go for it because my reputation was on the line. I guess it was my reputation; maybe it was my pride. Either way, I went for it.

The moaning led me to believe that I was doing something right. I started out flicking my tongue quickly and holding on to her thighs; she liked that. So then I decided that I was going to suck and blow. I think Dimples did that to me, and I liked it, so I went for it. That too was a winner. Lindsay began to squirm and squeal, and I started to think I was the shit. So I kept switching up between the flicks and the suck-and-blow, and then she started to reach for my hands. I didn't know why, so I kept going.

Go inside of me.

DO WHAT? If she could have known she was grossing me the fuck out! But I couldn't be no punk, so I did it. I took my index finger and my middle finger, and I went in. I CANNOT BELIEVE I JUST SAID THAT. I went in. Ew, that sounded so fucking gay! I did it, I did, but I said I was never going to repeat it! Oh my God!

Yes, Sentury!

While I was pretending to know what I was doing, I began to feel bad and think about Camden. Wrong timing, right? The more I began to think about him, the harder I started to go in on her. I ended up flipping her around and fingering her from the back so hard you would have thought I had a dick. That was horrible to say, and it was even worse to do.

Finally, she screamed, and her knees buckled—coming, I assume—and I pulled my fingers out and quickly went to the bathroom.

You really did it this time. Didn't you, Sentury?

I looked myself in the mirror, and then I looked down at my super-sticky fingers, and all I could do was shake my head.

You will pay for this one. I hope you are ready for it.

I had to stop talking to myself before she walked up on me, but I already knew that for every action, there is an equal reaction. Whatever the aftermath was going to be for my doing this shit, it was going to be epic.

Did you like it?

The question is, did you like it?

I loved it. You ready?

For what?

Your turn...

Nah.

Oh, I get it; you're a touch-me-not?

A what?

A touch-me-not.

Meaning?

A lesbian that doesn't like to be touched, but by the way you just fucked me, you know how to touch enough for the both of us, and I am fine with that.

(Silence)

I was so disgusted with myself I just got up and walked out. I am not a lesbian, let alone a touch-me-in-the-morning or whatever the hell it is. Camden will be back tomorrow, and this is what the fuck I have on my conscience.

I do this to myself. As far as I am concerned at this point, whatever happens, happens; it was destined this way anyway.

March 13, 2000

So…how about those Rams? Nothing? What I would give to have nothing to say these days. I knew that being in a relationship wasn't for me, and I should have just gone with my first instinct. I know what I said because I was there when I said it. I told Camden, "Look, I ain't never done this shit before. I am used to thinking about myself and not having to consider other people in my decisions." I told him that. I know I did. But it didn't matter, and I should have known that.

> *I have been out of town for the past four days. What do you mean you're busy? I am your man, Sentury. When do you make time for me?*

The story of my fucking life! I have to make time for my "man." I wasn't in the mood to spend time with Camden. I was having inner issues after my traumatic experience with Lindsay, and I didn't need him all in my ass.

I am coming over, Camden; just give me a second.

Whatever.

I don't have time for your condescending bullshit. We are going into the playoffs this week, and I already have a lot of pressure on my shoulders. I don't need you being a baby too.

A baby?

I am not going to argue with you either.
I will see you within the hour.

I dragged myself across campus to see what the hell he wanted. I have to stop right there because I sound as if I were annoyed with Camden, when in reality he had done nothing to me. Absolutely nothing. It was "just one of them days," as Monica told us a few years back. It is a woman's prerogative to be a bitch for no reason.

I know I had a reason, but he didn't know, and he really didn't need to know why I was acting like that. The skeletons in my closet have dangled enough in my rearview mirror for the past few days, and I probably needed some time with Camden to get me back to my happy place...maybe.

Your attitude has sure changed since you hung up.

Camden, don't be like that.

Be like what? Offended by that baby comment.

I apologize, but this is truly a stressful time in my life right now, and I need you to be there for me. You know we made it to the Sweet Sixteen. The first time Mon State has ever been represented; my draft number is going to be depending on this.

I thought you were rethinking the draft.

What made you think that?

Us.

What about us?

Our relationship.

Has nothing to do with me going to the draft. I have been working my ass off for this, Camden, and

no relationship is going to stand in my way. And if
that is something that you cannot deal with, then
maybe you need to rethink this entire relationship.

I didn't say that.

Then what are you saying?

I just thought, since I don't graduate until
December, you would wait for me.

(Silence)

That right there is the shit I do not like. I don't fucking get it. He thought, because we got together, I would lose focus on my dream, which is literally two weeks away from being my reality. He had the game all the way fucked up, and that was my cue to leave.

I will see you later, Camden.

Where are you going?

Back to my room!

Why?

Because that was a selfish-ass statement,
and I don't want to be here anymore.

Wait.

For what?

I'm sorry. I am just afraid of
losing you to the game.

What?

If you get drafted and you leave
to go play, then what about us?

The Alysé Diaries

157

Nothing, there is nothing about us. We don't end
because I am in the league. Would we end if
I got a job at IBM and had to move?

No.

Then what is the fucking difference?

If you go to the league, there may be
a girl there who you think is better
than me, and you might leave me.

(Silence)

Ever felt like pure and utter shit? He was worried about a bitch in the league. If only he knew what I was doing while he was out of town. I was frozen. I was stuck. It was like, wow, thank you, God. I knew there was going to be an aftermath, and it was going to be my conscience eating at my ass.

Come on, I apologize. Let's watch a movie.

I finally calmed myself enough to lie down and watch a movie with my "man," and then the foolishness began.

Stop it, Camden.

Come on. We haven't fooled around in a long time.

I am not in the mood.

Why? Because I was being honest about how I feel?

Because I am not in the mood.

Camden continued to try to push up on me and kiss on me, and I continued to move away. Not because I really didn't want to, but I really was into my guilt feelings about what I did to Camden by sleeping with Lindsay. I couldn't pull myself out of it, and he was being more and more aggressive.

Ouch!

So I ended up punching him and storming out of the room. I am not mentally in the place I need to be with Camden for us to have sex and kiss, and I am almost at the point where being together isn't the best thing for us either.

March 27, 2000

My career is over. In today's game I collided with a girl playing for Alaska Pacific University. Our knees bumped somehow, and when I fell, my knee was caught by hers, and I felt this rip and pop. The trainer said it is a torn meniscus and shattered kneecap. I was put on a plane back to Montana, and I have surgery tomorrow.

Did I mention that it was televised, and the entire country saw what happened? Camden and Lindsay have both left several messages for me, but talking isn't really what I want to do right now. In order for me to be drafted, I have to be healthy. I have to. There is no way that by May I will be physically able to even attend the draft, let alone ready to play.

I can't help but think this is Karma for all the shit that I've been doing. I threw the draft in Camden's face, and it has been taken from me in the worst way. I just need to prepare for this ride because I know it isn't over yet. Especially considering they have also announced my surgery tomorrow and where I will be having it. Thank you, ESPN…you have set me up for the ultimate trial this Karma ride will bring.

March 30, 2000

Today was my judgment day, so I am thinking, when I die, I will just get to bypass Saint Peter at the gate and keep it moving. I have said it before, and I will say it again—God knows what He is doing, and if you keep on playing with Him, He will MAKE YOU understand that He is the Almighty.

Picture it—Sicily 1923... I'm just kidding. I need some sort of laugh because this is no laughing matter. Picture it—I am doped up on pain medications and barely awake, and Lindsay walks into the room with flowers and a balloon.

Aw, baby.

I'm barely conscious, so I do not respond, and I continue to drift in and out of consciousness. I feel Lindsay grab my hand, and I can barely hear what she is saying to me. But none of it matters because it is time for another morphine shot, and I will be asleep anyways. As I begin to drift off, I see the door open, but I am so groggy I don't know who it is.

Now, everything after this point I thought was a dream until I really woke up.

Camden walks into the room and finds my hand in Lindsay's hand.

Aren't you the waitress from Red Lobster?

Lindsay looks up and gives a half smile.

Yeah, that's me. She's sleeping right now; can you come back another time?

Camden looks at her strangely and begins to walk towards the bed. He looks at me and then looks back at her.

I'm unsure about the impression you are under, but you can come back another time. I am her boyfriend, and I will be the one by her side.

Lindsay lets go of my hand and stands up.

If you were her boyfriend, where the fuck have you been? I was the one here when she got out of surgery. I have been here to help feed her and get her blankets when she was cold. I haven't seen you in three days.

Camden backs up from the bed. Lindsay then walks closer to him.

And I know you are lying because she told me weeks ago that you and she weren't together. Lame-ass nigga. Like I said, she is sleeping right now, and you can come back later when she is feeling better.

She told you what? Wait, when did you see her for her to tell you that?

Lindsay laughs and walks back towards the bed.

I've been seeing her every day since I served y'all. She even ate my pussy before she left for the tournament. Seems to me, if she was your woman, none of that would have happened. But it did, so who do you think I believe—her or you?

Camden looked as if he was going to cry. I felt myself moving, and I thought I was going to be able to speak, tell them to stop, and try to explain. With a defeated look, Camden placed on the table a card he had in his hand.

I guess you're right. You won.

Camden left.

When I woke up, I was alone, hence my inclination that it was a dream…until the nurse came in.

Girl, it must be hard being a superstar!

What do you mean?

        You got men and women fighting to be by your side.

Huh?

        I can't even get them to turn their heads and look at me, and they are fighting to sit next to you in silence while you are doped up on meds.

(Silence)

        Must be nice.

(Silence)

It was true. I would have been too damn lucky for it to have been a dream.

April 1, 2000

I'm all healed physically and emotionally! APRIL FOOLS!!!!! Ha ha! Yeah, I didn't find it funny either. Today was one of the most emotionally toll-taking days in all of my life. Including the day my dad died. Not only am I still in the hospital and still in pain, but when I woke up this morning, Camden was sitting in the dark, staring at me. He scared the shit out of me.

        Camden?

        You couldn't resist it, could you?

(Silence)

I attempted to sit up in the bed, but I was hurting so bad that all I could do was move the bed itself and not sit myself up. I could see that the flowers Lindsay had brought a few days ago were wilted. Camden stood up and looked out of the hospital room's window. I could see how heavily he was breathing, and I just waited for him to speak.

She is beautiful, isn't she?

Who?

Your girlfriend.

I'm sorry...

No need to lie. She was here, Sentury, and she's been here. I saw her here, and she told me what you did. So again I say, you couldn't resist, could you?

(Silence)

Camden's calm demeanor was freaking me the fuck out. It wasn't as if he'd turned around with a knife or a gun. I couldn't run, so I just had to sit there and take it.

Camden, listen...

I am not interested in your explanation.

(Silence)

I just want to know if you have gotten it out of your system?

What?

Sentury, let's be honest with ourselves. It doesn't matter—the sex of the person. What matters is that you cheated on me. And with that being said, I want to know if you have gotten it out of your system.

Camden had yet to face me, and I probably had about ten seconds until he was going to go postal on me. My only option to fix this was to tell him what he wanted to hear.

Yes.

Yes.

Yes.

*Good, I am going to leave now. When
I return, she better not be here.*

Camden walked briskly out the door, and all I could do was break down and cry. I was already in pain and long overdue for some meds, but the scene with Camden was emotionally intense for me. The entire room was filled with Camden's hurt, and the most fucked-up part about it all was that he still did not judge me for being with a woman. He didn't call me names or make me feel like shit for what I had done, which in turn made me feel more like shit because he truly didn't deserve my shit.

I hurt for Camden, and I know that all I can do is do what he asked of me and save my relationship. Today, the most important thing that he asked me was if I had gotten it out of my system. To me, that was more than Camden asking me about cheating; that was God asking me about this lesbianism that I continued to indulge in.

Have I gotten it out of my system? Have I gotten it out of my system? That is a hard question, but it seems to be stated so simply that I should be able to answer it with no issues. Do I think I have truly gotten it out of my system? No. Do I think that I have the potential to see another woman and lust after her? Yes. Do I want to be with a woman for the rest of my life? No. Do I want to jeopardize my relationship with Camden? No. Do I know what I have to do? Yes.

At the end of the day, everything lined up just as it should have. God took my distractions from me and made me face my faults head-on. He showed me a man who was everything

I needed and everything I wanted. He showed me a woman who was nothing but a temptation and a distraction. Though it would have been a nice idea to heed my inner feelings of conflict, I did not. This was nothing more than a learning experience for me.

What did I learn? Well, I have fought myself for the past year and a half, denying a part of me that has become more and more profound. I am not a lesbian, but I had a curiosity that was undeniable. To be quite honest, it is out of my system…for now.

Part 2

Promiscuous

*The reason that I can't find the enemy is
that I have yet to look within myself.*

—Craig D. Lounsbrough

October 25, 2005

I don't know why the hell I decided to go back to Montana; this shit is so beneath me! All LaTrice would talk about was going to this year's homecoming.

I don't see the purpose in going to a five-year reunion!

You may see people you used to care about! Like, I don't know, Camden.

Camden. Lord, please save me from the dramatics. I know I haven't written in here in a while, but I am not about to give a full recap. Camden didn't get over Lindsay. I don't know how that even works. I was sleeping with her, but he was the one who couldn't get over her. I think he became obsessed with her, to be honest. It was always about her.

I know you want to go to Red Lobster.

Not really.

You don't want to see your girlfriend?

Is that what this is about?

Isn't that what you want to make it about?

Aren't you the one who brought up Red Lobster?

Isn't that where she is?

I don't know, but I can call her and find out if it is that damn serious!

We didn't last much longer after graduation. Don't get me wrong, I was wrong for cheating on Camden, and I take full responsibility for that.

I am twenty-seven now! I do not have time for the blame game. At the end of the day, what happened, happened, and I didn't need to go back to Montana to relive it. Montana wasn't a breath of fresh air for me back then. It still isn't. A lot of shit happened there I would rather leave there. My dreams were crushed to death in Montana. My life changed in Montana. All the pain of my early twenties was in Montana! Why the fuck would I go back to Montana? Fuck Montana!

You have to face him.

Camden broke up with me while I was in Las Vegas getting things prepared to move back to Montana for good.

Can you talk?

Yeah, what's up?

There is no reason for you to come back to Montana.

Excuse me?

You heard me, Sentury. Don't act stupid. You have a degree now; it's not becoming of you.

What the fuck are you talking about, Camden?

I've been thinking…

Glad you don't get paid for that.

And you aren't the one for me.

(Silence)

Sometimes I think I can spend the rest of my life with you, and others I don't. Reality is, I'm not what you want, Sentury. Why are you wasting my time and yours? Go be with women.

I'm not gay.

*You keep lying to yourself and me. I don't
like liars. We are done. Stay there.*

I hadn't seen Camden since that conversation, and after LaTrice convinced me to go to homecoming, I wasn't even all too sure Camden would be there.

Oh my gosh! It's Sentury Alyse!

Campus lit up like a Christmas tree in Times Square once word got out I came for homecoming. I'd forgotten what it was like to be a campus celebrity. Damn, I think I missed it.

Can I take a picture with you?

People lined up to talk to me and take pictures; they had posters of me. It was so crazy. I navigated my way through the crowds to the booths in the breezeway. There were so many people it was overwhelming. I finally saw the booth for the class of 2000, and as I walked up to it, I was thrown off.

You came.

High off campus fame, I turned around smiling. It was Camden. Smile faded quick as shit! I should have recognized the voice, but I didn't.

Camden.

I didn't think you would be here.

I wasn't going to come.

I know.

Camden leaned in and hugged me, but I wasn't sure what to do. I didn't know if I should hug him back, or if I should continue to be in shock. I did a little of both. I gave a half-hug, half-twist, half-smile, half-frown deal. I think I was afraid that if

I gave in to my human-body reaction, he would feel something in me, and I just didn't want that.

Interesting hug.

Yeah, this whole thing is interesting.

Are you going to the Alumni Gala tonight?

Yes.

I'll look forward to seeing you there.

I didn't bring shit to wear to a damn Alumni Gala! I had no plans on being that formal! Why would I say I was going to that bullshit! I was so irritated with myself! I have got to do better. I left campus, and I went straight to the mall. There was nothing in my suitcase that I could possibly pull off at the gala. I've always heard the gala stories, and it was like Oscar night! I went to the most expensive dress store in the mall.

How can I help you today?

*Hello, I need one of your most stunning gowns
so that I can attend the Alumni Gala at Montana
State University tonight.*

*Oh, how fun! I have an associate that is also
going to that tonight; let me get her. Alana!*

Alana?

Fucking Alana! If I could have run out the store, I would have. I know there are probably 250,000 women in the world named Alana, but I also know my luck. That White girl with green eyes and freckles was getting ready to frolic her ass out of the back and ruin my already-stressful day.

SENTURY!

(Silence)

Alana hugged me so tight I had to push her back so I could breathe. Looking at her didn't do much for me (thank God). She looked about the same. Hair a little longer, face slightly chunky, eyes still piercing.

I'll be damned; it is really you.

Yup. In the flesh.

I hear you're going to the gala tonight.

Yup. I am.

Well, let me find something just as beautiful as you.

I sat down as Alana gracefully danced around the store, grabbing items she thought would be fitting for me. One by one, she selected gowns carefully, putting the ones back that she didn't think would match my style. I was impressed with her selection, to be completely transparent. Alana picked some pretty beautiful pieces that accentuated my body perfectly.

Wow, I love this, Alana, thank you.

It was really good to see you, Sentury, and I will see you tonight.

In my hotel room, I was a nervous wreck. Alana and Camden? He was the only one who knew about her, and I still don't know what he really knew—but, dammit, he knew something. I stood in front of the mirror and played out scenarios in my head. If Camden asked me to dance, what would I say? If Camden ignored me, what would I do? If Alana wanted to talk my ear off, what would I do? If Alana and Camden wanted to talk to me at the same time, what would I do? What would I do if what I would do didn't work? I was driving myself crazy!

I always had the option to not go! I could have stayed in my hotel room and avoided it all, but I didn't.

I have to say, you look beautiful.

First up, Camden.

Want to dance?

Per usual, my life is something straight out of a movie. Camden walks up to me and asks me to dance as Mario conveniently begins to sing "Let Me Love You." Of all the songs in the world, "Let Me Love You," a catalyst for pure emotional torment.

Why didn't you give me a chance?

What?

You heard me.

You left me, remember?

You let me.

The hell are you talking about, you didn't give me a choice.

The moment that you cheated on me you left me.

Well, if that wasn't a piercing moment, I don't know what is! Theoretically, he was right. The moment I stepped out on him, I emotionally left him. Not only did I leave him emotionally, but I gave someone else my body. A woman. I gave a woman my body. I guess to the male ego that could be a muthafucka to have to decipher and deal with. I am not too good with emotional shit (if you can't tell), so it took me a moment to regroup.

Did I say something wrong?

No.

Then what's the issue?

I loved you, Camden.

I loved you, Sentury.

That was it. That was the entire conversation. Honestly, I just didn't have it in me to have a long, drawn-out play-by-play of what happened years ago. Like, I am not the devil; I am not the same person. And to be honest, neither is Camden, so what is he holding on to? Why is this a conversation that he needed to have right then. Two total strangers (figuratively speaking) trying to connect to something in the past is asinine to me.

Seriously, think about it. Human beings evolve every day. That is a scientific fact. Every day, every experience, every minute changes who we are in the next moment. So if you calculate the amount of time since I'd seen Camden (I've already done it for you—2,009 days, or 48,212 hours, or 173,563,093 seconds, which-ever translates best for you), there has been significant change in both of us.

Why would he even want to feel that hurt again? If I hurt him so badly, why relive it for the hell of conversation? That just doesn't make sense to me. Once we said our I-love-yous and what have you, I needed to go get a drink of water. Not the fresh kind either. The spiked kind.

One gin, straight.

Hard night?

You have no idea.

I don't even drink gin, but that was the first thing out of my mouth, so I went with it. I had about seven actually. The guy was smiling and pouring, and I was pouting and drinking. At about the eighth cup, I started to feel it. I'm not a heavy drinker as it is, so once it hit me, that liquid courage, as they call it, came out.

Can I talk to you?

I stumbled straight up to Camden, who was in the middle of what looked to be a flirtatious conversation.

Give me a second.

I need to talk to you now!

I did not care about no damn woman all in his face. I'm his ex, and I come first, dammit! Well, that was an arrogant-ass statement! I liked the way it felt to write that though; I must keep it for future use. He needed to speak to me. Period.

What is so important, Sentury?

You need to hear me out.

Are you drunk?

What does it matter to you?

*You are. Sentury, are you
serious right now?*

*I'm just as serious as you were when
you gave me my walking papers.*

Sentury, look…

*No, Camden. I'm talking;
you're listening.*

I crack myself up! I couldn't even stand up straight. That gin was winning the war! Camden is the fool because, if the situation had been reversed, I would have left his drunk ass standing right outside, alone and looking crazy. But he stayed and listened to me.

I fucked up. I know it, but you were the only man I ever loved. I loved you in the midst of my basketball career, which had my heart. That is a big deal for someone like me. College served as a learning experience for me on so many different levels. You were my hardest lesson.

How?

Because you proved to me that someone could stand up to me. Someone who would, despite their love for me, choose themselves. I respected you for that, Camden, even if my actions showed otherwise. When you told me to stay in Las Vegas, that was a pain I'm unsure if I can put into words.

You didn't care, Sentury. This is the liquor talking. What did you drink?

That's where you're wrong. I did care. I cared a lot. I hated Montana, but I was willing to pack up and move here to be with you. You couldn't see the value in that because all you saw was your pain. I get it. I wasn't shit as a girlfriend. I wouldn't have wanted to deal with me either, but that doesn't change the facts.

What are the facts?

I loved you, and I never meant to hurt you.

That's all I ever wanted to hear.

Camden kissed me. Right then. Took my damn breath away—the amount of passion and forgiveness in that kiss. That was it. Forgiveness. In his kiss, I felt his pain leave, I felt his heart heal, and I knew in that moment that he would be okay. We would be okay. I'm only twenty-seven, so I can't say that I've spent a lot of time in my life on love. I haven't; as a matter of fact, I can count on one finger how many times I've loved, but I do know this is something that needed to happen. I may have been drunk, but energy doesn't lie. His energy was clear, and he now had closure.

October 26, 2005

WHO THE FUCK THOUGHT IT WAS A GOOD IDEA FOR ME TO DRINK GIN? Not only do I have a killer headache, but if what my brain is telling me happened really happened, I have made one of the worst mistakes of my life! Oh, I guess you can't read my brain, but I will say one word: ALANA.

I really need to get my bearings and think about what happened last night, but from the looks of my hotel room and the fog in my brain, I need to retire from drinking before I even started. Let me just think for a moment.

Hey, Sentury.

Alana. Damn it. I should have known that engaging in a full conversation with her while under the influence would lead to no good. I haven't even thought about Alana since college, to be quite honest. There was nothing to think about; I've had other shit on my mind.

How have you really been?

See, that was such a loaded question, especially for a drunken woman who just felt as if she had done something wrong. It led me down a rabbit hole.

And then I told him "I loved you, and I never meant to hurt you." Then he kissed me.

Did you like it?

Like what?

The kiss.

No!

Why not?

Because I don't want him kissing me!

Has your taste for him changed?

Taste for him?

Your yearning. Your desire. Your need.

*(Laughing hysterically) I never had any
of that for him in the first fucking place.*

You had it for me.

Damn that girl! I sobered up really quick, for a moment anyways. How in the hell is she always able to draw my mind back to that night of our encounter? She is so magnetic it is ridiculous. Even how the words flowed from her lips hit me like a sensual asston of bricks.

Crazy thing is, in the moonlight, she was actually very beautiful. Her postcollege weight fit her remarkably well. She wore one of the gowns she'd originally shown me. It was a very, very soft pink that made the color almost look white next to her white skin, but the freckles that accentuated not only her face but her body brought the color out that much more. Those green eyes though. MY GOD! Piercing is an understatement. The green in the moonlight was like emeralds in the highest on high of crowns. I was mesmerized as she moved her body closer to me and placed her lips near my drunken ear.

Come home with me.

Okay.

I'm not that difficult to deal with. She asked, and what else was I doing? Not a damn thing. I had no damn business doing this either, but, hey, I went.

You have a really nice place, Alana.

> *Thank you, I worked really
> hard to get it just as I like it.*

Her damn house looked like her! I mean, not really, but you know what I'm saying. It had the same vibe. There was nothing dark in the entire house, even down to outlines on the damn paintings. Light colors, airy feeling, just as if I'd almost walked into a cloud.

I felt woozy, so I sat down on the couch, which was just as soft as she looked. Moments later, "Nothing About Love Makes Sense" by LeAnn Rimes filled the room. I don't listen to country music! My drunk ass was just bopping to the damn song. It was the chorus that got me.

Boom! I started crying. Balling. Fell right over on the damn couch. If I could have slapped myself, I would have. *Sentury, get yourself together! In here, doing all these extras with this charismatic-ass White girl, you know better! She got your simple ass once.* These are all the things that my sober mind was telling my drunken, emotional self.

I wasn't listening though. I was ridiculously out of control with the waterworks. I am so embarrassed. I looked up with my running-down makeup and hair all over the place (I have no clue how that happened), and Alana was standing in front of me.

> *Let me help you.*

That was it. Alana turned on her Alana charm, which had already been on level twenty-five. So when she turned it up to one hundred, I was out for the count.

Alana stood over me and placed her hand so gently on my chest; almost like a magician, she pushed without touching me, and I lay back. It was smooth and deliberate. It was just as scary as it was sexy. LeAnn Rimes continued to sing in the background, but the songs blended together, placing me in a rhythmically induced trance as my eyes never left Alana. Alana was commanding in her movements as she threw her head back and unzipped her gown. Everything began to move in slow motion in that moment.

Do you like what you see?

To be honest, my vision was slightly blurred, so I didn't answer her. Alana's body moved to the music, and, damn it, that girl had every bit of Black-girl rhythm. Once my eyes finally focused, I realized she never had on any undergarments. Her breasts were beautiful.

Give me a moment; I just vomited in my mouth. I can't believe I said her breasts were beautiful. I mean, they were; for what breasts are supposed to look like, hers were perfect. She was also perfectly trimmed in her nether regions. I tried not to focus on these oddities as I needed to brace myself for what I knew was coming.

Let me be the first one to say, for someone who isn't gay, I sure don't have a problem letting the White girl take advantage of me. I know. No, I don't, but I know the shit is weird. I can't put my finger on it, but it is like a forbidden-fruit thing. I know I don't want it, but it is right here, dangling in my face. Am I not supposed to taste it? I tasted it before. It's familiar, and it doesn't jeopardize who I am because I am secure in that. It's something to do. She was something to do.

If I hadn't been drinking, I would have made a different decision; I'm sure of it. But since I was…why not?

It's been a while.

I can tell.

Alana didn't even waste time trying to get me out of my tight-fitting gown. She threw the bottom of that shit up so fast I reached down to see if it had ripped. No rip. Even in her aggression she was smooth. Two points for Alana.

Turn around.

I was slightly confused at this instruction, and the whole body-turning while the room had begun to spin was quite much. I found myself on my stomach, but bent over the couch, knees on the ground, with my chest and face buried in the couch. I held my breath, waiting for her tongue, which I anticipated to be cold, but it never happened. I closed my eyes and took a deep breath as I felt my body throb with anticipation, and there was nothing. I was too out of it to inquire, so I just kinda sat there as I realized Alana was nowhere near me. I tried to turn my head and locate her in the room, but as soon as I did, I felt her fingers inside me, and my focus soon changed again.

How do you like that?

(Moans)

Good.

Alana must have had two fingers working overtime because at every thrust it felt as if my walls curved to her and welcomed her in. I honestly think I either fell asleep or blacked out, because it turned into a complete cinematic dream sequence. I had never experienced shit like that in my life, and, to be honest, I'm not sure if that really happened or if it was a dream.

Picture it—Sicily 1912... Sorry, I think I am still drunk. Okay, so picture it. I'm on my knees, my face is smushed into the couch, and my ass tooted up in the air; Alana is standing behind me. Can you see it? Okay, great.

Now, picture this—Alana removes her fingers and begins to put them in her mouth while she uses her other hand to masturbate. Yes, my face is still down and ass still up. Now, picture Alana's moaning getting louder and louder as she suddenly stops and turns me over before pulling me down off the couch until I am flat on the floor. Alana stands over me and then drops into a split between my legs. All of a sudden, I am in a yoga position.

I swear to you! Let me look it up; give me a second. Okay, found it. She had me in a mix of the sleeping hero and the reverse plank. Let's just say my body ain't bent like that in a good long while!

Anyways, once she got into her position and the music got good to her—my goodness. Alana ground and slid and bounced, and did everything she needed to do to cause what I will call a mild explosion between my legs.

When I woke up, I was in my hotel room.

October 27, 2005

I'm sure that when I made the decision to go to a PWI (predominantly White institution), my sights were set on dominating in basketball, and that's it. There couldn't have been anything else appealing about going to an all-White school, especially homecoming. Let me take this moment to truly show my envy and appreciation for Black students who had the HBCU (historically Black college or university) homecoming experiences that I did not.

Let's first talk about the energy on campus the week of homecoming. PWI campuses are always filled with spirited people.

They wear school colors, pigtails, and shit. They jump around on campus doing chants and building up the football team for the game on Saturday. That's the purpose—making sure the football team is pumped up and has been encouraged to beat some rival school.

There is a high-school-styled coronation in which some eighty-year-old is crowned Miss Alumni and some blonde-haired, blue-eyed girl is crowned Homecoming Queen. They then get to pull onto the football field in their rose-decorated cars and are introduced to the entire stadium. That's it. A pep rally is held in the gym the night before the game, and after the game, there are usually a series of frat parties with kegs, drunk White girls, and overachieving White boys who use homecoming week as an excuse to no longer be corporate and to revisit their frat-boy days. Exciting.

At an HBCU, however, the energy on campus is something different. Let's start with the lineup for the week. Comedy shows (with famous people), concerts (with famous people), a big-deal coronation in which they crown kings and queens and celebrate the excellence that is the Talented Tenth (the concept defined by W.E.B. Du Bois, which is not taught at PWIs, but that is for another entry). An HBCU campus turns into the who's who of alumni and current students. People come out in their best attire because what you cannot do is look worse than what you did the last time everyone saw you. As the football game gets closer, campus is one big-ass family reunion. Cookouts, the Divine Nine (quick history—nine historically Black fraternities and sororities), campus celebrities, and Black people on top of Black people.

Oh, but the day of the game is the real show. The morning starts out with a parade for the masses, and whatever city the school is in is ready and willing to show up and show out in support. The entire queen's court arrives along with the band, the football team, the organizations, and they all lead the crowd straight to the stadium. At the stadium is the tailgate. Now, PWIs do tailgate, don't get me wrong, but ain't no PWI tailgate got ribs, chicken, and potato salad! At an HBCU tailgate, you getting BBQ, macaroni and cheese, top-tier drinks, and good music.

Once the game begins…again, a fashion show for the masses. While most of the older alumni will wear school colors and insignias, anybody under fifty is dressed to impress. Ain't no paint on the face and fat bellies out like the White folks. Black people be clean! The game is where you will probably see every ex you ever had, every man you had a fling with, and a woman too if you're like me (it's a joke—laugh, dammit). The football team comes out with more vigor than ever, but the real treat is the HBCU band's halftime show.

People come from all over the world to see these bands show up and show out. Remember the movie *Drumline*? That cute boy, um, Nick Cannon starred in it. That's your entire reference. Ain't nothing else to say. Those bands and drum majors take the field, and people forget the football team even exists.

The music fills the air for blocks, and it brings an entire community together. The band plays some new cuts from the radio, gives you a taste of the early hits of life, and then brings it home with a finale to die for. It makes everything up to that point worthwhile; it gives you a reason to come home.

Now, I'm not sure if you can tell, but my favor is for the experience I did not get, but can't cry over spilled milk, especially after the day I had today.

I found a cute-enough Montana State University hoodie, threw on some tight jeans, pulled my hair up in the tightest bun I could create, and headed to the stadium. The stadium was just as I expected, overpacked and undersaturated with anything worth my time.

Sentury Alyse!

People called my name left and right. I had on sunglasses for a reason, but who the hell am I fooling? I am the truly the tallest Black girl who has stepped foot on this campus in years. They know me! I stopped and smiled, kept walking, and stopped and smiled a few times. Then I realized if I kept walking around, I would have to keep pretending this was something I wanted to do. So I found a seat and sat my ass in it.

Let me honest, I wish I'd had more friends while I was in school. I had my teammates, but when you are the captain and you are the example, you don't have time for much. So I missed out on the fact that people forged bonds in college that last a lifetime. I was always alone in college, just as I am always alone on campus now.

Excuse me, aren't you Sentury Alyse?

Yes, and you are?

(Name Omitted)

Darling—well, that's what I'm going to call her—was one of the most beautiful Black women I ever saw. I was actually surprised that she was there.

You go to school here?

I used to.

She was older than I was, and I had never seen her before.

*Cool. Well, I'm sitting alone, so
these seats are open. Pick one.*

I like this one next to you.

That works too.

Darling was simply amazing. I mean, a delight. We sat there and talked about everything from her experiences in Montana to mine and my failed basketball career.

*When you got hurt, did you
think your life was over?*

Think? I knew it was.

Are you still alive?

(Silence)

*Well then, your life wasn't over.
Just that part of your life ended.*

I'd never really thought about it like that; I'd truly seen it as my life crumbled when basketball crumbled. I spent all these years slightly bitter about not being in the WNBA. I didn't watch games and wasn't supportive, all out of pain and shame. Darling changed my mind in two hours.

Sentury?

Hey, Camden.

*Hello, Camden.
Are you another one of her toys?*

THIS DUDE! Nobody asked Camden's ass to not only start talking, but run his mouth like some fucking diarrhea.

Really, Camden?

Is it beneath you?

No, but you are.

Camden didn't like that comment at all. He stormed away. Jealous, I'm sure, but of course I had to then explain.

About that…

Camden, your ex, I'm aware.

Wait. What?

Sentury, just because you were clueless as to who I am doesn't mean I had the same naïve experience upon sitting down with you.

I'm listening.

I saw you and saw it as my chance.

Chance at what?

You.

I have a date before I go back to Vegas. Who knew?

October 28, 2005

I can't lie. I am floating on cloud nine right now, and there is nothing anyone can say or do to bring me down. For this to be the night I want to be my last ever in life in Montana, it sure went out with a bang. Not a literal bang, a figurative bang, but a bang nonetheless. Look at me saying *nonetheless*. Darling says *nonetheless* all the time. Maybe not all the time, considering that we have only known each other for about thirty-six hours, but in our time talking, she has said it at least twenty times.

Sentury, why don't you tell me about you?

You're here with me.

Nonetheless, I want to hear about you.

Darling was what I would call invigorating. Full of energy and inviting. Anything she said I leaned into the word as if I was waiting for her to give me something. She wanted to know about me, and, dammit, I wanted to tell her.

My father died when I was six, and I feel
like I haven't had a parent since.

Your mom has passed on too?

Might as well. The woman who I knew as
my mother changed the day my father died.

Why do you say "died"?

Because that's what happened.

Do you not believe in the afterlife, heaven,
hell—you know, another realm?

I know that my father was in a casket, and
there has been nothing after that for me.

Nonetheless, do you not believe in the afterworld?

The afterworld has never really been a thought to me, other than going to hell for letting women play with my vagina when I was in college (plus that encounter with Alana the other day). When I think about my father's death, the resting place of his soul is really never on my mind. If you've ever lost a parent, then you understand the numbness of it all. If not, I honestly cannot explain it.

When you are born, a bond is developed with the humans who created you or stepped in to take your parents' place. There is a love that develops before the brain, a feeling before consciousness. That is something that does not change. A parent is a feeling that cannot be replaced, so when that is taken from you, no matter who is in your world, your parents will never be replaced. Because of this, the ability to fully comprehend the person not being in the physical world anymore is something that I do not have, so how in the hell was I supposed to articulate to myself or to anyone else where his soul may be.

Let's go get something to eat while
you explain to me what you think.

Honestly, Darling, I don't "think" anything.

You must think something. How do you
rest at night, knowing you have lost
the first man who ever loved you?

I don't.

What she was missing was that I do not live in the death of my father.

Let me explain that a little deeper. Death
is a state of being as far as I know.

So, you do acknowledge that there is a state
of something in that which you call death?

What I'm acknowledging is the fact that if someone
is no longer alive, they are dead, and that is a state of
being that is something other than what they were.

Are you getting angry?

No, why?

You're changing.

What does that mean?

It means exactly what I said. You're changing. As
this conversation progresses, your body language,
aura, and stance have changed. It has caused
aggression in you. I don't want to upset you, love;
I just want to help you unpack what you don't even
know was packed.

Damn it! She is like a fucking celestial being! The way she even handled me in this conversation. Hell yeah, I was getting mad! She was asking me about some shit I didn't want to talk about! She didn't even flinch! I had to look up the word *aura*— "the distinctive atmosphere or quality that seems to surround and be generated by a person." What does that even mean? No, seriously, what the fuck does it mean? She has to be celestial or crazy, because when I look at people, I don't see no atmosphere! Who does? When you look at people, do you see the atmosphere around them? Of course you don't; you're a notebook. Let me not tell anybody else that I just asked you this question. We can keep it between you and me. I did it again, huh?

> *This is all I want to say about this, Darling, and I am going to start with I'm not angry. Uncomfortable, maybe, but I am not upset.*

> *You're definitely upset.*

> *What'd I just say?*

> *It doesn't matter what you said. I feel it and I see it. Nonetheless, carry on.*

> *My father, in his human form, was my heart. He was all I ever loved and wanted. When he left this world—whether he went somewhere or not—he left me here on earth to deal with everything alone. I don't want to dream of an afterlife that involves him because that means I have to grapple with the fact that he chose a life without me.*

> *That's deep.*

> *Thank you.*

> *Dangerous, but deep.*

I let the dangerous comment go. I wasn't looking to make a night of going back and forth with an alien.

We decided that we should get a bite to eat before I went back to my hotel and she went back to wherever the hell she was going. I didn't ask because I didn't really want to know. If I would have asked, it would have put me in a position to then maybe have to invite her beautiful ass back to my room. No, thank you. I have had enough of the lady life this trip; I will save it for the next trip that will never happen.

Feel like burgers?

Burgers sounded safe as hell to me. There was no reason for me to think that walking into a burger joint at midnight would cause me anything other than heartburn. I'm getting old; don't judge me.

Lindsay?

Yes. It was Lindsay. I was smitten all over again. I could smell her before I saw her. You know the feeling of déjà vu? The moment you know you've been there before, you've smelled that scent in the air, and you remember the instant when you were there the first time, in your mind anyways. It hit me like a ton of bricks.

You know her?

Who?

That girl that keeps staring at you, and the one you can't seem to stop blushing about.

A fucking alien if I've ever met one! I couldn't hide it, and at this point, I didn't want to, so I told Darling I would be right back.

Can I speak to you for a moment?

(Silence)

Ouch. I can't even lie to you—when she just stared at me and didn't say a word, it hurt my feelings, kinda sorta. Wasn't a big deal. She was just as surprised to see me as I was to see her.

Lindsay, please.

(Silence)

She got up, reluctantly leaving her table of friends, who began whispering as soon as we got two steps away from the table. Across the room was Darling, watching so intensely she must have been reading our minds as we spoke.

Where have you been, Sentury?

I went back home.

I guess phones don't work in Las Vegas.

I didn't know you wanted to hear from me.

Why are you here?

Montana? Or this restaurant?

It's obvious why you are here to eat.

With a look of sarcasm and hurt, Lindsay nodded her head in the direction of Darling. I don't know that I cared enough to explain, but I did feel the urge to reassure her. Not sure about that either—why it would have been important—but, you know, whatever.

Lindsay, I just met that girl.

Figures.

What's your deal right now?

I'm sorry, Sentury. I'm being a bitch because
seeing you here with someone else wasn't
something I was ready for. I didn't even
know I wasn't ready until it happened.

If I would have known…

Yeah. I know.

I leave tomorrow evening if you…

I do.

That's why I am on cloud ninety-nine, not just cloud nine. Tomorrow I have a date with the only woman who kinda had my heart (there is Honey, but you know that's a special case). Oh, Darling—yes, she was too much for me. When I got back to the table, it was 101 questions about Lindsay, her sign, her birth chart, her aura, the change in my presence once I saw her, and all of that. I was too damn happy to have seen Lindsay to be dealing with the extra. Don't get me wrong, Darling is beautiful, but Lindsay is definitely more my speed.

October 29, 2005

Idiot! Yes, I am an idiot, and ain't no other word to describe me! There is no possible way in hell I could have thought that any of this wasn't going to go the way I planned. Shit don't work like that, not shit in my life anyways. I am huffing and puffing as if I were not an athlete, sitting on this fucking plane because I almost missed my damn flight! Who does that? There is no known reason as to why my ass shouldn't have been here on time—oh yes, there is. Lindsay!

What time is your flight?

Six.

In the morning?

That time has already passed.

Oh, that's right.

I should have known it was going to be some bullshit when I had to remind her it was nine in the morning, so the idea that I was leaving at six in the morning was dumb! Stupid! Idiotic.

So here was the plan; *was* is the operative word in this sentence. I had to check out of my hotel by noon. I was going to take my rental car in early, leave my bag with the airline, hop in the car with Lindsay, spend the day with her, and then be back in time to make the flight. Sounds seamless, right? Wrong!

I'm on my way.

I'm standing in front of the airport for at least two hours. I'm not sure if you know much about Browning, Montana, but I can tell you this much—it ain't that damn big! It doesn't take that long to travel anywhere. Period. In two hours, I could be knee-deep into Canada. But trying to get from point A to point B? No!

I'm stuck in traffic; do you see any taxis?

Sure.

I hop my ass in the first cab and have them take me to our favorite restaurant—Red Lobster. It takes me all of forty minutes max to get there. She's not there. Let's be honest here. It's fall, so it isn't the warmest weather in America at this very moment, and my belongings are at the airport that I am not at. Okay, sure, so I go inside, get a table for two, and ask for a nice hot cup of tea. Let's say at this point it is around 2:30 p.m. Still plenty of time for eating, fellowship, and even a kiss, if desired, before my flight boards at 5:20 p.m. Again, seamless, right? WRONG!

Would you like to order your food?

No, I am still waiting for my friend.

Okay. Well, let me know.

I will. Thank you.

At this point, I have called Lindsay so many times, but I have gotten no answer. My cell-phone battery is starting to dwindle, and I have no idea what I am supposed to do.

Lindsay, I have called you a million times. Where are you? It's damn near four, and we have to eat and then take the ride back to the airport! Where the hell are you?

Are you talking about the Lindsay that works here?

What?

That's who you're waiting on, right? The Lindsay who works here.

How do you know that?

She was here about an hour ago, and she said you were waiting for her.

Where did she go?

She left.

What?

She left.

What the fuck? Why?

I don't know. I thought she was coming back.

Just then, I looked down at my phone, and a text message has come through: *Have a good rest of your life. Lindsay.*

The waitress stood looking at me as if she felt bad for me. I am sitting there mad as hell because I'm hungry, I'm stranded, and I've been stood up! Did I mention that, before I could respond, my phone died? Dead. Where was my charger, you ask? At the airport with the rest of my shit!

Imagine having to not only deal with the emotion of being stood up, but having to beg the people at the restaurant to call a cab for you, without any contact information for them to give the cab company because your phone is dead, so they can't call you back. Then, finally getting in a cab, HUNGRY, and getting stuck in 5:00 p.m. traffic to the airport, arriving late, jumping out of the cab, and forgetting to pay because of the stress from all of the other things that have gone wrong. Naturally, the next thing to follow was backtracking and paying the cabdriver, running through security, and then being the person the fucking plane was waiting on—and all you've got to show for it is a text message that says, *Have a good rest of your life. Lindsay.*

Yeah, I'm an idiot.

November 3, 2005

I must say, I love my best friend. Like, I love her; there is nothing other than love that I have for LaTrice. Being friends with someone for so long results in an advantage that some people don't have. We know each other. We know the good, bad, and indifferent about each other, and there is no judgment. I know all her business, and she knows all mine. To take it a step further, she knows every secret, even the ones I don't want to share with myself. She knows.

White girl again? You like that pink pussy, don't you?

You're gross.

>*You keep sleeping with women with pink
vaginas, but I am the gross one? Right.*

Go to hell.

>*At this rate, I'm sure we will have box
seats in hell—the lezzie and the ho!*

We can say whatever we want to each other, and there is no offense whatsoever. Friendship is something that I value, especially with her. I do want to say, though, if I hadn't had LaTrice, I don't know what I would have done. When my dad died and my mom checked out, Trice was the only person who still treated me as if I was normal. Teachers, grief counselors, and anyone who knew turned me into the "girl whose dad died." LaTrice didn't. She and her family came to the funeral and the house afterwards. While everyone was wallowing in the sadness of the loss, LaTrice was not.

>*Want to play dolls?*

She took me out of that element and put me in my own. She was only six, but so intuitive; she knew who I needed her to be in that moment. And now, twenty years later, it is the exact same thing. I couldn't be more grateful for her.

>*Sent, come on, be honest with yourself. You
don't see that you are attracted to women?*

No.

>*Stop! You just told me an entire story about this beau-
tiful Black goddess that you've nicknamed Darling.*

And.

>*And, I wouldn't have called her a beautiful
Black goddess if you hadn't said the shit first.*

I never called her that.

Hello? I never called her that.

> *You might as well have.*

How?

> *(Terrible imitation of me) Trice, you should have seen her. She was a pretty shade of brown, and she talked like a celestial being, and she was articulate, and smart, and her hair, and this, and...*

I get the point, but I never said goddess.

> *Nevertheless...*

Nonetheless.

> *Interrupt me again.*

(Silence)

> *Like I was saying, you don't go around calling women beautiful with goo-goo eyes if you don't like women. I may say someone is pretty and move on, but you have a habit of seemingly falling for women you don't want.*

Who?

> *Lindsay.*

Next.

> *Honey.*

Next.

> *Darling.*

Okay, I see your point.

> *You don't, because if you did, you would stop and think about the things you are saying and realize they*

do not match with your actions. You could have slept
with Camden, but you slept with the pink vagina.

Stop saying that.

Pink vagina.

Couldn't have slept with Camden.

Yes, you could of.

How do you figure that, LaTrice?

Ow, you said my whole name. Say it again.

Stop it, Trice; this is serious, and I am trying to
hear you out even though I know I am not gay.

Camden was happy to see you, based on how you've
described his reaction to me, so had you not been
smiling with the White girl, and drinking, and
being aggravating as hell, he would have definitely
taken you home that night. You fucked that up.

I didn't want to go home with him.

Exactly my point.

What is your point?

You wanted to go home with a woman. Where is the
disconnect here? Are you embarrassed by it? Do
you feel uncomfortable talking about it? Because
you can't possibly be this fucking naïve and think
what you're doing and have been doing for years is
straight behavior.

Correction, before last weekend, I hadn't been with a
woman since college. That's about five years, give or
take, so in reality I haven't been doing this for years.

Are you stupid?

That's rude.

                                    Are you?

Am I what?

                                    Stupid?

No!

Leave it to Trice to send me into a mental and emotional tail-spin. In case you missed the debate, I really do not think I am a lesbian. I think that I enjoy the attention I get from women, but I prefer to be with men. That's it; that's all. No, I haven't been with a plethora of men, nor do I have an interest in doing so. Reality is, I have slept with more women to date than I have men. That didn't feel good to say, but that is the reality.

Camden is the only man I have ever slept with. Then when it comes to women, well, we know what my body count is looking like there. I still do not believe that I should be painted with a scarlet letter *L*! Hear me out on this, but I truly believe in this ideology.

Boy meets girl; girl likes boy; boy and girl sleep together. You following me? Girl meets girl; girl likes girl; girl sleeps with girl. Got that? Girl doesn't want a life with girls; girl wants a life with boys. This math will always equal straight, no matter how you add it up.

Let's explore this a little deeper. How could I really be a lesbian if Camden is the only person to have broken my heart? Riddle me that! I don't know about you, but that was my very first and, hopefully, very last heartbreak. Let's walk through it, shall we?

Heartbreak was a dark place that I never knew before Camden. It felt as if someone had taken my oxygen away and was giving it to me in rations. Gasping for air in a world filled with air had to be the single worst feeling next to losing my father. I remember when I hung up the phone after he told me not to come back to Montana. I was frozen. Frozen in time, frozen in the moment, frozen in the words. The tears began to fall, and I couldn't even control them. With those words, he ripped into my soul. I don't know if it was rejection or pain that I was truly feeling, but I do know it hurt, and it hurt bad.

I couldn't focus. It was as if something had come into my brain, put a brick wall up, and dared me to penetrate it. I stayed in bed for days, not that my mother noticed anything was wrong. She is in bed all the time, her damn self, so how could she possibly notice that I was not all right? LaTrice noticed—didn't matter much, but I felt better knowing someone would realize if I disappeared from the face of the earth. Not much better, but better.

I remember when I was in college and Faith Evans released her *Keep the Faith* album. One night I was up late—studying or coming back from basketball, I really don't remember. I put the CD in my stereo, and I let it go. Nice album, some cuts on there that made me move, and then I got to track fifteen. "Lately I" stopped me in my tracks. I remember now—I'd just come back from the shower and was studying late for a test in the morning. Seems like so long ago, anyways.

I found myself drawn to the sorrow of the song and, at the same time, pitying someone for having loved so deeply that this was the end result. There was one line that stuck out. I don't totally remember it, probably because I am blocking it out, but she said something about not wanting to hear her favorite song. I knew then I needed to cut the song off.

In 1998, it didn't make sense to me. How could one person make someone feel so low that even their favorite song didn't sound the same, the things they liked didn't feel good. Faith was looking for comfort from the exact person who hurt her. That was insane…until it happened to me. The love was so deep that the only person who could soothe her was the same person who made her feel like that.

I changed when Camden left me. I played "Lately I" until the song started to sound different to me because my ears began to pick up on tones that I didn't know were there. "Lately I" hadn't felt like talking to my friends, I hadn't stopped crying, and I didn't see an end in sight. I was so broken. I was fragmented. I went to work, I came home, I cried, I woke up, and I did it all again. Through it all, I wished Camden would call and tell me that he wanted me. How insane is that? The man told me what he wanted, but I convinced myself that eventually he would change his mind. Eventually he would wake up and miss me. I would be the one he wanted to spend the rest of his life with. I felt if I gave him a few days, this pain would end, and he would come back. Then I felt if I gave him a few weeks…then maybe a few months…then a year had passed, and when I looked at myself in the mirror, I didn't even recognize myself. I was missing from my own reflection. There was a person in the mirror, but that was it.

Deep, right? I am so happy that I'm past all that now, but in that moment, I couldn't see anything but hurt in my own eyes. There was pain from losing Camden; there was pain from losing my dad; hell, there was pain from losing myself.

The last time I played "Lately I" during that period, I was sitting on my bed in the dark, and I sang, then cried, then cried and sang. And after each line, I asked myself why. *Why won't you laugh the way you used to? Why are you no good to anyone? Why do you find it so hard to carry on? Why, Sentury? Because of him? Because of a man who has clearly moved on with his life. Why can't you? Why are you still holding on to him? Why has nothing been the same since he's been gone? Not because of him, it's because of you.* All of a sudden, it was as if I had been snapped out of it. I realized his hold on me was because of me, not because of him.

I said all of that to ask, "How could I be a lesbian if I can feel this way for so long about a man?" Doesn't make sense to me either.

November 7, 2005

Returning to work is never exciting. Nothing exciting to report. I love my job, but I hate the mechanics of it. I'm not alone, I'm sure. People think because I am an event planner in "Fabulous Las Vegas" that I live a fabulous life and have a fabulous work life. Not true. I work on the Strip, so yes, I do meet and see a lot of people, but there are so many event planners in Vegas, most of them well established. I get some of the midsize conventions, some receptions, things like that, but nothing to write home about. I do have a work husband though; he makes the days go by faster.

I made hot wings. Got blue cheese?

A man after my own heart—Matthew (Last Name Omitted). He is a beautiful representation of a man. Black and Puerto Rican, with that beautiful butter-pecan Puerto Rican coloring! Matthew and I are the same age; having someone to relate to makes the job much easier to stomach. He's married in real life, but at work he is my work husband.

*Sentury, can you let Matt know
that his wife is on line one?*

*Will you let her know he is with
me and will be with her shortly?*

I sure will not.

Thanks, hon.

It's all love and fun. Matthew and I have a lot in common. We both love the Buffalo Bills but have never been to Buffalo a day in our lives, which leads to our obsession with chicken wings and blue cheese. A true Buffalonian will tell you that ranch dressing does not go with chicken wings, and if you eat them that way, you're nasty! We have a problem with…well, more like an addiction to all things Buffalo. It's weird, and no one understands us, and that's fine too. Matt's wife thinks that it's surreal that he can be fascinated with a place where he's never been, but I get it, and we don't need her to understand.

I think my boss is going to put us on a project together; that will be fun. Wings for everyone!

November 11, 2005

I need to catch my breath. I need to catch my breath! I need to catch my fucking breath. My God, what am I doing with my life? Jesus, please tell me, because I don't know what I'm doing. Okay, okay, okay, okay, I got it. I just need to stop and think and calm down. I'm just getting home from work, and it's almost midnight! I work a nine-to-five. I'm usually home no later than five thirty, and that is if I stop at Jack in the Box! It's midnight! Okay, let me just play the night back.

I have the release forms. Do you happen
to have the actual venue contract?

Matt and I had to work late today to finish up all the logistics for our event coming up next week. My boss came to me this morning and got on my last nerve as only he can do.

Hey, Sent?

Yes?

The Kroger event next week.

Yes?

*Have you and Matthew compiled the complete list
of vendors, guests, VIP guests, and celebrities?*

Were we supposed to?

Did you read the Kroger contract?

Well...

*You need to have all of this on my
desk in the morning. Period.*

That led to Matt's ordering Buffalo Wild Wings, calling his wife, and telling her he was working late, and my throwing my hair in a ponytail, putting my iPod on shuffle, and making life happen. We started working about two in the afternoon, and around nine I started feeling delirious.

We need to take a break.

I agree.

I needed to give my brain and eyes a break. I lay back on my chair and closed my eyes. My iPod had turned off, and there was a peaceful silence between Matt and me.

What do you think about in moments like this?

Moments like what?

This. Peace.

I try not to think at all.

Why did I say that? Who made me think that I was some philosopher? This man wasn't asking me for a glimpse into my soul—or, hell, maybe he was. Shit, I don't know! That one statement sent me down a forty-five-minute rabbit hole about the things I didn't want to think about. Matthew hung on to every word in such a way it made me pay attention in ways I didn't know I wanted to pay attention.

What?

What?

Why are you looking at me like that?

Your soul is so beautiful.

What?

You've never heard that before?

How the hell do you see my soul?

I don't have to see it; I feel it.

You feel my soul?

Yes, and it is the most beautiful thing I've ever felt in my life.

He kissed me. It was such a sweet and deliberate kiss that I didn't even pull away. I wanted to feel it again, so I moved closer to him. His lips were soft and cool. In a soft manly way, of course, but yes. Soft.

What about your wife?

What about her?

You can't be in here kissing me and stuff.

Why not?

You're married.

(Name Omitted) and I haven't been happy for years.

You've only been married like three
years. Come on, Matt, really?

> *Sentury, I'm serious. I made you my work wife*
> *because you give me something that she doesn't.*

And what's that?

> *Fulfillment.*

The man told me I fulfilled him. As though he were saying that I made him whole. What was I supposed to do with that information? Act as if I never received it? Accept it—yup, I'm his fulfillment!—and just go back to work? I was in shock, and my brain was melting slowly from work, so I honestly didn't have the brainpower to even dissect all of what he was saying or meaning.

> *What else you got on here?*

Matt got up and went over to my iPod.

> *Oh, you nasty!*

What?

> *What's this "Bump N Grind" playlist?*

It's my sensual music.

> *Perfect.*

Erykah Badu's "In Love with You" filled the air, and before I knew it, I was swept up in his arms, dancing. He didn't even ask me if I knew how to dance, and for that matter, even if I wanted to dance. He was so demanding while being gentle. No, Camden was demanding. Matt took control in a gentle way that was beyond anything I had ever experienced, something I didn't know I needed.

As Erykah sang with that Marley boy, it seemed for that moment we were in love with each other. Matt knew the song, so he sang with the track. He sounded really good, made me want to sing.

Matt kissed me so passionately that I felt myself coming off my feet. I don't know if he was lifting me, or God was, but somebody made me float on air. He kept me in his arms, took me over to the chair, and placed me down softly. He got on his knees and pulled me to him to kiss me again. As we kissed, I heard my office door rattle, but I was so caught up that I didn't even move. Either he didn't hear it or didn't care, because that damn door swung open, and the janitor just stood in the doorway, looking me directly in my pupils, while this married man's tongue was down my throat.

Let's just say all the files are on my boss's desk as we speak, and I am going to sleep.

November 20, 2005

I am all that and a bag of chips! Do people still say that? Who cares? I am! Today was the Kroger event, and let's just say it went on without any problems in any way, shape, or form! Perfection, and it got the folks around the office talking, and in a good way for once.

Last night's event was amazing. Congrats!

Did you expect anything less?

From someone named Sentury, I guess not.

Exactly! I am epic; the name says it all.

I can toot my own horn should I want to! It's my party, and I didn't need to cry, but I would have cried if I wanted to. I can't take all the credit, considering my handsome partner in crime was by my side the entire night.

Something is different about Matt, like his...I don't know... how he acts around me now? I don't want to sound paranoid, but I do know I have been kinda weird since the kiss, but not because of him, because of me. We got caught! If we see that night janitor again, we are found out. He doesn't seem to be worried about that, at all, and that worries me too.

What are you doing?

When we were at the event last night, he was all trying to hold my hand and shit. And the thing about it is, it was subtle, so to the untrained eye he was just a sweet man.

Matt, it's people in here.

> *What do I care about them?*

What if one of them knows your wife?

> *And if they do? What am I doing to make them feel the need to report to her?*

Am I the only person in this equation that finds this to be ethically wrong?

> *Yes.*

Okay, so I know we didn't go all the way; it was a simple kiss and some body grazes at the event, but I feel guilty. I don't know his wife, she doesn't know me, but I feel as if I did her wrong. I did kiss her husband, and I completely and thoroughly enjoyed that. But if he isn't worried about it, why am I?

This is all irrelevant! My boss told me that with all the comments and feedback he got from the Kroger event, he may have something big coming up for me. Life-changing big, like amazing! I am so excited! I haven't felt this kind of excitement since playing basketball. This is a great feeling; I'm happy.

December 13, 2005

I'm officially a slut home-wrecker. There is no other way to say it. That's it; that's all. We can go ahead and hang my picture in the Hooker Hall of Fame. Hall of Shame. Whatever it is. There is nothing cute for me to say to describe my behavior. Nothing. I am just being honest. Ain't that what LaTrice told me—be honest with myself? Well hell, it doesn't get any more honest than this. I am just going to tell it as it was and document the moment I sold my soul to the devil. I wonder if there is a special place in hell for adulterers. Probably next to the lesbian and gay section! O Father!

Today started off like any other normal day at the office. I was damn near late, no big deal. I didn't start working for the first thirty minutes of the day, nothing new to see here. Matthew left a sweet note on my keyboard—bingo!

Dear Sentury,

I can't stop thinking about you. This is something I have never experienced before in my life, not even with (Name Omitted). I'm embarrassed to say this to you. When I got married, I was 21, fresh out of college, and we'd been dating since we were sophomores. My parents said that if I was a man, I would make an honest woman out of her. I didn't know she was pregnant. She told my parents, but not me.

I did everything I was taught. I got educated, I found a wife, and I married her when I was told to. My parents and her parents gave us the wedding people dream of, and I was just there. There was nothing else for me, except my son. I did it all because I was having a son. I loved her the way I did because she was going to give me a son. Then (Name Omitted) was born.

The first time I held my son, I cried. Sentury, I know you don't have children, but I will explain to you in a moment why this moment meant so much. I vowed in that moment to protect him and his mother until I had no more breath left in my body.

When (Name Omitted) was about 2, we had to rush him to the hospital because he seemed to be having a seizure. When we got to the hospital, my brother and I were both there. At first, I was confused because I hadn't called anybody, so I didn't quite understand why he was there, but I was relieved to have someone like my brother there with me in such a scary time.

The doctor came out and asked about the family, and all three of us stood up. Why wouldn't we? His parents and his uncle. The doctor had a plan of action. My son's brain was hemorrhaging, and once they drained the blood, they would need to do a transfusion. I was game. Let's go. How much do I need to give? My brother moved away from me, and at this point I was really confused because my wife turned her head.

Sentury, if giving blood was going to save my son, why the hell would they react like this? The doctor went to take me in the back, and my brother stopped me and looked at my wife. "Tell him," he said. My wife was silent. My brother had tears in his eyes. We had this stranger standing there with us, and my brother told me and this stranger that my son wasn't my son. I still didn't put two and two together.

I looked at (Name Omitted) and demanded that she tell me right then who the father of my son was! My brother had so many tears running down his cheeks at this point, and again I was so grateful for the chance for him to be there with me in this moment, because not only was the child I knew to be mine at risk, but my marriage was ending. He could empathize with my pain, and internalized it for me; that's what gave me comfort. My brother reached for my hand, and as his brother, I held his hand in solidarity.

"I'm (Name Omitted)'s father, Matt." My world ended that day.

Then I met you. From the day I met you, I knew there was something about you. I wasn't sure what it was. You are clearly beautiful, but there was something more, and when I got the opportunity to partner with you for Kroger, I needed to experience you and see if what I was feeling was true. It was.

I felt I needed to tell you the truth about my marriage before I asked you on a date so you had a clear view of what you would be walking into. This is my offer: If you are down, leave work early today. Go put on something amazing, and meet me in Downtown Las Vegas, and just experience me.

If I see you there, cool. If not, I understand.

Matt.

You never know what people are going through at home. Matt had come to work every day for the last year, while dealing with the fact he was raising his nephew and not his son. Dealing with the betrayal of his brother and that wife. That ho! I know I am not supposed to judge people; HOWEVER, all the men in the fucking world and she slept with the man's brother? How desperate could you be? Or maybe she wasn't desperate; maybe it was strategy. Either way, it was fucked up.

Back to me and my contribution to this whole fuck-ass web!

Let's be honest again. It's obvious I went on the date; I shouldn't have to state the obvious. This fine-ass man, who kissed as if he were of the heavens, invited me out on a date. In the city, in public, together. HELL YEAH, I was going!

I got extra sexy too. Going to work, I am business chic. But going out, I needed to dress to impress. I will take this moment to say that in reality, his story had disconnected me from the fact that he was still married, regardless of the status. I'm sure that was a part of the plan, but, whatever, I went. I had on my own version of the little black dress. I'm tall, so wearing things, like turtlenecks and miniskirts, elongates my neck and legs. Amazonian-like, especially wearing heels. For what seemed like hours, I stood in the mirror, perfecting this smoky-eye effect, and I let my hair hang bone-straight. When I stepped out of the car, all eyes were on me, but I was only looking for one face.

Wow.

Matt stood there looking handsome as ever, and, I can't lie, we complement each other visually like nobody's business. We strutted around DTLV arm in arm, smiling and just being. I can't remember the last time I was able to just be. He let me make corny jokes—he even laughed at some of them—and that made me feel as if in that moment we belonged to each other. It was one of the most amazing feelings I've ever felt.

The itinerary was as follows: dinner at Triple George (best chicken wings and homemade blue cheese in Las Vegas!), a private tour of the Mob Museum (moonshine and all), and then a show inside of the D Hotel. Once the show was over, I thought the night was at an end. Had that been the case, I would have been completely fine. Seriously, I would have been floating home on a cloud, but he pulled out a hotel room key.

I don't want this to end, Sentury.

Guess I didn't want the night to end either.

This has really been amazing, Matt.

*You mean you don't get this
treatment all the time?*

No! Not at all!

Stop lying.

*I have no reason to lie to you. As hard as it
is for you to believe, men don't chase me.*

Women?

Nope.

*You mean to tell me this is what you have to offer,
and no one has claimed it?*

That's exactly what I am telling you.

He kissed me. Again. This time it was crazy. I could feel what he felt through his kiss. He kissed me, and I felt beautiful. He kissed me and I felt worthy. He kissed me and I felt I deserved him!

It's been a while.

How long is a while?

Five years.

I'll be gentle.

I closed my eyes as he slipped my dress over my head. The feel of his lips all over my body was sending a tingling sensation down my back and causing me to prematurely moan. Then I started to think about Camden, and I started shaking my head like an idiot.

Are you okay?

Yes.

         Do you want me to stop?

No.

         What was all of that?

Yes, he was freaked out! I was freaked out. I didn't need Camden memories in this moment, and neither did Matt.

Matt had his own style, and I must admit it was something Camden could have never achieved. Due to the nature of our encounter and the fact that Matt has a wife, I am going to keep the details to myself. Maybe. Maybe not. Not. I need to be able to relive this with more than just vague details.

Camden—shit! See! Matt, I was with Matt. Matt placed his entire body on mine; he felt every curve and imperfection with his hands and his body. Matt said he wanted to "inhale" every part of this experience. And he did just that. He inhaled every bit of me with every movement of his pelvis, which instinctually moved with mine. I'd never felt anything like it, and I don't think I will again. Matt went slowly for a while; he said he was "warming" me up.

Shit got hot, too, when I was "warmed up" because Matt went into overdrive. Dude, he turned me on my side. My eyes got big as hell because I could see the floor on the side of the bed.

I'm falling.

         I've got you.

Pull me up!

He wouldn't! This was some acrobatic shit. As my head dangled off the edge of the bed, he stood, with one leg on the floor and his knee on the bed, and worked! The harder he thrust, the more I felt myself melting into and onto him. It was as if he were putting everything he felt about me into me and forcing me to see it firsthand.

When it was all said and done, I was spent. No energy. Matt stood by the window and looked at DTLV with a smile.

What are you smiling about?

> *This was perfect, and it's because of you.*

Because I gave you some?

> *Some? Speak better of yourself, Sentury.*
> *You didn't give me anything; we shared*
> *something together that we both needed.*

(Silence)

> *You just gave me a reason to tell my wife it's over.*

Fucking home-wrecker.

December 18, 2005

Today was my mom's annual holiday party.

> *Do you think this makes you straight?*

And my lovely, annoying best friend was in attendance.

> *'Cause you're fucking married men?*

The worst thing was trying to make her whisper while scolding me for my most recent decisions. Not that I look to LaTrice for approval or anything, but for once I do want to feel as if I am not on a path to self-destruction.

This year, my mom's theme was "Winter Wonderland." Everything was silver and blue. She had fake snow and ice sculptures, just a lot of crazy over-the-top, show-everybody-that-I-got-money bullshit. Each year, my cousins and aunts come from out of town. My mom's side of the family, never anybody from my dad's side. I asked my mom about that one time when I was in college.

> *They ain't done shit for us since he died,*
> *so why invite them to benefit from it?*

There isn't enough energy in the world to deal with my mother. Luckily, she considers LaTrice the good daughter, so, like me, LaTrice gets to work the event, not enjoy it.

Did you suck his—

Shut up! People can hear you!

Did you?

No!

Good, 'cause only real home-wrecking hoes suck—

Shut up!

—dick.

At least whisper.

I need details.

Girls, I need you to bring the ice punch out.

Yes, Mrs. Alysé!

Thank you, sweetheart.

You and mom can both kiss my ass.

Trice and I were worked our fingers to the bone this year and were fine with that. The least amount of time spent with my mother, the best. I don't want to hear your mom lecture. You live with my mother for twenty-seven years and then tell me how that shit works out for you.

I'm not going to ask you again.

What do you want to know, Trice?

How did you go from pink cats to mixed dogs?

You're sick.

Less lip, more details.

LaTrice and I slipped into the back of the banquet hall and spent about thirty-five minutes while I gave her every single detail. But I know my best friend; no matter how hard I tried to make it sound good, it wasn't.

Sounds romantic.

It was.

Wonder how his wife feels?

She cheated on him with his brother.

How do you even know that story is true?

What?

Where is the proof of that? Sentury, you are so damn simple!

What the fuck is happening right now?

You do know niggas say stuff like that to fuck, right?

You're telling me he made that up to get some ass?

Yes, dummy!

I don't believe that.

You the sidepiece now? Mary J,
"No Happy Holidays"? That's you?

Before I subscribe to that, let's see
what happens at Christmas.

Simple ass.

I really don't enjoy being called simple. I'm not simple! Naïve maybe, but I'm not simple. I sat there and listened to LaTrice tell me what a horrible human I was and how we used to have box seats in hell, but now I was going to have a floor seat. I don't really care what Trice says; he didn't make that story up.

That's not even the highlight of the night. The end of the night comes, and finally we slaves are allowed to come out of the dungeon and mingle with the rich folks. Mom gets everyone's attention; we all turn to gawk in awe at her, just as she needed. After her long, boring, and repetitive speech, she decided to bring me to the front.

My beautiful and single daughter, Sentury.

The crowd erupted with applause. I wasn't impressed. Mom went on and on about who I used to be and how mediocre I was doing in life now (not in those words, but you know). The crowd laughed at her jokes—at my expense, of course—and then cheered when she announced I was the most eligible bachelor-ette at the party. Still not the best part.

I managed to get away from all of the mangy old men and ugly young ones who were on the hunt at the party. While I was sitting outside, minding my business, I began to just take in the air; the night was particularly beautiful.

Beautiful night.

I know damn well this woman wasn't at my mom's party. Mom didn't do gays, and this woman was clearly gay. She was short, but masculine. Had on a tie and vest, some cowboy boots, and a shiny belt. I was intrigued.

Beautiful.

                                                              Like you.

I'm sorry, have we met?

                                                              No.

She didn't tell me her name. Fine with me. I had other things on my mind. I didn't need it to be complicated.

                    *This party was slightly boring
                    until the speech your mom gave.*

Who invited her? I know damn well my mother didn't invite an openly gay woman to her event; she had to be here with someone else. Come to find out, she was cool with my cousin Amy, and since they were in town, Amy invited her to the party.

Mom has a way with a crowd.

               You didn't want those men that were all in your face.

That obvious?

               Just as obvious as it is that you are attracted to me.

The. Most. Interesting. Part. Of. The. Night. There was a legit lesbian at my mom's homophobic event, and she was hitting on her not-gay daughter. Who knew adult life would be so eventful? She was cute, older, short, and I am going to guess she was about thirty-five. We talked for a little while, and then she got up to leave.

This was an experience, Ms. Alysé,
I hope this isn't our last conversation.

Just as this woman reached out with her hand to stroke my face—

SENTURY!

My mother and LaTrice were standing in the doorway, looking for me, and Mom spotted me. Completely fitting, right? I'm sure the surprise in my eyes, coupled with this gay woman's hand on my face, was the exact visual my mother needed to end her night. LaTrice's face was priceless. It was a mix between a half smile, disgust, and a pinch of embarrassment. My mother's face was pure terror.

The one screaming, yeah, that's my mom.

I spent the rest of the night getting glares from my mom from across the room and getting teased by LaTrice. As far as Mom's Christmas parties are concerned, this may have been the best one thus far!

December 25, 2005

If I weren't already scared of eternal damnation for my soul, I would say fuck Christmas. But I am, so I will just say today sucked. My mother is still pissed from the holiday fling last week. I can't even combat the argument with "I have a guy I'm seeing," because he is married. I spent my entire day being cursed out and accused.

You brought that girl, didn't you!?

Ma, I don't even know her name?

Is that what you are, Sentury? A homosexual?

Sure.

Don't play with me; that's not funny.

Then stop asking me that, Mom.

Not a gift in sight. My dear mother told me that when I embarrassed her at the party, she took my gifts back to the store. I don't think she bought any, but what do I know? I know today sucked, and I am excited to go to sleep and leave it right here!

December 28, 2005

Funny thing happened today. Not really funny actually, it might be considered odd. Met (Name Omitted), Matt's wife. Talk about an awkward moment. I'm sitting at my desk—headphones on, music good—going through the paperwork for my next event and minding my muthafucking business. I saw a crowd of people gathering in front of my desk, but it wasn't my business, so I didn't give it much thought. A few moments went by, and I saw two bodies facing me. I looked up; it was Matt and (Name Omitted).

Hello?

> *Sentury, I would like for you to meet my wife,*
> *(Name Omitted).*

My face had to look fucked up because Matt immediately began damage control.

> *Sentury takes care of me here at*
> *work; she's my work wife.*
>
> *Oh wow, nice. Thank you for making*
> *sure my husband is well taken care of.*

(Silence)

She was fine as hell too. Matt is fine, so I'm not sure what I expected his wife to look like. She is full Puerto Rican. Long, silky, jet-black hair. She has a small waist, but, my God, the hips, thighs, and ass on that woman. I'm sure Matt saw me looking at her. It wasn't even a comparison thing—she and I look nothing alike—but I recognized her sex appeal right away.

Which way is the bathroom?

As soon as she left us alone, I kicked Matt from under the desk.

Are you crazy?! How do you just introduce me to your wife like we don't have something going on? Furthermore, why are you parading her around in here like we don't have something going on? What's your malfunction?

> *As a husband, sometimes I have to do things I don't want to do.*

"*As a husband.*" He has me entirely fucked up! How dare he look me in my face and pull that "as a husband" card? "As a husband" you shouldn't be screwing in the bathroom on our lunch breaks, should you? Shit, did I say that out loud? It's the truth. I've been keeping it to myself, but my relationship with Matt is growing in ways I couldn't have imagined, and we have sex every day! Monday through Friday. No shame. Which leads me to further question his faculties about bringing this woman in my face.

How do you think this makes me feel, Matthew?

> *It should make you feel good?*

(Silence)

> *If I can bring the woman I am married to in front of the woman who I want to be with, what does that tell you?*

That you ain't told her shit, and you got her in
my face as your wife, and I'm the dummy.

Think more of yourself.

How about you think more of
me and get her ass out of here!

The nerve of it all is mind-blowing, captivating. He can't possibly expect me to answer his calls tonight! That's out of the question, but I am curious about (Name Omitted). If she doesn't know anything about us, her interest in me is misplaced.

What do you do here, Sentury?

The Puerto Rican princess perched her thick-ass leg up on my desk as if she owned it and looked me in my eyeballs.

I am an event coordinator with a focus on corporate
activities between fifty to one hundred people.

Sounds interesting.

It is.

What else is interesting about you?

Why?

Just trying to get to know you.

Why?

You don't need new friends? I always look
for friends in women, especially women who
I have such access to through my husband.

That was the weirdest shit I ever heard in my life! "Access to through my husband." What kind of access does she have to me through him? At this point, he doesn't even have any access to me. I heard this before about Black women, but she isn't Black; she's Puerto Rican. Close enough. Anyways, the saying: Keep your friends close, and your enemies closer. She was the epitome of that!

She looked at me and saw the beautiful Black woman that I am. Nothing more, nothing less. In her mind, if she becomes my friend, she can watch what I'm doing, keep one up on me. Trix are for kids, sweetie. I already got him. Our friendship, or whatever she's trying to establish, ain't even about to break up what Matt and I are doing, for now. Matt is fucking that up on his own; I don't need to give the Puerto Rican princess the assist under the basket!

Not sure what kind of access you're looking for, but here's my card. If you need an event done, call me. I'll give you the friends-and-family discount.

I grabbed my purse and walked out.

December 29, 2005

This whole time, I've been saying it's not me; it's not me. I am just trying to maneuver through life the best way I know how. But, lo and behold, it's me. What am I talking about? I'm so glad you asked because I have to get this out. I don't even know what to say about myself, but I had a dream about the Puerto Rican princess. No regular dream either, it was like a real nasty dream.

Matt was there the entire time. I think part of it was because I kept ignoring his phone call all night long, so his name and face were etched into my memory. (Name Omitted)'s face and body were etched into my memory as well. I'd subconsciously memorized every piece of her, from her smile to her hair, to how she walked. I even remembered the cadence in her voice.

This was the dream, and, yes, it will get weird. I apologize in advance, but blame my brain and not my heart. It started with

Matt asleep in his bed. I guess it was his bed. I've never seen their house, so how would I really know? Nonetheless (Oh, Darling!), Matt was asleep in his bed, and he was whispering my name in his sleep. It was such a sweet and sensual whisper that if I hadn't known any better, I would have thought he was in the room with me, standing over me, whispering in my ear while I was sleeping.

The room was dark, but there was an open balcony, so the moonlight came in and illuminated the room, turning it into something almost from Dracula's castle. Matt turned over in his sleep, and the moonlight hit his face; he looked as if he were made of porcelain. In the distance, I could see myself—well, a caricature of myself, because I'm not that damn goofy. The me in the dream was lanky and awkward; I moved as if I were unsure, almost as I did when I was like thirteen and had my growth spurt before anyone else. I was insecure and easily noticed; that's exactly as I looked in the dream.

Matt whispered my name again, and I finally stepped into the moonlight; my skin looked like his. I dramatically began to walk toward the bed; then I heard the Puerto Rican princess whisper my name from a different direction, which stopped me in my tracks. It was as if I were torn between the two voices. I couldn't see her, but I knew she was there.

I stood still for a while. I think my brain was trying to process what my choices were. I knew what I would get with Matt. I knew the sensual piece of Matt I would get, and I knew exactly how I was going to get it. The Puerto Rican princess, on the other hand, I didn't know anything about her, other than what had been presented to me. If I followed her voice, where would it take me and, furthermore, why?

Matt whispered my name again, but this time he was awake. Matt looked at me in such a beautiful way I began to move toward him again. As if he were the Pied Piper and I a child floating to his melody. The Puerto Rican princess moved into the light and then said my name with command and authority. I stopped.

(Name Omitted) stood in the moonlight, but all that could be seen was her silhouette. Darkness accentuated her curves in a way only an artist, not the human eye, could capture. Matt and I both were silent as she moved closer, and her hips propelled her body toward us in a mesmerizing way. When she got close enough to touch, one of her hands was between my legs. Instantly. I never moved. It was almost as if it had been there the entire time.

She looked in my eyes as she sensually rubbed me and crippled my body. Matt just watched, and when he moved, she waved her other hand, and he was lifted from the bed and floated to her. All the while, she's fingering the shit out of me, and I feel every circle, thrust, and pinch she is giving me.

Matt hung there, suspended in the air, watching his wife give his sidepiece the business. I tried to feel bad for Matt, but, damn, she knew what she was doing. I came. There were no ifs, ands, or buts about it; she did what she came to do with me. Matt started saying something that was inaudible, but she never spoke a word to him; she just kept saying my name.

She moved the hand that controlled Matt, and he started swaying in the air. Then she looked me in my eyes, smiled, and said my name again. BOOM! Matt hit the ground, and that beautiful porcelain face shattered into a million pieces on the floor. One piece that should have been his eyeball stopped right in the moonlight, and for a moment I could clearly see the moon in his eye.

That's when I woke up. I don't know what this means. I don't know if yesterday was just too much, and my subconscious used the dream to make sense of it. Yes, I like that idea; it really wasn't about the sex as much as it was about the mastery of the Puerto Rican princess and how she controlled the situation. In the end, Matt will lose because he has already lost with her.

That wasn't too bad once I got it all out, and now I understand it had nothing to do with me. That little hand play she was doing with me was her sitting on my desk yesterday and playing a game. Ha! Had me thinking it was me! I knew better!

December 30, 2005

Matt's still got me fucked up! He couldn't possibly think I was just going to get over his intentionally bringing his wife to the job then putting her at my desk, in my face, and making me talk to her! Is he ill?

You're still ignoring me?

Not to mention, his little stunt got me dreaming about his wife finger-fucking me! He doesn't know this, but I find it to be none of his damn business! He followed me from my desk to the break room, from the break room to the bathroom, waited outside, then from the bathroom to the coffeepot, back to my desk.

I'm not going away.

Obviously.

Why are you acting weird?

Why are you talking to me?

Because you are my woman, Sentury.

Correction. (Name Omitted), the Puerto Rican
princess is your woman. I'm just somebody you
used to know.

                Are we not even going to talk about this?

What is there to discuss, Matthew?

                                A lot.

He must think that I am a damn fool! His woman? When he gets smart with me, he always tells me to think more of myself. In that moment, I was thinking more of myself. Being his woman wasn't more; it was being less than his fucking wife!

                          We aren't divorced.

Clearly.

                          I can't just leave.

And why not, Matthew?

                            Because…

On second thought, don't answer that. I prefer not to
have to ask my man why he won't leave the woman
who embarrassed him. But what do I know? Maybe
that never even happened.

                          (Silence)

Think more of yourself, Matthew, and go find
someone else to lie to. I've closed that part of my
life, so you no longer have a place to reside here.

His face was priceless. If it weren't such a serious matter (I heard a few AKAs in the back of my head when I wrote that—I see y'all!), I would have laughed right in his face.

You truly think that the shit you pulled is cool.
That's a major issue for me, and because of that,
I need some time.

> *What is some time?*

Some means several pieces of, and
time is a measurement of the day.

> *Wow.*

He didn't know I had it in me. Today was not his day to attempt to play with me, and as my phone rings, I will sleep amazingly tonight knowing that I'm not being cheated on by someone else's husband.

January 1, 2006

Happy New Year! 2006! That sounds crazy to me! I remember when 2000 was coming, and they said the whole world was going to come to an end. Y2K. Prince had released "1999" in the eighties, so the world was playing it up until that last hour of 1999. Reality set in really quickly when midnight became imminent. Half the world was in church praying that they would live through the stroke of midnight, while the other half was drunk out of their minds and hoping, if they had to go out, they would go out with a bang! Midnight hit, everybody held their breath, and then it was 12:01! Hahahahaha! How stupid were we?

I appreciate the famous Y2K scare because it has made me take the last six New Year's Eve experiences to the max! Last night was no exception! I convinced LaTrice to let me pick the place, and after a few dead ends, we ended up in the Odyssey, only the premiere gay club in Las Vegas.

> *New Year's with gay people. Yay.*

Neither of us had ever been in a gay club before, so why not! Let's be honest; the gays know how to party better than anybody else on the planet. We were not disappointed! The music had us dancing all night long! They must have played Mariah Carey's "It's Like That" fifteen times, but I was not complaining!

I came to have a party!

I see!

Trice was pretending that she was uncomfortable, but the music got to her, and she began shaking her groove thang too! It made my heart smile because, at the end of the day, having fun was the main goal, no matter whom we were having fun with!

Oh shit.

Oh, how I was sadly mistaken. As we were dancing and having a blast, I spotted Honey. I hadn't seen Honey in a while—like, we know this. My heart dropped in my stomach so fucking fast!

What? What's wrong?

At this moment, I am hiding under a barstool. Imagine that! My long ass managed to fold smoothly under the stool, and I refused to move.

It's her!

Who?

Honey!

Honey?

Yes!

Like, the Honey?

Bingo!

So, what the fuck are you hiding from?
Get your ass up! Go over there, and face her!

Next thing you know, we are literally fighting under the barstool. As she is trying to pull me out, I look up, and Honey is staring down at me with a look of utter confusion. I immediately acted as if I had fallen. Lying completely out on the floor and grabbing my head. LaTrice was too undone, but I did not care. I could NOT be found out hiding from her. Honey kneeled down to assist with getting me up.

Never thought I would be seeing you here, and
damn sure couldn't have paid me to think I would
see you here like this! Are you okay?

No, this bitch isn't okay!

You must be LaTrice. I've heard a lot about you.

She talked about me? Interesting,
she barely even mentioned…

I am happy to see you!

Really?

She is. Trust me.

Trice got up and walked away. I was fine with it, honestly. Honey looked amazing. Something about this woman I just can't shake. Her spirit is pulling me in, but I guess it must have already pulled me in because I'm here, and this is what she makes me feel, and that doesn't happen overnight.

Can I be honest? If I were gay, Honey would be the woman I would choose to be with. Her heart is something I've never seen or felt. Granted, there hasn't been a whole lot of interaction, but you know when a good person is a good person. That's not something that you need years to figure out.

Honey is the type of person to give someone her all and ask for nothing in return. When I was in college, she would send me boxes, and we weren't even talking. I was with Camden, and I would get a random box delivered to the dorm. Candy, cards, stuffed animals. She was sweet, and I know that I was a hot-ass mess, especially then. So for her to look past my behavior and still show me that I was cared about is something I will never forget.

One time Camden asked me where I got a particular bear.

Who got you this?

Not you.

Obviously.

Do you like it?

I'll like it more if I know where you got it.

A secret admirer.

A chick.

If that's what you want to believe.

Okay.

He wasn't wrong, but it was none of his damn business. He probably thought it was from Lindsay, or maybe not. I may not have gotten caught with her at that point, but nevertheless, or nonetheless, subconsciously Honey became more and more important to me without our ever saying a word to each other. That's powerful to me. The best thing that could have happened was seeing her last night.

Can I get you a drink?

LaTrice found her a happy-go-lucky gay man on the dance floor, and she was occupied, so Honey and I found a corner, some drinks, and had a talk.

I think I owe you an apology.

I think you do too.

Let me get it out.

Go ahead, beautiful.

Why are you still so gracious with me? I was a bitch.

You weren't a bitch; you were conflicted.

You understand?

You haven't given me my apology yet.

Oh. Sorry.

Is that the official apology, or the apology for not giving me the official apology?

Second option.

Okay, go.

Okay! Honey, I think you are a beautiful person, and I should have never treated you a way that made you think I was something I wasn't.

(Silence)

What?

That's what you are apologizing for?

Yeah, what else is there?

Honey got up and walked away from me. What did I say? That was the issue. She thought I was gay. I wasn't, so shit didn't go as she planned. I didn't see the issue. I looked over at the dance floor, and I saw LaTrice looking at me as if I were crazy. I shrugged my shoulders and went to finish my drink. Trice kept staring at me until I looked back. This time she was pointing in the direction of Honey. We had the most volatile silent argument ever, and she won. I sulked for a moment, and then I slowly walked over to Honey.

Can't take a joke.

That would work if you were joking.

I want to try again; this isn't easy for me.

I don't expect it to be, but I expect you to be an adult.

I can feel her heart in every word she says. I am such a fucking idiot. I keep hurting this girl, and she doesn't deserve it! I am just trying to apologize. I wasn't trying to do anything else, yet, and still, here I am, fucking it up.

Honey, I was wrong. You didn't and still don't deserve the things I said or did. You are such a beautiful...

Stop.

Why?

Because right now, in this light, you are captivating, and I want to pretend that for this moment you are mine. And if I have to listen to you tell me I can't have you, it will take away from my fantasy.

(Silence)

This is why I think she is so amazing. Who the fuck says some shit like that? Just some beautiful shit. How do I reconcile the fact I am this woman's fantasy? What the hell am I? She looks at me, and she sees beauty without words; she recognizes something in me that I don't even think Camden saw. To bring in the new year next to her was such a breath of fresh air. I basked in the fact that she wanted to have that moment with me, and I didn't have to do anything but exist.

Happy New Year!

The clock struck midnight, and we toasted our glasses to the new year. Trice smiled as she watched Honey watch me. I didn't get a kiss, but what I got was worth so much more. I was seen; 2006 is going to be great!

February 9, 2006

I did it! I did it! I did it! It is very rare that I am proud of myself, but I am damn proud today! So, remember the Kroger event a few months back? Yes, the one I did exceptionally well, that's the one! I knew that my boss was going to talk to a few of the higher-ups and get me a spot, but I didn't know how or when it would happen.

Sent, you got a moment?

Sure.

My boss calmly and casually came to my desk and asked me to come to his office. I immediately started thinking about everything I could have done wrong, so I could have my damage control perfected by the time we turned the corner. We walked into the office, and it was the normal office—nothing on his desk that said I was in trouble—so I panicked.

You're firing me?

Excuse me?

You brought me in here to take me away from the group in case I made a scene, right?

What the hell are you talking about?

*You don't have a write-up on your desk. You
are standing here, looking at me really weird,
so there is something going on.*

Yeah, you got a promotion.

I don't think it's fair when I work my ass— What?

Promotion.

I don't really get embarrassed; however, that was pretty fucking embarrassing. That's how you know someone has done some dirt—when they start acting as I did. I ain't done shit, but still.

Wow, I don't know what to say.

*Me either. Did you really
think you were being fired?*

Yes.

That's crazy.

*I'll admit I feel a bit foolish, but, hey,
makes the day more flavorful.*

Do you want to know what the promotion is?

That would be wise.

*You are going over to the 500-plus groups reser-
vations. This puts you in the league with sorority
conventions, smaller cons like Daisy Con and Color
Con, you know, the larger small events.*

I am the planner?

Yes.

Wow.

I did it. I don't know what else to say. This was all a part of my plan. I need to get to the thousands planning, but being at the 500 puts me right where I need to be. Proving myself is what is important in this type of job. It's who you know and positioning, and I am now positioned.

News of my promotion spread faster than my actual understanding of what happened. With that came a bunch of congratulations—"you are amazing" and "we are going to miss you and Matthew."

I knew you would get it.

(Silence)

He knows damn well I am still not talking to him. We haven't talked in almost two months. There was nothing I needed to hear from him, so he was wasting my time and his own. Not a smart cookie.

Thank you would be nice.

Kiss my ass is nicer.

What is with you, Sentury?

I am beginning to feel like you rode the short bus. Did you?

You can be cruel.

Only when provoked.

You never gave me a chance to talk to you.

Call the Puerto Rican princess; she will listen.

I am trying to clean off my desk and blow this Popsicle stand, and he is in the way.

Tell me what?

I'm going too.

If I were high, he would have blown my damn high! I got the promotion; I didn't want the promotion with Matthew's ass! I know he helped me with the Kroger event; I get it. He is a jerk! Handsome as hell, but that whole wife stunt was a piece of work for me. I can't just let him get away with doing that to me. We will be working even closer together, and that makes me very uneasy, but I will figure this out. I am still proud of myself; he is just a fine-ass bump in the road.

February 14, 2006

Happy Singles Awareness Day! I really had a good time today... with Honey. I really want to begin a friendship with her; I think that is the least I can do. When I was in college, I wasn't really secure about much of anything, and Honey came at a time that was just inconvenient for me. She deserves true friendship and generosity, and I know I can be that.

This feels like a date.

It is a date.

A Singles Awareness date between two single people.

A date.

I planned a whole excursion for Honey and me. My connections at my job give me benefits that the common person cannot get. Like free air-balloon rides at dusk, dinner at the top of the Eiffel Tower restaurant at the Paris Hotel, and ending the night with a gondola ride in the river at the Venetian Hotel while a weird White man with an Italian accent sings Bobby V's "Slow Down" to us.

> *This was perfect.*

What was perfect about it?

> *There was no expectation.*

Explain, please.

> *Sentury, why do you have so much doubt in the inevitable?*

Explain that too, please.

> *Okay. Let's start with the expectation; it will be less to retain.*

Let's do it.

> *We came out tonight as friends.*

We did.

> *When you go out with your friends, there is only the expectation that you will have a blast, enjoy yourself, and make memories.*

This is true.

> *That gave us the opportunity to openly enjoy each other, without expecting anything but enjoyment from each other.*

I like that.

> *Now, the doubt in the inevitable.*

Yes.

> *You enjoy me.*

I do.

> *You reached out to me for us to spend*
> *the most romantic day of the year together.*

When you put it like that…

> *Did you?*

Yes.

> *All of your decisions and movements have put us*
> *on the course of one day experiencing each other in*
> *more than a friendly manner.*

How?

> *Sentury, you like me.*

I like her? I like her. That is such a loaded thing to say. In the world of gay women, admitting that I like her in any capacity would have been taken to mean I like her enough to explore the possibility of a relationship with her. That's not the type of like I have for her. Granted, if I were gay, a lesbian—you know, one of those—I would stand by my statement in the past; I would be with her. But I'm not gay. I won't be; I don't plan on it. I am just a woman who has slept with a few women, but I have no desire to take one home.

> *You are very comfortable around me.*

Should I not be?

> *You should be whatever makes you feel safe.*

Good.

> *I make you feel safe?*

Yes, you really do.

That's not odd to you?

No.

Sentury, you aren't slow, so please kill the act.

(Silence)

*You have a comfort with me. Like a sense of protec-
tion, not the I-can-be-myself comfort. Everything
in your spirit points to me. Why won't your mind
let you go there?*

Great question. I can't lie; I really enjoy how Honey carefully challenges me to think. I had no real excuse; she was right. Everything about my body language said I was attracted to her. Everything in my movements gravitated to her. Of course she noticed this, but that didn't mean that it was something to be spoken about or acted on. I feel as if I am not making sense, as if I am making excuses rather than facing it. I'm fine with that.

I'd picked Honey up—such a gentlewoman—so once we got back to my car, we started the drive home. The feeling in the air was somber, almost as if someone had died. I wondered if it was my fault, trying to shift my energy from something evident to something uncomfortable.

Do you fear being gay?

What's there to fear?

That's what I'm asking you.

Can I think about it and come back to you?

*Only if you promise to truly think about it
and search deep in your spirit for the answer.*

I promise.

I am going to sleep on this, but it's something about the way she makes me feel that makes me want to keep my promise and answer these questions with a clear mind and heart.

February 16, 2006

If I could take a deep sigh and write it in the same way that I am feeling it, I would. Sigh. That's so ugly, but it is truly how I am feeling. After Honey asked me the other day about being scared to be gay, I had to really think about what that meant for my life. Not everything is as black-and-white as it sounds, and this is a harsh reality that most people don't have to face.

I've spent so many years of my life saying what I wasn't, but acting as if I was. Why? While convincing myself I was just doing random things, I truly did not give myself the respect or time to process what my actions truly meant. I wonder how many actual lesbians go through this. The thought process of fear, shame, and walking in a lie, rather than walking in the truth.

The bottom line of the bottom line is I have slept with more than one woman, more than once. There is no way around this; there is no get-out-of-jail-free card, nothing. I have had sex with women. It wasn't just in college. Over the years, I've continued to dabble, and that's just what I considered it, but why?

I have so many whys to ask myself, but I don't have the answers. At all. So, to add Honey and the question of fear to the mix has sent me into a self-reflection moment. I may have never admitted it, but I enjoy the attention of women. Women pay attention in a certain detail that men don't.

Don't get me wrong, men have been sweet, but there is a connection between two women that is sensual and delicate, yet powerful and commanding. Women naturally pay attention to detail, we are naturally intuitive, and we just have a flare for romance that you can't pay men to have.

The women I have dealt with have made me feel more like a woman than any man ever has. Not saying that the men I have dealt with didn't give me the same feeling…no…actually, that's exactly what I am saying. Though I have been with men who told me I was beautiful and made me feel somewhat special, they have nothing on the way women have made me feel.

Saying that out loud is weird, but I promised Honey. I promised I would go deeper than the surface for this, and I have to. I have to stop hiding from myself and lying to myself so I can come back to her with something that is genuine and well thought out. So yes, women have made me feel more beautiful, wanted, and loved than men. Period.

Back to the original question—what am I scared of about being gay, if that is the truth? If it is real that, though I have an attraction to men, I am more comfortable with women, what is it that I am scared of? Are you fucking kidding me? I am scared of all of it! It freaks me out! People will see me as something different, something misunderstood, something feared, and I will be treated as such.

I see and hear how people refer to lesbians and gay men; that shit ain't cute! People are nasty to the gays. They are downright disgusting, and I am supposed to fall into that? I know what that sounds like, but reality is, if I had a choice, no, I would not willingly fall into the cruelty of being an outright lesbian.

What about my family, my job, the people around me? How will they treat me? My parents didn't talk about homosexuality when I was younger, and if they did, they didn't do it around me. Since the death of my father, nothing nice about anything has come out of my mother's mouth.

That dyke! He's a faggot!

Derogatory at its finest comes from that vile woman. I could only imagine how it would go if I sat her down to tell her that I, her only daughter, her only child, was in fact a lesbian.

> *You're going to hell! You disgusting child! All that*
> *your father and I have done for you, and this is how*
> *you repay us? Blasphemy.*

That was probably a nice rendition, however accurate. I would lose the last parent I have left. Not that it's a major loss, but every child needs her mother, no matter what. That's what it is, and that's what it will be. Having your parent turn their back on you because you're different elicits a different kind of fear. It falls in the pits of your stomach and causes a sense of nausea that is unmatched. My mother hasn't been a "mother," but I think it would change me, and I am not ready for that change. So, fear number one is losing my mother. None of that other shit matters.

Fear number two is public rejection. Can you imagine being on a date with the love of your life, and everyone you pass turns their nose up as if you have baby shit smeared on your face? Every time you walk into a restaurant holding the love of your life's hand, someone turns their back to you or even tells you that you can't come in because it is a Christian establishment, and your very existence goes against everything they believe? This is real. People hate what they do not understand or agree with. Not that agreeing with whom I love is anybody's fucking business. It happens.

To be made to feel as if I cannot be in love in public is petrifying. There are some brave souls who endure for a stance. I am not that brave, and I can admit that. Not afraid to admit it at all. I am not brave enough to hold a woman's hand and walk into a movie theater and sit with her, side by side, in love. I know that

B. Danielle Watkins

244

I've done some similar things, but that was when I was hiding from myself, when in some sick, twisted way I thought if I didn't acknowledge my behavior, no one else would either.

I think my biggest fear of being gay, fear number three, is another woman rejecting me. It is one thing for a man to walk away from something, but for a woman to walk away means something deeper. It would be devastating to begin or pursue a relationship with a woman and have her wake up one day and realize you are no longer whom she desires. To hear the words that you aren't what someone who is a mirror image of yourself wants would be crushing.

I am everything you are. Yes, every person is different, but a woman next to a woman is two women. Nothing will change that. In my experience with women… Let me take a moment and celebrate my ability to say that in a positive space. Go me! In my experience with women, we were more alike than we were different. Minus the White girl, she was different. But with everyone else, we were reflections of each other. A yin and a yang. Two sides of the same coin. How would it look if one day George Washington wanted to part ways with the American bald eagle? That would be a sad-ass day for a quarter. I don't know if I would be able to take a woman telling me I wasn't enough for her after we had accentuated each other prior to that.

I decided to take this conversation from my brain to the out-side world. LaTrice is really the only person I can talk to about this because she won't judge me. She thinks I'm gay as it is, so bouncing these ideas between her and me makes sense.

> *Let me get this straight, you fear being what you've been because you're scared people will know?*

Theoretically.

> *You want to know what I think about that?*

There would be no other reason for me to come to you.

Fuck them.

(Silence)

If somebody's worried about who you're sleeping with,
then they wanna fuck you, and that's just what it is.

So, if I came out as gay, you wouldn't care?

You are gay.

No, I'm not.

Okay.

Okay what?

You're still lying to yourself, and
I don't have time for the bullshit!

I came to you for an honest answer about the fears
of being gay!

You got it! You can keep pretending with yourself,
but for me, I know you are gay. I don't see any-
thing else other than you, Sentury; the rest of that
shit doesn't matter. The sooner you realize that
shit, the easier your life and everyone else's life
around you will be.

LaTrice didn't really give me what I was looking for. I wanted more of an in-depth discussion of my fears and how they affect day-to-day life. It's in Trice's personality to be dismissive about things that don't benefit her. I believe with my entire heart, if the shoe were on the other foot, she would have a girlfriend, walk around in public with her, and not give a damn, or in her words, "not give a fuck what someone had to say." That didn't do me any justice, so I called Honey.

Hello, beautiful.

Hey, can we talk about my homework?

> *Of course.*

I did some thinking.

> *Okay.*

I'm scared of the backlash.

> *That's a normal fear.*

Is it?

> *Of course it is, Sentury. Can you imagine the fear
> I had when my mother found out I was gay?*

No.

> *It was horrible! She yelled and screamed, and
> I cried. I didn't know how to face my father and my
> brothers, but I did. I had to. There was no way
> I couldn't tell them.*

What do you mean?

> *If I didn't tell them, I wasn't giving them the real
> chance to know me, and that was doing them and
> myself an injustice.*

But what about the fear?

> *I had to face it because this is my life. Let the chips
> fall as they may; when they fall, I'll still be a lesbian.*

That was by far one of the most profound things I'd ever heard. How dare I continue in the mindset of this selfishness? I'm not even sure if Honey realizes how her question was really something that I needed for more than one reason. Honey is an oasis in the desert of ignorance, and I appreciate her. I appreciate her patience. I appreciate her willingness to teach, her willingness to accept, and her willingness to wait. I am beyond afraid, and I don't know if that will ever change, but one thing is true. Honey is the woman who is teaching me more about myself than I ever could have imagined, and that is a friend you don't let go.

March 1, 2006

I hate Matthew! That's it; that's all! Ain't nothing else I can do or say because he has tried to fucking ruin my life as if I did something to him. I should have known something was up when he was sitting at my desk and waiting on me this morning.

Why are you here?

You might want to be nice to me.

I have no reason to be nice to you.

You want to rethink that?

Move!

Why didn't I find that the least bit strange? Let me just tell you what happened. I am at my desk, minding my business after he was being a weirdo in the morning, and I am working on my next event. The HR manager and my boss walk up to me.

Ms. Alysé?

Yes?

Can you come to my office?

I've never been called into the office, so that was a cause for alarm, but I got up and slowly followed them down the long hall. When I got my promotion, I lost my shit, so I decided to keep my cool this time because I was completely wrong before.

What's going on?

This lady was looking at me as if I were a murderer, and my boss wouldn't look me in my eyes. Anxiety began to swell right up in my chest.

Can you tell me about your relationship with Matthew?

I don't have one.

Your past relationship.

There wasn't one.

Ms. Alysé, please don't make this difficult.

What are we talking about?

That bitch went and told HR that I was sexually harassing him and causing problems with him and the Puerto Rican princess. Are you fucking serious? He came on to me! He wanted me! HE WROTE ME A LETTER!!! I ran back to my desk as fast as I could to try and find what I did with that letter. At this point, the whole office is whispering because he has planted seeds in anyone who would listen, including the daughter of my mother's sorority sister.

I just realized something! I bet that's why his bitch ass was at my desk; he was looking for that letter to stop me from showing it! Joke was on his ass because I hid it in my folders. I grabbed the letter and then had to walk by all of those who were watching me and rolling their eyes. I saw Matthew watching me intensely with a sinister smile. I could have spit in his fucking face.

What is this?

It's the letter he wrote me!

What?

*Yes, this is how everything started. I did not
harass him!*

Ms. Alysé, I'm sorry.

Save it.

I stormed out! I was over it and over that job, so I grabbed my shit and walked out. The real fun happened when I walked into the house.

Slut!

Mom?

That bitch at the job called her mama, who called mine and told her what was happening. I was blindsided. Yes, I acknowledged that that girl worked there, but never in my wildest dreams did I think she would tell her mother my business and then her mother would tell mine! The shit was squashed! When I gave that woman the letter, there was nothing else to talk about. He was in trouble; I wasn't!

*How could you embarrass my
name in the streets like this?*

*Mom, I am grown, and I didn't
even do anything wrong.*

You were sleeping with a married man!

He was married; I wasn't!

What does that mean, Sentury?

*It means exactly what I said. I didn't
have anybody to be loyal to, so his
decisions were his and his alone!*

Who raised you?

You.

Could you be any more disrespectful?

Mom! You are yelling at me like I am a child. I am twenty-seven years old! I am working, I have a degree, and I am living my life! It really isn't your fucking business!

And you go and curse me in my house?

Being a slut is better than the dyke you keep accusing me of being, right, Mom?

(Slap)

You hit me!

I should be whupping your ass right now! Don't you ever talk to me like that again in your life! You live here in my house! I pay the bills! You run around selling yourself, and you think you can just treat me any kind of way? You can't! You won't! Get out of my face!

I can't believe that my mother hit me! I guess we never really talk enough to know each other. Damn, that was a reality check. My mother and I don't talk, and when we do, it is volatile and ends in violence. I miss my father so badly; I just don't think things would be like this if he were home. Hell, if he were home, I probably wouldn't even be scared to be gay if I were gay. Daddy would balance out this unstable-ass environment I am in. I need my dad. I need my daddy. I can't keep on like this.

March 2, 2006

I visited my dad's grave today for the first time. I've been crying ever since. You don't know you're hurting so deeply until it is in your face. My father died in 1984. That is a lifetime ago for some. I'd never seen his headstone. My mother never took me back to the grave. I had to ask the cemetery where he was buried, and it's been so long they almost didn't know. The groundskeeper put me in his golf cart and took me to a far corner of the cemetery, and my daddy was lying there. Alone.

You can tell my spastic-ass mother hadn't been out to the graveside in years. The headstone was full of moss and mold, there were some old plastic flowers in the attached vase, and it just felt cold. The groundskeeper told me he made sure the area's grass was cut down, but that was it. It was up to the families to maintain the rest. Then he got on his cart and rode off. I wasn't sure what to do, but I at least had sense enough to bring some fresh flowers.

The plastic flowers had to be twenty years old. They were disgusting to touch and dry-rotted. It made me mad to think my mother had left my father out there like that all these years. I tried as hard as I could to remove the moss with my hands, but each time I touched my father's name engraved on that stone, I felt light-headed. I finally just sat down. On top of him.

My father was under me. That was such a wild feeling. It felt as if I were sitting on top of my father's coffin underground. It reminded me of that conversation I was having with Darling at homecoming. The actualization of what my father's death meant to me and what I thought about where he was—he was right here.

> *Hey, Daddy. I'm sorry it took me so long to get here. I honestly don't think I wanted to see you like this ever again, so I selfishly didn't come. There is no excuse. Mommy hasn't been here either, but I guess you know by now she hasn't been the same since you left. I wonder how much of life you've seen from where you are?*

Daddy, I'm suffocating here. There is nothing that is helping me to breathe, and I lost my breath when I lost you. The air hasn't been the same since. I think I lost myself then, and all these years later I still can't find my footing. I just don't know what direction to go in, Daddy, and it is making me weak. Not physically, but something is off inside of me, and, Daddy, it hurts. It hurts a lot.

I just needed more time with you; you should have been here. Mom needed you too; now we are a mess. Our relationship is a mess, she is a mess, I am a mess, and we are both hurting for you.

I came today because I wanted to see if it would make me better, make me feel closer to you. It didn't; it made me worse. I don't even know what I'm doing here. You're dead! You've been dead! What comfort could I get from talking to a piece of stone?

You left me, Daddy! Why did you leave me? What did I do? Why couldn't you wait? Tell heaven or hell no! It wasn't time.

I can't stop crying. My life feels so heavy right now. I can't shake this feeling; I can't shake the pressure on my chest. Nothing is right for me now, and I can't even explain why. I need a break from it all. I need a break from life! I don't want this life!

June 8, 2007

It's my birthday! Twenty-nine years young! I know it's been a while since I've written. My life last year was rough. What I now recognize as a stint with depression, 2006 proved to be a test for me. I just read my last entry in here, and I don't even recognize that person. I was so lost. I was blaming my mother for my pain, which stemmed from my father's death. I was wilding at work, sleeping with married men, and fighting my urges to be a lesbian. I was in a bad space to be so young.

Today I feel like a brand-new person! I see life differently. I miss my dad, but not in an unhealthy way, and I am in a relationship that has made me happier than I could ever dream.

Honey and I are together. It is the craziest thing I've ever experienced, and I would want to experience it with no one else. Honey is perfect. The world wants you to believe that perfection doesn't exist, but that's just not true. There is someone who is perfect for everyone, and I have her. I am so filled with love for her. So here is how it happened:

Last September, I had a mental breakdown. I had to take leave from my job, and I checked myself into a facility. I wasn't allowed to have my cell phone, and the only number I seemed to remember was hers.

Honey?

Sentury? Where are you?

I started crying immediately! I was so fucked up! My baby was so sweet, and she listened. For a week, she let me just cry and talk about nothing, and cry some more, and not make sense. Once that week was over, the doctors diagnosed my depression, gave me some medication, and released me.

You're not taking that.

Honey was first—before my mom, before LaTrice—to come to my side when I got out. Not that LaTrice didn't try, but Honey was already there. The first thing she did was tell me that she was not going to watch me medicate myself into a fog, and that we were going to find natural ways to pull me out of this depression.

The first thing she did was get me out of the house. We would go to the park and meditate, sit on the grass, and just breathe. She never said anything; she just led me. She started checking in on me, making sure I was getting enough sleep; she helped me find another job. Anything that would cause me stress, she shielded me from it, including my mother.

> *Who the hell are you, and why are you in my house? With all due respect, ma'am, I am (Name Omitted), and right now your daughter needs me. What she doesn't need is your cynicism, stress, and negativity. She's not well. I want nothing more than for you and her to be happy together, but this right here that you're showing me isn't it. I will be here until she doesn't need me anymore.*
> *(Silence)*

That was my mother's introduction to Honey. Pure protection from all that would send me in a downward spiral, and it worked. The pressure I was feeling was lifted. I looked in the mirror, and I started to see someone whom I loved, not someone I feared. I began being able to meditate alone, exercise, and I found joy in just being in Honey's space. She was so amazing and so sweet.

Around January, we were taking a trip to Big Bear in California, and while we were driving, I started to study her. I always thought she was beautiful, but the clarity in which I saw her made her captivating. Her skin was flawless, and as beautiful as she was, there was a masculinity to her and a softness that was refined. Her smile lit up a room, and to just be around her and feel how she loved me was a dream.

We got to Big Bear, checked into our cabin, and began to relax. Honey picked up some groceries, so she began to cook. I sat in front of the fireplace and just lost myself in the crackles.

What do you see?

You.

I'm back here.

But now I can see you.

I kissed her. It was I who did that. I turned around, I saw what she meant to me, and I realized in that moment she was so much more important to me than I'd allowed myself to feel. I wasn't ready for sex yet. I didn't want that with her. I wanted to experience the intimacy of our connection without the sex, and it was beautiful.

We've been together for six months, and as happy as I am, I haven't told anyone. I know—that was a curveball, right? I just had so much praise and adoration, right? Yes, that has not changed; however, I need to protect her and myself. Honey deserves a woman who is completely out, and right now I can't afford that. It could send me back into a depression, and she understands that.

Bitch, where you been?

LaTrice and I haven't seen each other since I started dating Honey. It's not that I don't want to include my best friend in my happiness. That's not the case at all, but I don't want to be made to feel any kind of way about anything. Trice will spend her time telling me that she knew this was going to be the outcome, and, honestly, I still don't know if I'm gay or if I just fell in love with Honey for being there for me. Or even deeper, if I fell in love with her because she loved me.

I need to be sure about all of this before I present us to the world as a couple, so that I am strong enough to defend us. In the world, there is a lot of hate for what we are. There is a fight right now happening in California to ban same-sex marriage. It's called Prop 8 or something like that, and next year it will go on the ballot if they vote for it in the primaries. This is a real thing. I know I am hiding—hell, Honey knows I'm hiding—but I honestly need to position myself for the life I want to live forever.

Honey is my today, my right now. I don't know what's going to happen. Am I wrong for enjoying the ride? Am I wrong for loving her for loving me, and allowing myself to finally experience happiness without fear or hindrance from outside influences? I'd like to think I am not wrong for keeping my happiness private, and as long as she's okay, we are okay. I love her.

June 15, 2007

I've been wondering for a while now if I've ever made love before, and as of last night, I know now I hadn't. For a long time, I didn't even know there was a true difference between making love and having sex. It's all sex. Let's just put the shit out there. Sex is an act. The act happens in both situations, with or without love, and up until this point, I have only had sex. Making love proved to be a totally different experience with a totally different outcome.

I have a surprise for you.

Yesterday morning, my baby called me and told me that she had a surprise for me, and that she would be picking me up from work. Granted, I drove myself to work, but if Honey said she was coming to get me, I wouldn't say no.

Where are we going?

Just as she said, she was outside waiting for me when I got off at three thirty. I jumped in the car and gave her the sweetest kiss in the world, and we started driving. Please note, I am the only person who gets off at three thirty at this new site, so I don't have to worry about hiding my relationship. No one saw me, in case you were wondering. I love kissing her. It makes me have butterflies; it makes my spirit roar. I just…anyways…

I have a thing for cheap motels. It may sound weird, but I don't care! Unlike the resort-style hotels here in Las Vegas, run-down motels on the side of the road offer nothing. That's what I love about them. Think about it. You are on a road trip, and you come across a VACANCY, FREE HBO sign. The motel looks as if several serial killers have rested there, the pool is black and nasty, and the attendant barely speaks English. You following me? You get into the room; it's clean, but there is a residual stench that comes with a place like this. But you walk into the room, and all you have is you. There is no distraction, and there is no flare. There is a bed, nightstand, maybe a desk with a Bible in the drawer, a tube TV, and an iron anchored to the closet.

I love this so much because it forces you to spend time with whomever you are with. It makes you face each other, and for me, it is more intimate than any $200-a-night space. Give me a $29.99 motel out in the desert, one that has a VACANCY sign with half its lights burned out, one in which the only thing in the room that works is the Jacuzzi.

And that's exactly what Honey did. We drove to the Clown Motel in Tonopah. Right up my alley. Exactly what I expected it to be—nothing. Honey had packed a bag for me, which I found to be super thoughtful, and we checked into our room. The room was small and filled with clown pictures. A mini fridge in the corner made it a "suite." We'd driven three-and-a-half hours to spend this time together.

Free HBO!

(Laughter)

I hadn't even realized Honey was paying attention to me when I would go on and on about staying in a place like this. This is what I mean about her being perfect for me; my girlfriend thought enough about me to do this for me, just to see a smile on my face. Wow. My girlfriend. The possession in the word *my* before *girlfriend* is unnerving, but in an amazing way.

I love you so much.

Aw, Honey, I love you too.

No, Sentury, you aren't hearing me.

I heard everything you just said.

But listen to my heart.

I put my head to her chest, and I realized that our heartbeats were in sync. It was mesmerizing. I closed my eyes, and I pictured both of our hearts in our chests beating in synchronicity, dancing around together in the universe, and then I exhaled at the same exact time that she did. It scared the shit out of me; I won't lie. I popped up and looked at her.

What is this? What's happening?

You've never been in love before?

I guess not.

Does that mean you've never made love before?

You know I'm not a virgin!

Baby, that's not what I'm asking you.

(Silence)

Everything thereafter was like a dream. The first thing she did was pull out the Alicia Keys *As I am* CD. "Like You'll Never See Me Again" filled the room. I sat on the bed and sang along to the song as Honey ensured the door was locked and turned the lights out.

I thought we were going to wait.

We did.

Honey kissed me, and I swear to God I saw fireworks in that muthafucking room! I think my clothes just melted off. I have no recollection of taking them off. Honey was so gentle in how she handled me, and I could feel her love in every caress she gave my body. Considering I'd been with so many women before, I was anticipating the usual—some fingers, some tongue, something along those lines.

She pushed my leg up and then pressed her body against mine. In that position, I felt helpless. I couldn't control what I was feeling. Alicia sang in the background, and I realized Honey had the song on repeat. She was making love to me as if it were the last time, and she wanted to feel and experience every bit of it. As she pressed her body against mine and began to grind, I realized that our nether regions were rubbing against each other, and I allowed myself to embrace it.

The passion with which Honey handled me was unparalleled. Right as I was about to scream, she stopped and put my leg down. As if she knew it was coming. She then pressed her entire body against mine, and I could feel her breasts. It was the first time I realized she had breasts. I know that sounds weird, but she's masculine, unlike any of the other women I'd been with. She wears sports bras, as I do, and her breasts are hidden. I could feel the fear in the trembling of her breath on my body, and it made me want her so bad. I could feel her hands exploring my inner thighs, and I moaned at the thought of her digits entering me. I quiver now thinking about it. Damn.

Okay. Whoa. I got myself together. Okay, where was I? Yes, she stuck her fingers inside me.

You feel just as good as I thought you would.

I don't know what the hell she was doing, but I liked it! I didn't even realize she'd slipped down and added her mouth to the equation. The combination was explosive! Like. Yeah, not to be too graphic, but the kind of explosion you have to clean up after when it's done—but I wasn't done because she wasn't done. Honey and I made love for hours. Like six hours or some shit. Even then, I didn't want it to stop. As we lay in each other's arms, watching the sun come up in the window, Alicia was still singing.

Why did you choose this song?

                                                    You don't like it?

I love it, but for about eight hours now, she has told
us to love like we will never see each other again.
A. Keys has worked a whole shift.

                        I wanted our first time to be special, and I feel
                        like the message behind this song is clear.
                        I wanted to experience it with you.

Forgive me, what?

                        I wanted to cherish what we had in case we never
                                                    have it again.

Why do you think I deserve what you give me?

                        For the exact reasons you think you don't.

And then we went to sleep. I made love to my girlfriend in a cheap, dirty motel, and I loved it.

August 2, 2007

I am in the Windy City! Having a new job gives you new opportunities and benefits. Now that I work for Belmore International,

I get to travel and plan events. I don't go often, but when I do, I love it. I miss my boo, but she knows I've got to work, and it gives us time apart. I've been here a few days, and I think I've got about a week left. Considering this is my first time in Chicago, I am probably more excited than I should be.

Today, I met with the company that I am organizing the event for, and I learned it was a fundraiser for a local politician. Easy enough. A young Black woman making waves in politics. Even better.

Hello, my name is Sentury Alysé.

> *Nice to meet you, Sentry. I hear you will be*
> *heading the organization for the fundraiser.*

I'm here to help.

(Name Omitted) caught me off guard; I didn't expect to meet her so soon. We sat in her campaign office and discussed the overall layout of the event, which I am going to have to come back for, and then I thought the meeting was over.

Have you eaten?

I didn't realize it was already seven when the meeting ended, so when (Name Omitted) invited me to dinner, I was like "you bet."

> *May I please have a bottle of your best*
> *wine and some calamari to start the night.*
> *Sentury, you do eat calamari, don't you?*

This woman was giving me Pam Grier vibes, a real Foxy Brown-type chick. That's what I am going to start calling her—Foxy. She's pretty too. It's rare in politics to see a Black woman represented with such beauty and class. I know she's got to be a snake because politics is a snake pit. She and I are about the same height, but, I'm telling, you she looks just like Pam Grier, 1978. She's striking; because she is so tall, its noticeable. She also speaks in a very deliberate dialect. She has the politician thing down pat.

So, how long have you been a politician?

Do I make you nervous?

No. Why would you?

Usually, women are intimidated by me.

I have no reason to be intimidated by you.
I don't want anything you have.

I like that.

Good.

We spent a few hours in the restaurant just talking about every-thing—how she got started, what I do, my basketball career, the WNBA, and even when she used to ball. We talked so long that eventually we looked around, and we were the only customers left; the staff was cleaning up around us.

How long are you in town, Sentury Alysé?

I leave Thursday, but then I will be back
the Tuesday before the fundraiser.

Do you know anyone in Chicago?

Nope.

Good, now you know me.

I think I would like that.

I know I would. See you soon.

I let Foxy know that I had work to do—for her, no less—so I couldn't be kicking it with her every night. I am trying to keep this job. I think we are doing dinner on Wednesday. That gives me just enough time to get everything done for the fundraiser before we hang out again. Let me get to work.

August 4, 2007

I am a magnet for women. I don't know when this started, but it doesn't matter where I am; somebody is going to fall for me. Who, you ask this time? Foxy. Yes, the snake politician has thrown her hat in the ring! I have a woman back in Las Vegas, but what does that mean in Chi-Town?

I've been waiting forty-eight hours for this dinner date.

To my surprise, Foxy showed up at every meeting I had this week. The caterer, she was there; the DJ, she was there; the host, she was there. In the moment, I figured she was just hands-on with her shit. It's hers. Why wouldn't she be? I would! As I secured each piece of the puzzle, she watched and nodded in a sign of approval, and by the time I finished my meeting locking in Mayor Daley as the special guest, I was looking for her approval.

Meetings with mayors and things, you seem
to be fitting into my world like a glove.

I'm about the mark that an event leaves on
those who attend, and this guy has been
a mayor since I was like nine or something.
Seems like a guy to have around.

You know Chicago history?

I do my research.

I wonder what you know about me?

My final meeting was with the florist, and when I noticed that Foxy wasn't around, I found myself disappointed. About what, only God knows. Honey called as I was leaving the meeting, and I guess it was evident.

What's wrong, babe?

Nothing, why do you ask?

You sound disappointed. Is everything okay out there? How is work?

Oh, nothing. (Name Omitted) wasn't at this last meeting, and I was hoping she would be.

Why?

Needed her approval, I guess.

It's her event; I get it, but don't let it get you down. You land at seven in the morning, right?

Yeah.

I'll see you in the morning. I love you.

You too.

Honey wasn't what I wanted right then, which was weird because she is my entire security blanket. So for her to not give me comfort in that moment was alarming for me.

What's on your mind?

Then I found myself sitting at dinner with Foxy, and I was in a funk. I couldn't understand it, and rather than hiding it, I had the nerve to question her.

Where were you this afternoon?

Excuse me?

The florist. Where were you?

The way she smiled at me…I realized I'd fucked up.

You realized I wasn't there.

Of course. You've been at everything else.
Why wouldn't I notice you weren't there?

I wanted you to miss me.

Excuse me.

Sentury, I'm attracted to you, and you won't give
me the time of day. Have you not noticed?

(Silence)

I am a lesbian. I thought you knew; you did so much
research. What did your research about me yield?

(Silence)

As I was checking myself, my phone started ringing. Honey's beautiful face popped up on my screen. Foxy and I both looked down at the phone. I tried to cut it off quick as hell, but she'd already peeked at the word *Honey* on the screen.

You need to answer that?

No.

Your girlfriend?

No.

Oh, you're single?

No, I'm straight.

(Silence)

I know. I know. I just pissed you off. I make myself mad some-times. I didn't know what else to fucking say. This woman was looking at me in my eyes as if searching for signs that I was available so that she could try to get with me. I couldn't do that to Honey. I didn't want to.

The rest of the dinner was mad awkward. She didn't have much to say, and I could tell I hurt her feelings.

Are you disappointed?

You're beautiful, Sentury. I shouldn't have assumed.

*Thank you, but that doesn't mean
we can't be friends, right?*

Unfortunately, that's exactly what it means.

She dropped a one-hundred-dollar bill on the table and walked out. I'm sitting there looking stupid. Honey called back; I ignored the call again. Wasn't in the mood. Lovely work trip. Just fucking lovely.

August 10, 2007

My mother is a piece of fucking work! She never ceases to amaze me. Let me be clear. She has no idea about me and Honey; however, the fact that she thinks she is a matchmaker makes my spleen itch! Jesus, give me strength! Let's discuss today's mother antics.

Sentury, come down here.

I'm off of work because I am getting ready to head back to Chicago in a few days, and my boss wants to give me some me time before I am there working nonstop. Amazing man. My mother, on the other hand, couldn't care less that I am relaxing.

Mom, who is this?

I get downstairs, and there is a man looking at me. If I were Squeak in *The Color Purple*, I would have been saying, "Harpo, who dis woman?" I was stuck looking between my mother and this man.

Isn't he handsome?

Who is he?

Don't be rude.

Hello.

Hello.

Who are you?

Sentury! Excuse her; she has no manners. Give her about ten minutes, and she will be ready.

Ready for what?

Sentury, can I see you in the other room?

Mind you, I have on a wifebeater and some basketball shorts, my hair is all over my head, and I ain't going nowhere, so where'd she get this shit? Mom pushes me into the dining room and starts that whispering-between-her-teeth bullshit.

Don't you embarrass me!

What are you doing?

Setting you up with a real man!

I didn't ask you for that!

The only person I see you running around with ain't for you, and since you like married men so much, he just got a divorce.

Oh, is that how you are acting today?

You need to grow up, Sentury. You will be thirty
years old, and you need to settle down, get out of
my house, and live like a respectable woman.

You think I am going to do this with Mr. No Name
out there.

You damn right! Now go upstairs, fix yourself up,
and go to the basketball game with this man.

Mom…

What did I say?

She's going to tell me I'm almost thirty, but treat me as if I'm three. Make that shit make sense! I get upstairs, and my loving, unassuming girlfriend is sitting on my bed.

You got to leave.

Huh?

My mom is setting me up on a date.

(Laughter)

Babe, I'm serious.

(Silence)

My mom has a man downstairs, and he is taking
me to the UNLV game tonight. She asked me not to
embarrass her, so that means I have to go.

What about me?

You got to go, babe. I don't know. She's wild.
She just gave me this whole speech about being
almost thirty and growing up and sleeping with
married men…

Sleeping with married men?

Besides the point.

> *So I am supposed to be okay with you going out on
> a date with a man in my face? This shit is silly.*

*I'm going to a basketball game with a man whose
name I don't know, and it's not a date.*

> *(Silence)*

I got dressed. Nothing fancy—UNLV hoodie, some jeans and Js. Honey and I both came down the stairs. My mother and Honey already don't really deal because of when I was sick, so they glare at each other from time to time, but today Mom was smiling as Honey glared.

Nice to see you again, (Name Omitted)!

My mother is beyond petty; she makes me sick! Honey stormed out, and this guy, Mr. Handsome, was looking confused. I gave a half smile.

Ready?

> *You kids have a good time!*

It was the weirdest thing to get in the car with this man whose name I still didn't know. We rode all the way to UNLV in silence, and as we pulled in the parking lot, I had to say something.

What did my mother put you up to?

> *She said you thought I was attractive, and now
> that I was divorced, we should give it a try.*

Wow.

> *What?*

She's unbelievable.

> *It wasn't true?*

B. Danielle Watkins

Sir, I don't even know your name.

                                                        Wow.

*Let alone, know that you used to be married
or want to talk to you after your divorce.*

                                                     Jason.

What?

                                        My name, it's Jason.

*Thank you. I've been calling you Mr. Handsome
since that's how my mom presented you. "Isn't he
handsome!" She makes me sick.*

                    *I must say, I am disappointed I was lied to, but you
are beautiful. Even if it isn't real, you're the best
date in the streets, so let's enjoy the night.*

(Silence)

I was surprised at how well he took the fact my mother was a liar, and even more impressed that despite what I had to say, he wanted to continue the "date." I wasn't tripping; we all know I love women's basketball, so it was a win for me.

I'm sure you were better than everyone on the court.

He knew how to soften me up. We spent much of the game comparing my basketball career to those of the players on the court. He was knowledgeable about my career, and I know it was no thanks to my mother.

How do you know all of this?

                    *You don't just go out on dates with people
you know nothing about, do you?*

(Laughter)

I forgot who I was talking to.

I see you have jokes.

Just saying, is that a thing?

Must be.

I found myself flirting with this man. Jason. Mr. Handsome. My time with him was light and fun. There was no pressure, and that was cool for me. Not saying there was pressure with Honey, but with Honey, when I was out with her, I still had an uneasy feeling. People didn't look at me strange when I was with Jason, so there was a sense of relief in that moment.

I can't take you home on an empty stomach; that isn't gentlemanly. You like Chinese?

Did my mom tell you that?

Maybe, maybe not.

Then the answer is maybe, maybe not.

He took me straight to P.F. Chang's! My favorite restaurant ever! By this point, Honey must have called twenty times, and I had a million (really six) text messages from her. It wasn't that I was ignoring her, but in that moment, I couldn't answer all of her questions and give her the attention she needed without taking away from my time with Jason. I feel bad even saying this, but reality is, I was enjoying my time with Jason more than I enjoyed my time with Honey. I felt free, and it was something I hadn't felt in over half the year. I needed this.

I enjoyed our time together.

I did too.

Too bad this date wasn't commissioned.

Yeah, too bad.

What are we going to do about it?

I don't know. What are we going to do?

He gave me his number and a goodbye kiss. When I walked in the house, my mother was standing there waiting for a debriefing. But I was still upset with her, despite the turn of the evening, so I didn't give her the satisfaction.

You're not going to say anything?

(Silence)

I never called Honey back. Just didn't think I was in the right headspace to deal with her. I will call in the morning; by then, she will be calm, and I will be clear.

August 18, 2007

I'm beyond exhausted. This has been the longest trip of my life! I love what I do, but a bitch is sleepy! One of the hardest things about coming to Chicago this time was leaving town while Honey and I aren't on speaking terms. That whole debacle really put us in a strange place, and I guess it's because we've never had a real argument.

You're going to act like we have nothing to talk about?

We don't.

You went on a whole date, Sentury!

That I didn't sanction.

Did you go?

Yes.

You sanctioned it.

We weren't exactly seeing eye to eye when I got out of the car at the airport. Nothing against what she was saying, but how can she blame me for doing what my mother told me to do? I didn't go find this man in the streets and ask for a date.

Why couldn't you answer the phone?

(Silence)

I didn't like being questioned; that was something else I learned during this whole thing. Every time she asked me another question, I got more and more irritated, to the point that I felt as if I needed a break from her while I was in Chicago.

What do you mean, a break?

I'm going to work for (Name Omitted), and I can't be bogged down by arguments with my girlfriend about men who don't matter.

(Silence)

On that note, I haven't spoken to her since I landed in Chicago. I texted her to let her know I was safe, and I got a stale-ass "K," so there was nothing else for us to talk about.

Hello, Sentury.

In other news, (Name Omitted)—the lesbian, Foxy Brown, slimy politician—was a whole different story. Her fundraiser was amazing, thanks to yours truly. The who's who of Chicago were in attendance, and they were all flapping their money around to endorse her for the state senate. Foxy was beaming with pride as she walked around from table to table, greeting people as only politicians can and thanking them for their generous donations.

You are really talented.

Thank you. You seem to be good at what you do as well.

Something like that.

What do you mean?

Depends on what we are talking about,
politics or something different.

(Silence)

That was my night—Foxy threw out hints every time she got a chance, and I dodged them as if I were in *The Matrix*. As the night began winding down, I found myself alone by the bar, wishing I could take my heels off, sit down in a quiet corner, and hear myself think.

What are you drinking?

She'd spoken to everyone who was important enough to speak to, so it was time for her to direct her full attention toward me.

Woo Woo.

What the hell is that?

Vodka, peach schnapps, lime juice,
and cranberry juice on ice.

Sounds sweet.

It is.

Bartender, a Woo Woo for the lady. Put it on my tab.

After ordering me a drink, she walked to the front of the room to give her thank-you-and-good-night speech. It started off very political—can you tell I don't really do politics?—but it took a turn toward the end. Please imagine me standing by the bar, feet hurting, drinking my Moo Moo.

None of this could have been possible without
the beautiful and incomparable Sentury
Alysé. Sentury, come up here, please.

Caught off guard is an understatement. The crowd was clapping and looking at me, and I was shaking my head no, but her pushy ass was waiting for me to move. I moved, but I didn't like it. I walked slowly to make sure the entire city of Chicago didn't know I couldn't walk in heels, and I meandered my way to the front.

Sentury Alysé is the first woman to ever turn me
down. I find her to be talented, mysterious, and
beautiful, and I am going to use this moment to
ask her again if she would consider going on a date
with me.

I have never in my entire life wanted so badly for something to be a bad dream. I closed my eyes really tight and opened them up superfast, but nothing changed! She was still standing there, looking like Pam and gazing at me as I stared at her, the crowd waiting for me to answer.

I leave town in the morning.

There is always tonight.

Okay.

What the fuck was I supposed to do? Say no in front of all of these people? The crowd erupted in cheers, and the gay folk in the crowd gave her more money! She came out of this fundraiser with well over $200,000; I am sure of it! I don't even know why politicians need money. I should find out why they need loads of cash to work for the government that is paying them. Sounds like a scam all the way around, and I want no part of it. I didn't donate shit.

You're not tired?

No, are you?

Hell yeah!

Straight women get tired. I never would have known.

Ha ha, very funny.

Sentury, I know you're not straight.
Unlike you, I've done my research.

Excuse me?

Montana State University…basketball team.

That's me.

Yeah well, I know you lied to me.
So am I not your type?

(Name Omitted), what are you talking about?

Stay in Chicago an extra day.

I can't. But can I tell you something?

Sure.

If this was a decision I could make, I would
make it for you in a heartbeat.

(Silence)

What I can say is, after all these years of being swept off my feet by women, I have learned a line or two! I told her that shit, and she floated off as if I'd made her night. I will never see that woman again. I had a relationship at home I needed to focus on, and my feet were fucking hurting; I couldn't deal with Foxy right then. So I didn't. Pretty girl, wrong time. Had she caught me in her younger days, I would have fucked her! Believe that!

September 4, 2007

If lives were movies, my life would be a box-office smash hit! Coming off a holiday weekend and a liquor-induced stupor, I am looking back at this weekend and asking myself, *What the fuck was I thinking?* I am sitting here and writing this as I replay the weekend in my head. *Who the hell lives like this?*

Starting from the beginning, I think I'm single. I'm not sure how I feel about it because I think I just realized what truly happened. Ouch! I need to retrace more steps than what I am retracing. Let's start with Friday.

I need to see you.

> *Now, you give a fuck about me?*

Honey. Honey. Honey. When I got back from Chicago, you must know that it was all over the news that a lesbian politician in the Chicago area asked her fundraiser planner on a date in front of the entire crowd.

I can't control that!

> *You can't seem to control anything*
> *that concerns me as your woman!*

I love you!

> *No, you don't.*

Yes, I do; don't tell me I don't! That's not fair, and it's not right.

> *You are on the television, smiling and shit in Chicago, in the face of a bitch who wants you, and don't lie and tell me you didn't know she did, because I know damn well you knew!*

I didn't!

> *Bullshit!*

This argument lasted for weeks. My story never changed, and never will. I am sticking to it.

I bet you never even told her about me.

In that moment, I realized I wouldn't win the argument. I knew that, so I tried to ease it over.

Wasn't her business.

Bullshit!

Babe...

Don't call me that!

Honey...

Don't call me that either. Matter of fact,
don't call me shit. I'll call you.

I didn't hear from her for a few days after that blowup. I get it; she was mad. I wasn't the most forward about her or my relationship with anyone, so her anger was just. I am not going to sit here and say it wasn't; however, she had horrible timing.

Ms. Alysé?

Who is this?

(Name Omitted)

Oh, hi.

I'll be in town Friday.

The universe and God tend to play off of each other every now and again. How ironic was it that I was waiting to hear from Honey, and the woman who caused this entire fight was coming to town and hitting me up? I feel as if no mistakes were made, and I don't want to go against what the universe and God have planned for me, so I just went with it, whatever it was going to be. But never did I think that meant I was going to lose Honey. I am going to cry about that later.

I'm going to go to her job.

> *This is way too much for me right now. Not only did I have to find out about you in Chicago and being a gay on television, but I am finding out almost a year later that you have been in a whole relationship with a bitch, and you never told me!*
>
> *Imma fuck you up.*

LaTrice was right on schedule! If adding insult to injury were a person! I know I was wrong. I was hiding shit. I got to Chicago, and I was careless. But I needed my friend; I didn't need her to tell me some shit I already knew.

I wouldn't talk to your ass either!

Trice!

I wouldn't! You ain't worth the trouble you cause, Sentury! Let's run down the list: you had a nervous break-down, got with a woman, told nobody. Honey got you to be a brand-new person, job included, but then you go on a date with a man, in her face, then go to Chicago and seduce a politician...

I did no such thing.

> *Shut up! You go to Chicago and seduce a politi-cian. Then brought your ass back here and had it on your shoulders like you didn't owe this woman an apology. Then took your ass back to Chicago and didn't talk to said woman, but then allowed the seduced politician to embarrass you and your secret girlfriend on national television!*

When you put it like that...

> *When I put it like that, what? It sounds exactly like it is! A fucking mess! You are a mess! I am sick of the shit!*

Trice!

> *Don't Trice me! You're so fucked up, and you need to see yourself for who you are!*

And who is that, LaTrice!?

> *Don't get cute with me! You're a bitch! You are selfish, and you are hurtful as fuck! You are leaving a true trail of tears behind you, and you don't even realize it. How many people do you think you can hurt before somebody comes and rips your heart out your fucking chest?*

You think I don't know I am hurting people?

> *I don't know what the fuck you know; I know what I see! You hurt me because you didn't think you could tell me what you were doing. I don't know what that was about. And then, on top of that, this girl took care of you! Nursed you! Stood up to your mother for you! And you are treating her like a piece of shit for no reason! You lack accountability, and I am going to give it to you.*

But...

> *Ain't no but! You better hope she is at work to talk to your stupid ass, and if she does talk to you, you better hope she has mercy because you don't deserve her!*

Trice was right. Everything she said was right. There was nothing I could say. I got in my car, with tears in my eyes, raced over to the Hughes Center, and rode the parking lot, looking for Honey's car. Just when I was about to give up, I saw her car, and I parked mine in front of it. Like clockwork, at five Honey came out, walking toward her car. When she saw me in front of the car, she stopped in her tracks. In her face, I could see the confusion and pain fighting with each other. It took her a moment, but she slowly approached me.

What are you doing here?

Can we talk?

Not here.

Where?

I don't know, Sentury. I am not ready to see you!

Babe, I'm sorry.

Get off of me.

I'm sorry, can we talk? Please?

Meet me at Flex tonight.

The club?

You want to talk, right?

Yes.

Meet me there.

I didn't want to hash out my relationship in a club, but after the tongue lashing I got from Trice, I was willing to do anything. Trice was right. I didn't deserve Honey, and she needed to know that.

I went home, got dressed, and headed to the club. When I got there, I realized she never told me a time, so I started calling her. She wouldn't answer the phone, so I started sending text messages asking her where she was and when she was heading to the club. Nothing. Not a word. The longer I sat there, the more uneasy I got about the entire situation. I don't know if I knew something was happening, or if I knew I was losing the woman I loved.

You look beautiful. Did you do this for me?

As if my nerves weren't already bad, Foxy was in the club. Jesus, just take me now! She had an entire entourage with her, and they were all in my face. I kept looking at the door, but Honey never came in. And the more drinks Foxy bought, the less and less cognizant I was becoming.

You love Moo Moos, I see.

They don't taste like liquor, so it works for someone like me who doesn't like the taste of liquor, but likes the feeling.

Why do you keep looking over your shoulder?
Who are you looking for?

No one.

Good, then you can focus all your attention on me.

Huh?

That's what I came here for.

What?

You. I came to claim you.

At this point, it was going on midnight. I'd been sitting at the bar since seven, and nothing about this night was going as I expected. Honey never answered my call, and Foxy kept liquoring me up.

Things get pretty fuzzy after that. I remember leaving the club in Foxy's car. Shit! My car must still be at the club! Fuck! How did this even happen? Okay, okay. I know we went to the Trump Hotel because that is where I woke up this morning. Think, Sentury! Think! What did you do?

Oh my God! I fucked her. I know I did. I can taste it. Oh no, no, no. This isn't happening; this couldn't be happening. Why don't I remember this?? Did she drug me? Oh my God! I can't. I just can't!

I didn't mean it.

Part 3

Transcendent

Love goes very far beyond the physical person of the beloved. It finds its deepest meaning in his spiritual being, his inner self. Whether or not he is actually present, whether or not he is still alive at all, ceases somehow to be of importance.

—Viktor E. Frankl

June 25, 2009

It's the day that music died. Michael Jackson died. I haven't written in this thing in so long, but after such a loss, I needed to just get this out. I never thought it would happen, or it would happen so soon. I never thought I would lose him. It's something I just can't comprehend, and the world is in mourning. It hurts.

May 14, 2012

It has been a long time, and I feel as if I have reconnected with an old friend. Wow, so much time has passed; so much has happened since my last real entry. I see I made time to acknowledge the king though, but even then, I didn't say much about what was going on in my life. It's been too much to go play by play, but I will say this: I have accepted all of myself and being a lesbian is included.

Yes, I am a lesbian. I have accepted this about myself, even if those around me will not. I spent years hiding, playing, wading in the waters, but I had to sit down with myself and really think about what was making me happy. I spent a couple years abstaining. Staying away from everyone, men and women, because I needed to rid myself of all distractions and see what it was I really needed. It wasn't easy for someone like me. Reading this journal, going back through my journey (see what I did there), and seeing where I am now—God has brought me a long way.

I truly believe I was using sex to cope. Cope with my father's death, cope with the lack of relationship I had with my mother, cope with hiding from my own sexuality; I was coping with coping. I was self-destructive, and I didn't have respect for myself or the people around me. I caused so much pain and suffering in the lives of so many people because I was not settled within myself. Even my depression stemmed from a lack of ability to cope.

At thirty-three years old, I am so thankful that I've come to terms with myself now. There are people in their fifties who can face themselves in the mirror and say to themselves, "You need to own your part in the destruction in your life and move past it." It's not easy, and I don't recommend it. It's scary, and it hurts. It's not something that anybody wants to face, but I did it. I did it. I fucking did it. I cried it out. I prayed it out. I talked it out. I faced my fuckups so that I could grow past all the bullshit and just be Sentury.

Who is Sentury, you ask? Thank you for asking. Sentury is a beautiful Black woman who is statuesque and powerful. I am feminine, but I am a tomboy and will still kill somebody on the basketball court if need be. I am a woman who loves women. I love women, and there is nothing wrong with that. There is nothing wrong with me. Sentury is sexual. I like sex. Yes, I had an unhealthy sex life, but sex is important to me. Sentury is love. The moment I learned what love was, I realized it was all in me. I may have had a fucked-up way of showing it, but it was all I knew at the time.

Sentury made mistakes, many mistakes; I did shit I can't take back. I said shit I can't take back. I fucked up relationships with people who didn't deserve it, and that's all on me. At the end of it all, Sentury is human. I will never be perfect, but I am so grateful for my journey thus far, and I am excited to be in the space I am in now.

As for the lesbian thing, I have come to that conclusion, but I haven't shared it with others, and that was a personal choice. When I was on that journey of self-discovery, I realized being a lesbian was something I wanted to keep to myself. Not as I'd done so in the past; I wasn't hiding. No. I was giving myself space to understand it, so when I had to explain it, I could stand strong in my truth. I didn't want to tell people and then crumble under pressure. I needed more time and coming into my own meant holding on to some things.

I haven't dated anybody in years—like since Honey. Saying her name hurts me something terrible. That girl didn't deserve any of what I gave her, and I lost her as, just as I should have. When I was going through my painstaking realizations, I realized I learned my biggest lesson from Honey. The sun doesn't rise and set on my ass. At all. As a matter of fact, the sun doesn't give a fuck about me. Every day, the sun rises and sets without a care for anyone. Honey gave me the world…until she didn't. I expected her to come back, and she walked away from me, clearly and cleanly, because she knew her worth, and I didn't. I appreciate her for this lesson, and I miss her deeply.

Tomorrow is my father's birthday. My mother and I are better, but I know when I sit her down and tell her who I am, it will get bad again. I am okay with that. I would rather start over in my truth than continue in a lie. Tomorrow, I plan to tell both of my parents who I am and let Daddy's personal new year be my own rebirth.

May 15, 2012

Happy heavenly birthday, Daddy! Today was trying, but it was to be expected. I feel as if such a weight has been lifted from my shoulders, and if I could face this, I can face anything the world has to throw at me. Today was also the first birthday since my father's death that I didn't yearn for him; instead, I celebrated him. I went to Daddy's grave with balloons and flowers; I played his favorite song, "Cherish" by Kool and the Gang, and danced next to his grave, smiling because I was in a space where I could. Before I left, I even told Daddy who I was.

> *Hey, Dad, before I go, I just wanted to let you know something. I have been going through so much it is unbelievable, but I'm okay now. I'm a lesbian. I know you don't love me any less, and now I love me even more. Happy birthday, Daddy. I'll love you forever.*

The ride home was amazing! I had my music playing, windows down, and I smiled and cried at the same time. It felt good. I knew that telling my mom wasn't going to be as easy, but I felt as though going to the graveside first was going to give me the strength I needed to face my mother. It did.

Hey, Ma.

                                        Hey, Sen.

Can we talk?

                                        Sure.

Have a seat.

                        Oh God, are you pregnant?

No, Mommy, just sit down.

                        Jesus, you called me Mommy.
                        Do you have cancer?

Lord no, just sit down.

                When I finally got my mother to stop thinking I had stage four cancer, she looked at me as if she hadn't seen me in a long time.

You look different.

                                I feel different.

What's going on, baby? Talk to me.

Mom, I have been battling some demons for a while now. After my depression, I needed to do the work on myself so that I could beat it.

Amen.

While I was working on myself, I had some realizations about myself, and who I wanted to be moving forward so that I could be happy with myself.

Okay.

Mom.

Yes.

I'm a lesbian.

(Silence)

Over the years, it was just a thought, it was an accusation, it was everything other than my reality, but the truth under all of that pain is I am a lesbian.

(Silence)

I was hurting so bad, Mom. Things between us were horrible. I was still grieving Daddy. There was so much on me that I couldn't see clearly, but I see clearly now. What I see is that I have an undeniable attraction for women, and I prefer them over men.

How could you be so fucking disrespectful?

Huh?

On your father's birthday, you sit me down to tell me you're a dyke?

That's so derogatory, Mom.

Dyke! You sit me down to tell me my
child is laying down with women?

                    I haven't dated in a long time, Mom.

So, this is something you've been doing?

                    Are you listening to me?

Yes, I hear you very loud, and what I'm
hearing is that you don't care how your
behavior reflects on this family.

                    Mom, I have to live my life for me.

What about me?

                    What about you, Ma? You lived
                    your life; I have to live mine.

What about God?

                    He loves me.

Bullshit.

                    Mommy, I love you, but this is me.

Get out.

                    What?

Get out.

                    Mom…

You will not live in my house, as a grown-ass
woman, and lay up with women when you feel like
it. You have until the end of the month.

                    I love you.

I can afford to live alone; it's not a big deal to me. I haven't
had my mother most of my life, and if she wants to put me out

for standing up to her, that is more than okay. Am I hurt by her reaction? Eh, not really. I expected worse, to be honest. Mom is all about appearances, and if I am different than the expectation, then I am the enemy. It's cool. I'm happy, and she will get over this. And if she doesn't, that's fine too. I'm happy.

June 1, 2012

Today was crazy! Not only was it my move-in day for my new apartment, but I ran into Honey. Trust me, it was the last thing I expected, but at the same time, it made me so happy. I moved into a spot about three miles from the Strip, which is beautiful because from my balcony I can see the Strip. At night, the view is breathtaking; however, the apartment is on the other side of town from what I've ever known.

Enter Honey.

How can I help you today?

Hello, I need wooden things for my bed
— to keep it up, apparently.

Slats?

Sure.

Right this way.

I had to go to Home Depot because I bought a bed that didn't come with all the pieces. Who the hell sells a bed that you've got to go out and buy shit to go with it? Annoying! The movers put my bed together, I sat on it, and the shit collapsed. I cursed those people out! I had to apologize after the fifth time they put it together, and then they told me about the wood things I needed. I felt guilty and tipped them well because I talked to them really badly.

Anyways, at Home Depot, I had a little man helping me figure out what all I needed. On my phone, I had to pull up the bed I bought and figure out the measurements; it was a complete nightmare. But as I was walking out of the store, I dropped all of the wood. Everything I had in my hands just fell as if someone from the heavens had slapped them!

Sentury?

If I weren't already embarrassed that I had butterfingers, my one-who-got-away, whom I hadn't seen or spoken with in like five years, is standing over me with her girlfriend and looking as if she's seen a ghost.

(Name Omitted)*? Hi.*

Do you need help?

Wood was on the floor. Heart was on the floor. Face was on the floor. Just clean my whole life up off the floor. In true Honey fashion, she came to my aid. She looked different. More beautiful, as if that were something that could even happen. We are older now, so we are more established in life and doing better, making more money, and, my God, it looks good on her.

Tonya, this is Sentury.
I've heard so much about you.

I'm sure there are better stories in the world than
the ones about me.

No, there aren't.

(Silence)

There is a Mariah Carey song for this occasion. Let me grab my iPod. *Emancipation of Mimi* album, "Circles." That's my fucking life! The entire second verse spoke to this situation as if I'd written it myself!

I literally was choking on tears as they walked me to my car to help me put the wood and shit in there. I tried my damnedest to not face them; I wanted to just say thank you and drive off, but, no, Honey didn't allow that.

You live around here now?

Her girlfriend was looking as bewildered as I was. Why are we asking such questions? This was a chance meeting. Everything that I had been wanting to say if I ever talked to her again wasn't about to come out without a river full of tears, in front of her girlfriend, so it was better that she just let me leave. Everybody but her in the equation knew this.

Yes, I just moved in today.

That's crazy. Where?

In the Oasis condos on Karen.

Seriously?

Yes, why?

We live there too!

Jesus, strike me down! How in the hell did I manage to get a place in the same complex as my ex, whom I am aching for, and her current? Is that the definition of Karma? It couldn't be; the world of Buddha and them couldn't be so cold.

Which unit are you?

Fifty-seven.

I'll come by later and help you unpack.

Okay. Nice to meet you, Tonya.

(Silence)

B. Danielle Watkins

294

This girl hates me, and she just met me. Why did Honey have to be so Honey? I cried all the damn way home. An ugly cry. Gut-wrenching. What did I expect, she was going to be single for the rest of her life? I probably will be, but she deserves someone to love and for her to love and experience. I had it. I fucked it up. I lost it. It's my burden to bear, and I didn't know how heavy it was until she knocked on the damn door.

I brought dinner.

She walked in the door with my favorite food—P.F. Chang's. Honey knows the way to a girl's heart. She was acting as if nothing ever fucking happened. I was dying on the inside. I wanted to bring the shit up, but it was so nice to be with her I didn't want to mess up the vibe. I was going through some shit on the inside, and she was just smiling and unpacking and singing along to the music.

About an hour in, her phone began to ring, and I knew it was her girlfriend. Nobody's girlfriend would be okay with their partner buying dinner and heading to their ex's new apartment. Nobody. Not a soul in the world. I wouldn't.

Was that Tonya?

Yeah.

It's okay if you need to leave; you've done enough.

No.

No?

No.

(Name Omitted), *I can handle it. I promise.*

Call me Honey.

(Heart melted)

There was a nostalgic tone to her voice when she told me to call her Honey. Unbeknownst to her, I never stopped calling her Honey, so it came naturally. By this point, her energy had shifted, and I was thinking it was because of the phone call from her girl.

If she wants you to come home, Honey, I get it.

I need to say something.

I knew my life was about to get slightly harder in this moment. Her face was serious, her tone was serious, and the food was gone.

I'm sorry.

What!? I'm sitting here, going through all of these motions, and she was apologizing to me. I couldn't believe it. That made me love her even more because it was such a selfless reflection of how she ended our relationship. She spent about thirty minutes just explaining her reactions to the politician and my not being out. How she ran from it, rather than facing it with me. How, for all these years, she had been too embarrassed to reach out, so she changed her number and let me live.

I was stunned. I didn't know what to do with this. I didn't know if I was supposed to profess my love for her or say things happened as they should have and let her go live the life she deserved. I didn't say shit. It was safer.

Can I come by sometimes?

Of course.

I love you, Sentury.

I love you too.

She kissed my cheek and walked out. I closed the door so dramatically I was angry with myself for my own behavior. I leaned against the door and cried, and in my mind, she was doing the exact same thing on the other side of my door. Whether she was or not is beyond me, but that is the story I told myself. In my mind, she ached for me the way I ached for her, but at the end of the day, there was a love there that we could do nothing with.

I want love, but I think to want a love with her is selfish. I may be wrong in my thoughts, but I didn't know how to treat her when I had her. So how dare I think that it's okay for me to act on the love that remains? I would much rather walk away as friends and allow her to love freely without the fear of being hurt by me again. Maybe I will find somebody else. Somebody I won't compare to her. Someone I can love freely.

No lie, it cuts me up to know not only that she is with somebody else, but that she loves her. My God, I had to say that out loud. Honey—my first love, my entire heart, the woman who taught me more about myself than I could teach myself—has someone else whom she loves, and it's not me. Ouch! I guess in my imagination, when she saw me, her world was supposed to stop and rearrange itself because she was still in love with me. That's that sun-rises-and-sets-on-my-ass thing. It's real! It's fucking real!

I love Honey from a place that cannot be touched, and I always will. I appreciate the fact she even thought enough of me to apologize. To me, that was such a sweet gesture because, yes, she left me, but look at what the fuck I was doing. Even I would have left me.

In my new place, alone and aching for a love that's a couple feet away—that's some shit I could never have imagined. I'm going to sleep.

June 8, 2012

Happy thirty-fourth me! I have been in my own place, the first since I was in college, for about a week now, and I think I love it! It's not too bad living in the same building as my ex-girl-friend either.

Happy Birthday!

LaTrice moved to Louisiana, so my life is slightly different without her. But she is always the first person to call me on my birthday.

Have you heard from your mom?

No, but I might not. I'm okay with that.
This is all still pretty fresh for her.

Have you seen Honey?

She woke me up this morning.

Excuse me?

Considering Trice is gone and the situation with my mom, it seemed natural to give Honey a key to my place in case of emergencies. This morning I woke up, and she was standing in front of me with a cake. She had candles lit and was standing there just smiling.

Happy birthday, beautiful.

LaTrice was too outdone.

So, she wished you happy birthday before I did?

You were the first call though, Trice; you were still first.

How does her girlfriend feel about all of this?

I don't know. I've only been here a week.

How many times have you seen her?

(Silence)

Every day, eh?

How did you know?

> *I know you. Have you told her*
> *you are still in love with her yet?*

No.

> *Why not?*
> *I don't want to. I want to be friends.*

She is using her key unannounced, wishing you
happy birthday, and stopping by daily. You don't
think she already knows?

> (Silence)

Honey is just being a friend. We said we would be friends, so that's what we are doing.

> *What're your plans today?*

When she brought the cake and I finally got out of the bed, we sat at my table and had red velvet cheesecake for breakfast.

I don't have any.

> *It's Friday!*

I know.

> *Are you off work?*

No.

> *What about tonight?*

Nothing planned.

> *We are going out!*

Just like that, I had plans for my birthday. I would have done just fine picking up some P.F. Chang's, coming home, sitting on my couch, and watching *The Boondocks* reruns until I fell asleep! Honey had other plans in mind.

Is Tonya coming?

If she wants to. If not…we're out!

When I got off work today, I raced home. It was like a little kid on the first day of school; I was super excited to hang out with Honey. I had this new red dress that I bought for an event for work that ended up being cancelled; it was just waiting to make me look good. I stood in the mirror for about an hour and perfected my makeup. Hair is always laid, so all I had to do was brush it back into place. Then I just waited.

I think I have PTSD because waiting for Honey reminded me of being in the club and waiting for her all those years ago; it didn't feel good. I started pacing the floor, checking my phone, and pacing some more. About nine, I heard a faint knock at my door. When I opened it there she stood, tears in her eyes and not dressed to go anywhere.

Can we reschedule?

I took my heels off when I saw her because I knew she was in no condition to go anywhere.

What happened?

Tonya and I just had the worst fight ever!

Why?

Because of you.

(Silence)

Let me say this: you don't know how strong you are until you have to be strong. I was sitting in my house, looking at the woman I crave silently, and watching her cry about the woman she loves. Man, young Sentury wouldn't have taken this too well; let me just put that shit right on the table. Ain't no way in hell the old me would have been able to separate the emotions well enough to be a friend to Honey.

In that moment, she needed to know I loved her, but she didn't need to be bogged down by my love for her. Oh, that was good right there; I'm going to say that again. She didn't need to be bogged down by my love for her. I needed to check myself immediately so I could be who she needed me to be in that moment.

Honey, I'm sorry.

> *Sentury, I won't apologize for loving you.*

You don't have to.

> *I mean to her. I won't apologize to her for loving you.*

(Silence)

> *You came before her, and that doesn't negate the love I have for her. I love Tonya. I wanted to marry her, but now I don't know.*

Why?

> *Can you marry someone and love someone else?*

Yes, you can.

> *What?*

Honey, if you loved Tonya enough to marry her before you saw me in the Home Depot parking lot, you still love her enough to marry her.

The pain that shot through my chest when I said that shit! Not that I didn't mean it, but reality is, if she marries this woman, it solidifies there will be no more us; I think for both of us that was a hard pill to swallow. I fought tears as I held her in hers. My love hurts, so I hurt. I hurt for her, and I hurt for me. It was as if we both knew what this would mean.

I don't want to ruin your birthday.

As long as I am with you, I'm happy.
Best birthday ever.

Sentury, I am so sorry.

It was by far one of the most emotional birthdays I've ever had, but still special. Through our tears, we learned a lot about each other silently, and I appreciate that the most. In the end, being her friend is far more important to me. Yes, I would love to have another chance to treat her right and be the woman she needed me to be, but my time has come and gone; I think that chance has long passed. I wouldn't be a friend if I didn't encourage her to fix it with her girl. Now, if that doesn't work and the universe gives us a space to be back together, you damn right I'm jumping on that. But right now, we are friends, and that's the birthday present I needed.

July 9, 2012

I love my job. Over the years, I have been in some fantastic venues and have planned some amazing events. I am currently in the City of Angels and in the presence of some music-industry royalty. At the forefront of it all is the sexiest woman I've ever laid eyes on: Siobhan Rei.

Hello, I'm Siobhan Rei, and you are?

Sentury Alysé.

I like your name.

I like yours too.

My mission in Los Angeles is to land the contract for Capitol Records, which would give Belmore the first right of refusal for the planning of all Capitol events—album releases, pre- and post-Grammy parties, and any other Capitol activity that required planning. If I land this contract, I would then be the overseer of it as the executive planner for Capitol Records. The person I needed to impress to do it—Siobhan Rei.

Siobhan Rei, I just love how her name looks in print. I can't imagine just calling her Siobhan. She's the top PR rep for Capitol Records and is forty-five years old, a mix of Black and Japanese, and a masculine-identified woman. Yes, she is a lesbian. She has been in the music industry for over twenty years and has worked with artists like the Bee Gees, Neil Diamond, Paul McCartney, Ice Cube, MC Hammer, and even Nancy Wilson. When I say music gold, she is music gold! She may be the head of PR now, but she has done everything from merchandising to sound engineering.

Your presentation was fantastic.

I have been in Los Angeles for three days now, and today was the final meeting to get Siobhan Rei to say yes to Belmore.

> *Aside from the corporate bullshit that you drum up to suck companies into spending their money, tell me why I should endorse Belmore, a small company that is not local, when there are several more reputable companies here in LA?*

That's easy.

Is that right?

Yes.

Then why?

Because none of them have shit on me.

(Silence)

This sexy-ass woman leaned back in her seat, looked over at her assistants, and then back at me... I GOT THE CONTRACT!

Dinner on me.

I can't even catch my breath; she was amazing to deal with. From the professional setting to once she loosened up her tie and was laid-back at dinner. She took me to Roscoe's Chicken and Waffles, and it was as if she weren't famous anymore; she was just Siobhan Rei, a mixed-race girl who likes chicken and sticky rice and grew up in Compton.

You've never wanted to leave this area?

Why leave LA? There is nothing else like it.

I can get that.

You prefer Montana over Vegas?

Hell no.

See.

What?

You were raised there, but you still prefer it.

*I'll leave Vegas. Today, I just got a contract
in your city. Imagine that.*

It don't get no better.

I'm obsessed. Everything about her. And she's older than I am; that's fine. I mean, she doesn't know I'm obsessed or that I'm planning our lives together or anything like that, but she is amazing. She has a degree from USC (University of Southern California) in marketing and a masters from Berkeley—like, she's educated, cultured, and down-to-earth. I am enamored with her.

You have a look in your eyes.

Do I?

You like me?

What?

You are into me.

This is business.

But this is personal.

I have lesbian eyes apparently. I didn't deny it, though, because I knew she was single. If she's single, and I'm single, then we can be single together, which means we've gone from single to taken. It is totally against company policy for me to do this; however, to court the new client is not against company policy.

When can you be back?

Depends.

On?

Business or personal?

Personal business.

Next week.

I'll see you then.

Can you imagine me on the arm of Siobhan Rei? I can. I am stunning—let's just put the shit on out there—and she is fine as hell. We would be the talk of any red carpet, as she deserves to be. I even called Honey and told her about Siobhan tonight when I got back to my room.

Guess what?

> *What happened?*

I got the contract!

> *I am so proud of you, Sentury! That is amazing!*

Guess what else?

> *What?*

I have a date with Siobhan Rei.

> *Siobhan Rei?*

Yes.

> *The Siobhan Rei?*

Yes.

> (Silence)

She and I are still navigating this friendship thing. I know she wasn't thrilled to hear my excitement about having a date with another woman, but at the end of the day, we are both pushing the other to be happy. So with that in mind, she gave her well-wishes and told me she would see me when I got home.

Siobhan Rei invited me to the RCA West listening party for Elle Varner's album next week. Perfect market- and competition-research opportunity. I will hop on my flight in the morning, head to work, and make my arrangements to come back and accompany her.

July 19, 2012

I am living a dream. Wow. I can't even believe this is my life. Let me start by saying Elle Varner's new album, *Perfectly Imperfect*, is amazing. That listening party was something out of the movies. Elle even sang "Refill" for us, and she has a beautiful in-person voice. Some people don't sound like themselves when they get on stage; in the studio, they get fixed up so much their voice is unrecognizable on stage. Siobhan Rei was the dream date. She picked me up from my hotel in a limo and took me over to the club on Sunset Boulevard, where the event was being held.

How would you like to be introduced?

Sentury is fine.

Ms. Sentury Alysé, it is.

Let's start from the beginning. We walk into the club, and of course she knows everybody. But with each greeting, she introduces me to the person she is speaking to, holding my hand and all.

This is Ms. Sentury Alysé.

The respect in the room for her was unspoken but high, which bled into how they greeted me. Nobody asked me what I did; it was clear it didn't matter because I was there with Siobhan Rei. Record execs from other companies had their own VIP tables toward the front of the room, and we were front and center.

As the night went on, more and more people came by our table, spoke, shook my hand, complimented, and stared. I am sure she has slept with some of the women who came by the table to get a look at me.

You good?

Yes, why?

You're on display, and I wasn't
sure if you could handle it.

What made you think I couldn't?

This isn't your lane.

It is now, right?

Damn.

What?

*I like how you handle your own
with me. You aren't scared.*

Is there a reason to be scared?

Nah, but it's a thing. You see this; you see me.

All I see is you.

Enough said.

Once Elle took the stage, the entire mood changed. Siobhan Rei moved closer to me, making me feel as if I were the only girl in the room. Siobhan Rei's presence is undeniable. Her personality fills a space, so when she moves in on your space you have to stand your ground to make sure you don't lose yourself in her. I'm trying to be lost in her, but in a different way. In a room, she needed a woman who could shine just as bright as she did, and I was up for the challenge.

For a debut album, this is hot. I wish we'd signed her.

I love this song.

Elle sang "I Don't Care," and Siobhan could see I was feeling the song. Next thing I know, Siobhan had Elle sing it again! She had the power to tell that girl to run it back one more time so I could hear it again. The album doesn't come out for another month or something like that, but I was already sold. I could have waited for the album, but I didn't let on; I acted as if I expected that of Siobhan.

Thank you.

You like the song, right?

Of course, I do.

Then you should have heard it again.

You're right.

It made me feel powerful; she empowered me. I'm so in love. I can't tell her I'm in love though; she isn't that type of woman. Women fall all over her often, and you don't want somebody who wants you in this industry. This is the type of woman whom you have to keep on their toes, and I have that down pat.

You going to continue to act like you don't want me?

Once the listening party was over, Siobhan Rei and I went to the after-party and danced until there was no one left on the floor.

Do I make your heart race?

What?

Do I?

I must make your heart race.

What?

You're asking me all these questions. Reality is, you are trying to project onto me how you feel about me, and I'm not biting. Sorry.

That drove her insane! I was like a little girl on the inside, but I read the vibes, and I knew what I needed to do to get what I wanted. I have the biggest crush, and I've only known this woman for a week, but we have spoken daily since I left LA the first time.

Then we were on the dance floor together and looking into each other's eyes.

Want a drink?

I don't drink.

Good girl?

Smart girl.

Explain.

*I don't want to have to mask
my actions by liquid courage.*

Is that right?

*This way, all of my actions are understood to be
mine and mine alone.*

When we got back into her car, she was all over me. It felt good to not be in a drunken stupor and to actually feel and enjoy the sensuousness of what was happening. We were naked in the back of the car before the driver turned the corner. Siobhan Rei's sex was different. It was rough; it was seasoned.

With our nine-year age difference comes a lot, and experience was one of those things. Now, we know I have had my share of sex. I'm no Virgin Mary by far, but she is an old lesbian with old-lesbian tricks up her sleeves.

What is that?

We are in the middle of heavy making out and petting, and she reaches under the seat and pulls out a satin bag. Inside of the bag was a plastic dick. Wait a damn minute!

You ain't never been strapped?

No.

Fuck yeah!

Baby! She put this contraption on and slid that black plastic dick inside of me, and it was as if the world stopped. Siobhan Rei looked me in the eyes as she thrust in and out of me like a madwoman. I was so wet it was unbelievable. I am embarrassed to say that. When I was having sex with men, dick didn't do that to me! I didn't even like dick, hence how we got here. The sex got intense. The louder I moaned, the harder she went, and unlike a man, ain't no stopping when you come. That thing stays hard. We fucked. Period. Upside down, around, sideways, backwards. She was tossing me around like a rag doll, and I was loving every minute of it.

By the time we finished, we had been sitting in the parking lot of my hotel for a while. I was embarrassed the driver heard us, but, shit, it was so good I didn't even mind. I haven't had sex in five years; my body needed it. The way Siobhan Rei did it was the best way to be reintroduced to the lesbian lifestyle.

Will I hear from you?
Probably not.

A good fuck or not, I know the game I need to play. I may be sprung. I may still be wet. I may want to do it again, but I damn sure ain't telling her that. The way she made my body feel and the way she looked at me as I exited the car made me feel beautiful, and nothing can take that away. But, damn, if I could feel her again, I wouldn't mind at all.

August 31, 2012

I have been so busy I forgot I had a damn diary, journal, sounding board…hell, notebook. I realized my mother gave me this diary when I was eighteen years old. Had I stayed with it, it would have been filled years ago, but, due to life, sometimes I write, but sometimes I don't. This diary has grown up with me. Wow. The things you don't know matter…until they do. I like flipping through and looking at what I went through or didn't. I clearly had more time in college than I do now to detail my entire life, but I am grateful for this diary now, even if I don't write in it every day. Oh well. No time to be sentimental.

I have phenomenal news. My plan with Siobhan Rei paid off. When I left Los Angeles last month, I had nothing to say to Siobhan Rei. She never got my personal cell number on my business card, and I was only responding to business-related emails. There was nothing else to discuss. It was as if we never even slept together.

Not going to lie. I was dying a slow, terrible death on the inside. I want this woman so bad I can taste it, but I can't tell her. I can't tell anybody. I can't put it in the universe because she might hear it.

You're floating on air around here. You got a boo?

Honey noticed it. She knew I had the date with Siobhan Rei, and she was waiting for details—for her own selfish reasons, I'm sure.

How did it go?

Oh, it was cool.

That's it?

Yeah.

Nothing else?

You should get Elle Varner's album when it comes out.

What about the date?

It was work.

(Silence)

I know she truly doesn't want to hear about me and Siobhan Rei's fuck fest, just as I don't want to hear about her and Tonya when she comes over to vent. So I saved her the vulgar details of my first strapping, and I changed the subject just as my doorbell rang. Honey and I both looked at each other.

Expecting someone?

No.

Honey beat me to the door; the protector came out instantly, and I will admit it gave me butterflies. But I felt the air change when she opened the door to twelve men, each carrying twelve white roses, coming down the hallway.

Sentury Alysé?

The men filed into my apartment and placed roses in every single open space they could find. Honey's face was priceless, as was mine. Each attached note had a different quote about being beautiful.

1. "How dare the world define beauty. God defined beauty when he made you! You are beautiful; you are a true beauty just the way you are!" (Rachel Hamilton)

2. "If you feel beautiful, then you are. Even if you don't, you still are." (Terri Guillemets)

3. "You can take no credit for beauty at sixteen. But if you are beautiful at sixty, it will be your soul's own doing." (Marie Stopes)

4. "You're a beautiful flower; fall fearlessly." (Akash S. Bansal)

5. "Because you are beautiful. I enjoy looking at beautiful people, and I decided a while ago not to deny myself the simpler pleasures of existence." (John Green)

6. "Your beauty cannot be ignored; it is something unbelievable because it not only pleases my eyes but also warms my heart." (Author unknown)

7. "Of course. You are beautiful. And I shall always keep you that way." (Sam Robins)

8. "Because of your smile, you make life more beautiful." (Thich Nhat Hanh)

9. "I just wanted to let you know that I think you are beautiful and amazing and wonderful and everything I wish you could be." (Author unknown)

10. "Every single thing about you is beautiful." (James Frey)

11. "It's quite peculiar for bees and butterflies to not notice a beautiful flower like you. You're so beautiful." (Author unknown)

Then it was the last one.

12. "Meet me in New York." (Siobhan Rei)

Honey and I stood in awe. I was fucking amazed. I personally looked up the cost. If my calculations were correct, it ran her about $3,500 before delivery. So I am going to say it cost roughly $5,000 to ask me to come to New York City. I looked over at Honey. My heart hurt for a moment. She silently went from bouquet to bouquet, reading the cards. When she got to the last one, she turned and looked at me. I couldn't hide my excitement.

You going to go?

Hell yeah.

*Date in LA must have gone
better than you thought.*

Must have.

That was hard. Let me stay true to my feelings. All the infatuation in the world doesn't make up for my love for Honey. Accepting we are what we will be doesn't change that, and anytime she is hurt, it hurts me to the core. As Honey started gathering her things to leave, Siobhan Rei called me.

Your phone is ringing.

That's not important right now.

*Sentury, yes, she is. I can see it in how you're
moving. You love all of this. I am in the way.*

Honey…

Have fun in New York. Be safe, please.

Honey walked out, and my heart broke. I felt as if we'd broken up all over again. The woman of my absolute dreams was blowing my cell phone up, and I was fighting tears, knowing that this could be the beginning of the end again with Honey. I had to get myself together because I needed to still play the role with Siobhan Rei.

*How did you not only get my cell number,
but my home address, Ms. Rei?*

All that matters is I found you, right?

At this point, yes.

> *Are you coming?*

When?

> *Tomorrow.*

Tomorrow?

> *Your flight leaves LAS at noon; bring a party dress.*

I have a flight tomorrow at noon. Siobhan Rei is flying me to New York City. I am freaking out, but I so deserve this. I need to pack!

September 3, 2012

I have a girlfriend. If I could draw hearts all over this book, I would. I think I'm in love too. New York City was perfect. I'd been to New York a few times in college, playing basketball, but I never got to experience that which is NYC.

When I landed in New York, there was a car waiting for me.

> *Ms. Alysé?*

I got into the car and rode from JFK to Manhattan. I am green about it all, so I did not realize it was an hour-and-a-half trip. Riding through the boroughs of New York was fascinating to me. The closer I got to Manhattan, I could see the quality of life changing. Traffic was crazy, but I appreciated it because I was having a mild panic attack thinking about Siobhan Rei and what this trip could possibly mean.

It was almost three when I got to my hotel. I didn't know what name the room was under, but when I got out of the car, someone was standing at the door with flowers. I walked by. Ain't for me; ain't my business.

Sentury.

It was Siobhan. She was waiting for me with the most beautiful bouquet of sunflowers and roses I've ever seen.

Wow.

Impressed yet?

I'll let you know.

I was impressed as fuck! That could have been the whole trip for me, and I would have been just fine! We stayed in the Waldorf-Astoria; I'd only seen that hotel in *Coming to America*. Normal people don't stay at the Waldorf-Astoria. It was gorgeous. Straight out of the movies, random stars walking through the lobby as we made our way to the elevators. I looked as if I didn't belong. I don't look like money. I look like a reformed basketball player in heels. I walked as if I belonged though—couldn't tell me shit—and Siobhan Rei beamed as she guided me through the crowd.

When we got upstairs to the room and we walked in, it took my breath away. The whole back wall was glass, which provided a stunning view of Times Square. The room itself was huge. It was like an apartment, but not even a studio apartment; it was a luxury condo. Siobhan Rei had a dress laid out for me on the bed, and there were other women in the room.

What's going on?

> *Someone like you deserves a glam team; they are going to prepare you for tonight. I have a meeting.*

She kissed me and walked out. I was standing there looking at those women who were staring at me, and I had to check myself. *Bitch, you are this life; embrace it.* That's what LaTrice would have said to me. My self-talk was more, *Oh my God, oh my God, what am I doing? This is way above my fucking pay grade, I'm a fake, and Imma be found out!* Luckily, I have a good poker face. One of the women handed me a mimosa, and I placed my bags down and let the glam begin.

After I got out of the shower, they went to work. One was doing my feet while the other had my hands, another was in my hair, and the makeup artist was checking foundation colors. It was a bit overwhelming. I wonder if this is how Beyoncé feels when she is preparing to go to the BET awards and stuff. I was being pulled in every direction, but all I could do was imagine what the night held in front of me.

In my head, we were going to a red-carpet event, reporters would be calling her name, she would be telling them I was her woman, and I would smile and pose for the camera. Looking like Naomi Campbell. I think I favor her slightly anyways, so with all the glam, it only made sense to think she was my muse. After the event, which really didn't matter, I imagined us having an intimate dinner before a night of making passionate love on the floor with the hustle and bustle of Times Square illuminating the room. Dramatic, yes—even cinematic, yes—but I felt as if at this point anything was possible.

You look amazing.

When Siobhan walked back into the room, I was ready. Let me try and give you a full visual. Times Square lit up in a panoramic view. I am standing in front of the mirror with a Christian Dior Bodycon dress, all black. My hair is up in a tight, slick bun, black nails, high heels, and my face is beat to the gods. All I did was smile.

You belong in my world.

I am in your world.

Our first stop was Broadway. I am not a theater head, let's be honest. Las Vegas may be known for its shows, but theater culture is not a part of that equation. I wasn't sure what to expect of Broadway, but it was amazing. We went to see *Sister Act*. How cool is that? Raven-Symoné played Deloris Van Cartier! I lost it! *Sister Act* was one of my favorite movies in junior high, so it brought back so many memories, and then to see little Raven in the lead role was like wow, wow, wow. It was so amazing. Five stars. I don't even know if I am qualified to give ratings, but the show was fantastic.

Have you been stalking me?

Why do you ask?

You seem to know a lot about what I will and will not like and are accurate. Either you're psychic…

Or a stalker.

Heard that one before?

No, I just like to finish beautiful women's sentences.

Oh, pardon me.

You're excused.

After the show, we had reservations at Sardi's—again, a place I'd only seen on television. Kermit the Frog went to Sardi's in *The Muppets Take Manhattan*, and I love that movie. So at this point I'm like, *Yo, this is scary*. She is hitting marks on films and things that would cause a nostalgic reaction in me. *The Muppets Take Manhattan* was the last movie my father and I went to see before he died.

Be honest with me; who have you been talking to?

Why do you ask?

*You are taking me down memory lane of my most
loved films, in this beautiful city, and it's not making
sense. There isn't enough coincidence in the world
for this.*

> *How is it making you feel?*

Like I'm in a movie.

> *All the world is a stage…*

And everyone has their part—Madonna.

> *Another coincidence?*

At this point, I am thinking to myself this bitch is playing with me. I wanted to get mad, but it was so sweet and so deliberate I started to not want to know how she knew so much about me. The food at Sardi's was too good—like, where do they make food that good in the world? Who knew? Kermit didn't eat, so I never imagined.

You're trying to make me fall for you.

> *Is it working?*

Is that what you want?

> *If I haven't shown you what I want by now,
> then I don't deserve what I want.*

Every time Siobhan Rei kissed me, it sent shock waves through my body. No woman or man has ever put this much thought into getting my attention. In college Camden did the thing with my dad's pictures on campus, and that was sweet, but this was deeper. This was Siobhan Rei taking a glimpse into my life and bringing it to date in a modern, relatable, tangible way. I was able to feel my childhood in my heart and experience these places in real time, and I had never said a word to her about those memories.

When we got back to the hotel, it was late. The hotel was still, but it felt as if there was more. When she stuck the key in the door lock to our room, this music started. Startled me, but when the door opened, a small band was there, and Melanie Fiona started singing her song "Like I Love You," the acoustic version. I was floored. That was it. I cried. She'd gotten me. I'm not even a fan of this woman, but for her to be in my room, singing to me—because Siobhan Rei is Siobhan Rei—was the icing on the cake of my perfect night.

When Melanie finished singing, I learned she and Siobhan Rei are godsisters, and that made me feel a little better because all these stunts and shows Siobhan was pulling out of her pocket were throwing me for a loop. The band cleaned up, and finally, after midnight we were alone. You know what happened next, no need for me to lay it all out.

Now, imagine two naked women's bodies entwined on the floor, with the lights of Times Square the only illumination in the room. Just as I'd fantasized earlier, but more beautiful.

How was your night?

Breathtaking.

I'm not talking about the sex.

Me either.

I'm glad you enjoyed yourself.

I've never experienced anything like it.

This would be your life if you were my woman.

What?

I want you to be mine, Sentury.

I can't do that.

                                                            Why?

My job.

                    Fuck that job. Do you see this? You don't need that job!

I need to think about this.

I got up from the floor, naked and all in a panic. I had been floating on a cloud at the thought of Siobhan Rei, but I know what that comes with. My job has a strict policy; you can't sleep with the people paying your bills. That's just what it is. There is no way around that, and if they find out, I'm fired. Gone. Ain't no discussion. Nothing.

                        What do you have that I can't give you?

My own.

                                                    (Laughter)

That's funny to you?

                        No, your need for independence is what's funny to
                                                                me.

I just met you, and you're willing
to wife me and take care of me?

                                                            Yes.

(Silence)

I realized I was naked in the middle of this conversation, so I went looking for my clothes. I knocked over a lot of shit in the meantime, and Siobhan Rei's jacket fell too. A pair of diamond earrings fell from the pocket. I only saw them because the light hit them just right and they sparkled.

B. Danielle Watkins

Your yes gift.

What?

Those will be yours when you say yes to me.

I was defeated. I said yes, for now. And for now, I have the most beautiful woman in the world calling me hers. Even if I wake up tomorrow and I change my mind. All of that happened, and when I close my eyes, she will still be mine.

September 9, 2012

When people are supposed to be happy for you, they usually are not, and that shit sucks! I was thinking that coming back to Vegas and talking to the two people closest to me in life (Honey and LaTrice) would have led me in a positive direction with this situation with Siobhan Rei, which really isn't even a situation. We are together; the only thing that needs to happen is I need to figure out my job and living situation.

Are you fucking stupid?

I get no breaks from LaTrice, and as a best friend, I guess that is what is supposed to happen. But I am finally happy. Why can't she be happy for me?

This sounds like some controlling shit, and I ain't never known for you to be controlled.

She is not controlling me!

She told you to quit your job, and she just met you last month. She don't know shit about you; sounds to me like she found herself a fool.

LaTrice!

Sentury!

She knew a lot about me.

That is creepy!

But you just said "she don't know shit about" me!

Sentury, you are smarter than this. I swear you are. Yes, she did her research, and she found out things about you that I don't even know. How she found this out is beyond me, but the fact that she searched so deep to get such intimate details about your life, and just met you, is a big fucking red flag for me.

Why, Trice?

Why isn't it one for you, Sentury?

It took me all of these years to accept who I am...

And now that you are a happy gay, you settle down with the first bitch who fucks you good with a plastic penis?

It's not like that.

It's exactly like that. All the lesbians in the United States of America, and you have decided that you got the best one, after only thirty-five days of knowing her.

She makes me feel good!

What about (Name Omitted)?

Honey has a girlfriend.

So, you are stupid!

What?

That girl loves you!

She is in a relationship, so what am I supposed to do? Wait?

You should do something more
than what you are doing.

You are confusing me.

That's not difficult these days.

What are you saying about Honey?

I'm saying that if she had her way, she would be
with you, but circumstances have changed that.
And rather than you pick up on the signs, you are
frolicking around with Siobhan Rei, about to find
your ass on the cover of TMZ!

How do you know that about Honey?

It don't matter to you, right?
You got who you want.

Trice, that's not fair.

What about your job?

I won't need it.

You are willing to depend fully on this
woman for everything. And you don't
find this the least bit controlling?

No.

I can't do this with you.

What?

You are making one of the biggest mistakes of your
life, and I can't just sit around and watch it happen.

LaTrice, what are you saying?

If you go through with this, you don't need me either.

My best friend of almost thirty years told me that if I continued with this relationship, our friendship would be over! How could she be so heartless? What about what is good for me? What about the fact Siobhan is making me happy? LaTrice has been in my ear about accepting myself for all of these years, and now, when I need her the most, she turns her back on me? If that's how she wants to be, fuck her! Fuck LaTrice! Fuck her with a sick dick! I was furious with her!

In my rage, I called Honey. As it was, I needed to talk to her, but LaTrice's accusations about Honey were putting me in a bad mental space, and I needed to know where she got that information.

What are you talking about, Sentury?

Do you talk to LaTrice?

Where is this coming from?

Answer me!

Why are you yelling at me?

Did you tell her you would rather
be with me than Tonya?

(Silence)

Did you tell her that?

Why does it matter, Sentury?

I'm with Siobhan Rei now.

(Silence)

Say something.

You don't know her.

Why does everyone keep saying that?

You don't.

She wants me.

Sentury, I want you!

(Silence)

So, you are going to give this stranger the life you refused to give me?

(Silence)

I am struggling, fighting, trying to be your fucking friend. I love you, and you are going to give it all up for this woman you barely even know.

Honey, I…

I know. You think that because I am with Tonya, this is as far as we will go. You don't know the future, and neither do I!

I just need you to be here for me.

When wasn't I there for you?

I love you.

I know.

I cried when I hung up with Honey. My soul wept for her. I had to make the decision between my best friend, my happiness, and crushing the woman who taught me to love. Nothing about this decision is easy for me. I have gone my entire life making sure shit was good for everyone else and hurting myself.

I spent my college years being someone I wasn't and falling into endless dead-end relationships. I spent my twenties trying to figure it out. I am thirty-four, I am in a space where I need to live for me, and those who are not with me, well, they just aren't. Everyone isn't meant to spend your entire life with you. Some people serve their purposes, and then they move on; if they don't, the universe removes them for you.

I love LaTrice, but if she cannot support me, then she can go. I am going to do this. I just decided. Siobhan Rei and I are in a relationship, and that's what it is going to be. I will go to work next week and see what the policy really says, and then I will go from there. But at the end of the day, this is my life, and I am going to live it how I see fit.

Part 4

Relinquishable

The relinquishing of the lesser is the gaining of the greater. Give up all and you gain all.

—Sri Nisargadatta Maharaj

September 11, 2012

I have always been a policy-and-procedures person, no matter the situation. And in this situation, I call bullshit! I can list several client-employee sexual relationships happening at my job right now...well, my old job. But the reasoning and the manner in which they gave it to me today was discrimination. Siobhan Rei said I needed to let it go, but no. Fuck that. I have a right to be handled with the same dignity you handle everyone else.

My boss claims that someone from the higher-ups contacted him with pictures of Siobhan Rei and me in New York City. Unless it was the paparazzi, it's a fucking lie! We never took pictures...ever. I don't understand where this is coming from. There is something that doesn't make sense to me.

Siobhan Rei and Capitol Records is our largest account, and you enter into a lesbian relationship with her?

Is it the relationship or the lesbianism?

We didn't know you were like that.

Like what?

That.

A lesbian? Why did you have to know that?

If we had known, we would have sent someone else. We thought you were safe.

What does that mean? How does who I'm sleeping with affect my job performance?

How could you possibly do what is in the best interest of the company when the woman you are laying with is working for the other side?

In the employee handbook it states: "Fraternization is frowned upon in the workplace. Client-employee relationships, if any, must be discreet, and if the employee's performance is questioned in alignment with the relationship, the company withholds the right to discipline up to, but not limited to, termination." We just landed the account; my performance hasn't happened yet, so it can't be questioned!

Do you think you can keep this relationship a secret?

Why should I have to?

For the sake of the company! Sentury, you don't know what you've done!

I know exactly what I'm doing.

I am placing you on unpaid administrative leave until we know what we can do further.

You are shitting me.

Please collect your things.

I am fucking pissed! I know it's because of my lesbian relationship; the shit is cute until it's some shit they don't understand. I know for a fact my boss fucked the CEO of Casers Entertainment—who is a woman, a client, and they have a kid! A kid! Ain't shit discreet 'bout a little punk-ass kid running around with my boss's face! But they put me on leave. Me! I landed the biggest contract that fucking company ever got, and they put me on leave? Who is going to handle the account? They better not put Sandy on it! I know that's what they better not do!

Why are you upset? I told you, fuck that job.

Siobhan Rei was cool as a fan when I called her. I got a surprise I was not looking for.

I told him.

What?

She called them and told them she'd started a relationship with me. The first thing I thought about was LaTrice, and I couldn't even call and tell her this shit. I am not saying my baby is controlling. I am just saying that she took it upon herself to call my job and tell them something she knew was bothering me.

I did this for us.

How?

I can't have my woman worried about shit that doesn't matter. You were worried about the job, how they would react, and what they would do. A good company wouldn't give a fuck, as long as the job is done and done well. Belmore is clearly a fucked-up company. What they don't know is, because of this stunt, we are pulling out of the contract, which I haven't signed yet.

Wow.

Don't question me. There is always a method to my madness. You are mine, and anything that belongs to me will be taken care of.

It's unpaid leave.

You have 5K waiting on you.

What?

FedEx. Go pick it up. Pay your rent. You're good.

(Silence)

LaTrice poisoned my mind! There is nothing controlling about what she did; she was protecting me. I'm really going to be okay.

I just got such a sense of calmness. Siobhan Rei is a grown-ass woman, and with that grown-ass woman comes shit such as sending me money to pay my rent up and punishing my company for hurting me. They say that it's not about how long you know a person; it's about the strength of the connection.

Siobhan Rei and I have known each other for two months, but dating for roughly one, and she has done more for me in this month than anyone I have ever dated. That speaks volumes to me about the people I've dated in the past and the choices I made before I was clear. In my clarity, I see her, I see her intentions for me, and I see my life with her.

Ever since I accepted that I am a lesbian, I've wanted nothing more than a woman like Siobhan Rei, someone to make me feel safe. Emotional safety is important and something that I can't take for granted. Being Black, a woman, and a lesbian is an anomaly walking around the world, as it is, and one of the most unprotected species on the planet is a Black woman. How do I walk the streets as a lesbian Black woman and feel safe physically while battling emotional demons? It's not safe.

To be with someone who has mastered guaranteeing the security of their partner is a woman's dream, and time after time in only a month, Siobhan Rei has shown me she is the dream in living color. Yes, I'm pissed about Belmore International basically firing me, because ain't shit positive about being on leave without pay. We all know what is coming next, and I can fight that with litigation because it is clearly discrimination. Yeah. I can do that. I win the suit, and—boom!—I've got my own money, not depending on Siobhan Rei for it, and we are together without distraction.

My heart is so full. I'm ready. I am finally ready for the life Siobhan Rei has to offer.

September 19, 2012

It did it. I came out to the world. Siobhan Rei surprised me and came to Las Vegas this weekend. We went to Lake Las Vegas and lived it up on a yacht. I took mad pictures because this is my woman, this is my life, and that's it.

How do you feel about me posting our pics, babe?

You're my girl, right?

Yes, baby.

Why would I feel a way about it?

I grabbed my laptop and sat down on the deck of the boat. It was a beautiful setting. The sun was setting on the mountains, and there was a certain calmness. I took this as a sign from the universe that it was time; everything was aligned. I opened Facebook, and I took a deep breath. I named the photo album "H.E.R." Handsome, endearing, romantic. The first picture I posted was a selfie of her and me; I'm kissing her cheek while we sit on the beach. I captioned it, "You and me against the world."

I only posted about twenty pictures because, honestly, I don't need people all in my business; it was just a small kind of an announcement thing. I was announcing my relationship, as well as coming out to the world. If you knew, you knew. But not a lot of people knew, and if I was going to be on Grammy red carpets and seen by the world, I needed to make sure I was clear in my stance.

When I woke up this morning, I had over one hundred comments on the pictures.

You're gay? WTF??????

Who is this woman? Are y'all like together??

Wow!

I've seen her before. You with someone famous?

That's Siobhan Rei! She is fine as hell. You know her?

I know your mother is disgusted by this, because your father is turning over in his grave.

Congrats, Sent! She's super cute!

I knew you were gay, you been lying all these years, and you are exactly what we knew you were.

If you're happy, that's all that matters, Sent. Do you; be happy!

Y'all are both beautiful; this is amazing, Sentry. I am so happy for you.

This is wild!

I scrolled through the comments on my phone like a kid in the candy store. I had text messages and phone calls coming in from people I hadn't spoken to in years, trying to see if it was a joke, but I wasn't for the fanfare. I made my statement, and all they needed to know was right there at their fingertips.

Cute pics.

I know, bae!

Now what?

What do you mean?

Are you happy?

Yes. Are you going to put them on your page?
Want me to send them to you?

No.

(Silence)

> *I don't do the social-media relationship thing.*
> *They will see you when they see you. I know*
> *I'm with you; you know you're with me. To me,*
> *that's what's important.*

She's an old lady. She was born in the sixties—it was the late sixties, but the sixties nonetheless—she is old school. It made perfect sense to me. I'm young; that's what's in. What works for me will not always work for her, and vice versa; surprisingly, I understood that with no question. That's what I'm talking about—how easy the relationship comes. I know if I were with someone my age, I would have immediately gotten suspicious about the lack of desire to show the world our love, but I get it. I think I'm falling in love. I don't even know what falling in love is, but I think I am.

Just as I was basking in the thought of falling in love, I get a text message.

> *I saw your post. You look beautiful, and you look happy.*
> *I'm glad you are able to finally be you.*

Honey. It's rough having soul ties to someone you are not with. Let me tell you! That shit is not fun—sitting next to somebody who fills you with so much joy, but slightly still yearning for another. I say slightly because if it was a strong yearn, I wouldn't be here. I don't think. Honey and I had our time! Timing may have been off, but we had our time, and we all know that love doesn't just go away because the relationship ends.

B. Danielle Watkins

Unlike so many others, Honey and I have the rare experience of friendship after love, and it is not easy. We have to watch someone we love and care about deeply go through this life with someone else, but that's okay. It's okay. It happens. We aren't the only couple in the world who still love each other. The world has been spinning for millions of years, and this shit has been a theme.

How many movies have I seen in which someone loves someone else, and shit doesn't go as planned? *Brown Sugar*, prime example. What's Sanaa's character's name? Sidney. Sidney and Dre. They grew up together, loved each other deeply, but it wasn't for them. Dre got married, Syd was dating, and, yes, it was hard for them, but they did what they needed to do to be happy. I am getting choked up just writing this. I forgot I loved this movie.

Syd and her cousin, Queen Latifah, sat at Dre's wedding and watched him marry another woman. That's strength, and that's real when it comes to wanting the friendship more than a relationship. Granted, at that point in the movie, Syd and Dre had really never dated before, maybe just a fling in college. But what's the difference between them and me and Honey?

We were young when we were together, and now we need to do what's best for us; that's maintaining our friendship at all costs. At all costs. I can't lose her again. I won't survive that. I love her greatly, and that's okay. It's okay for me to need her and be with Siobhan Rei. Honey deserved this, but I have to do it correctly now so that I don't make the same mistakes with Siobhan Rei that I made with Honey.

I never responded to Honey. Emotionally, I wasn't ready. I needed to remain present with Siobhan Rei; she deserved that. She's something good for me.

September 23, 2012

I am sick to my stomach. I don't know if it's because I am now a motherless child, or if it's because of the reason I feel like a motherless child. My mother, former mother, came by my home today, in true my mother fashion.

You won't be satisfied until you kill me!

Nice to see you too, Mom.

Of course, Mommy caught wind of my Facebook grandiose gesture the other day. I knew she would; I wasn't trying to keep it from her. She already kicked me out of the house for being gay. What else could she do to me?

If I was dating a new man, would I have to tell you that?

No.

So why do I have to tell you I'm dating a new woman?

Because you're dating a woman!

That's it! We are dating. I'm not engaged or anything like that.

But it's a woman!

And again, I ask…if I was dating a new man, would I have to call and get your permission?

No, Sentury, be real!

I am being real, Mom. You need to get a grip; it's not a big deal!

You are parading this woman around like I am already dead. My friends see this and see what you're doing, and when they call me, I look like an idiot! I know nothing! All I know is my daughter told me she was gay, and I didn't believe it!

You didn't believe it?

> No!

Then why did you kick me out?

> I never kicked you out, Sentury!
> Stop saying that!

Are you bipolar?

> You are so fucking disrespectful!

Mom, you kicked me out of your house, and you
are telling me it never happened, and now I'm
disrespectful. You need meds.

> You think this is funny? I'm done with you.

You've been done with me.

> You eat pussy, you're nasty, and no
> daughter of mine would be like this.

Mom, that was extreme and gross.

> You need to hear extreme and gross to
> understand the longitude of this situation.

Meaning?

> You have two dead parents as
> far as you are concerned.

(Silence)

> If this is the life you want to lead,
> lead it, but leave me out of it.

Get out!

> Gladly.

My mother stormed out of my house with such anger and
venom. I am trying to keep it together because I have lost a

lot in a short amount of time. LaTrice, my job, my only living parent. If I'm not careful, I will fall back into that dark space, and there is too much going for me right now for that to be my reality. I have an amazing relationship with an amazing, rich, beautiful woman. I need to keep my eye on the prize. Keep it together, Sentury.

I have to vomit.

I'm back. Had to get that out, this pressure on my chest is unbearable. I know my relationship with my mother has been fucked up, but to tell me I should consider myself having two dead parents, when she's alive across town, is extreme. She's just mad. She will apologize soon, and we will rebuild. Yeah. She just needs to deal with her grief over Daddy and her image of me; when she does that, we will be better. Things will get better. It will be better. Everything will be better.

September 25, 2012

There's something to be said about a woman who can go through anything and accept everything. Whether good or bad, there is something to be said. Unfortunately, I don't think I'm that woman. Not anymore. I feel myself unraveling, and I'm unable to find my footing. I remember when I went to the psych ward in 2007; they gave me some mechanisms to use if I started to feel myself head back to that place. I don't remember them all, but I have been trying the ones I do.

Getting out in the sunshine, taking long showers, listening to music, and breathing—none of it is working. They also told me to make contact with people whom I love and who love me. That is depressing in and of itself; those people are few and far between. Honey is out of town, fixing things with Tonya, as she should be since the chance of our being together has gone from seventy percent to zero. I don't go to work anymore, so I don't see people. Siobhan Rei, she's sending me into a bad space on top of the bad space I am already in. I'm supposed to connect, but the one person I want to connect with I CAN'T FIND!

Yesterday I was feeling lower than low. I looked in the mirror, and I didn't recognize myself again; it scared me. It scared me so bad I panicked. I grabbed my backpack, threw a few things in it, and hopped on Interstate 15 headed toward Los Angeles.

I realized, after about fifty miles, that I have no fucking clue where Siobhan Rei lives! She's my girlfriend, and I couldn't just go to her house! Immediately I started calling her as I drove through the dark, hazy desert.

> *You've reached the voice mail of Siobhan Rei. Leave*
> *a message if you must, or you can call my assistant,*
> *and she can get the message to me sooner. Love.*

My eyes were welling up with tears, but I had no reason to be upset with Siobhan Rei yet. My emotions were just all over the place. I hadn't had a chance to tell her about my mom and her visit, and I was still hurting over how my job handled me. Calling her assistant wasn't what I needed, so I called Siobhan again. If she sees I've called more than once, she will know it's some sort of emergency; whatever she is doing, she will call back because I'm her woman, and I need her.

Twenty-five calls later, I was shaking so badly I couldn't even drive. I wasn't even halfway to Los Angeles. Maybe I was. I don't know where I was. It was dark, and I was sitting on the side of the road and bawling my eyes out.

> *This is Jordan.*

Hello, Jordan, this is Sentury Alysé. Can
you please get me in contact with Siobhan Rei?

Who?

Sentury. Alysé. Her girlfriend.

(Silence)

Hello?

I will let Ms. Rei know you called.

No, you don't understand…

(Disconnect)

Why wouldn't her assistant know who I was? Shouldn't there be a list of people who can get through? Your parents, accountant, girlfriend…you know, the important people. *I don't like how that girl talked to me! She sounded young too! Ugh!* My heart was racing, I had anxiety out the ass, I was crying hysterically, and I was in the middle of the desert, probably Death Valley, which was befitting the situation.

I got myself together and pushed on. I had to get to LA. I had to see her. I had to make contact so I could feel better. That's all I wanted. I know Siobhan Rei is a busy woman; that's part of what I love about her. She's a businesswoman. My businesswoman…whom I couldn't get in contact with.

Irrational as it may be, I thought that by the time I arrived in Los Angeles, Siobhan Rei would have called me back, I would have her address, and I would be safe in her arms for the night.

Two in the morning, I cross the city limits, but still no call. Nothing. I had to check into a hotel.

Ma'am, are you okay?

I will be.

Do you need a hug?

Please.

Strangers can be so kind. Be kind to people; that's what they say. You never know what a person is going through. This young man in the lobby with his family stopped me and asked me if I needed a hug, and I just started crying. His mother was weirded out, as she should have been, and ushered her family off, leaving me in my own puddle of tears. I wiped my face and went to the counter.

Do you have a room available?

One night or more?

Just until the morning.

ID and credit card, please.

(Hand cards to clerk)

Sentury Alysé? From Montana State?

I'm sorry, have we met?

I went to Montana State too!
You're a legend. Are you okay?

What's your name?

Nariah Wood.

That's a beautiful name. I will
be fine, Nariah, thank you.

All these years later, to someone, I am still a legend. I needed that. I needed someone in that moment, and God sent me two someones. Not that that took the place of my baby. I wanted my baby, I wanted her to touch me and tell me she got me, but they comforted me in unknown ways.

I went to my room, and I called Siobhan Rei one more time.

You've reached the voice mail of Siobhan Rei. Leave a message if you must, or you can call my assistant, and she can get the message to me sooner. Love.

Siobhan Rei, it's me. I need you to answer the phone. I'm in LA. I'm at the Cecil. Call me.

I'm pretty sure I cried myself to sleep. When I woke up this morning, I was sitting straight up in the bed as if I had just sat down. Unconsciously, the first thing I did was grab my phone, expecting a missed call from Siobhan Rei. Nothing. There was nothing. At that point, I had been calling her for over twelve hours. I began to feel the heaviness in my chest again as I wondered why I hadn't heard back from her. What did I do? Is she mad at me? Did she change her mind about us? What is going on?

I called Siobhan again.

> *You've reached the voice mail of Siobhan Rei. Leave a message if you must, or you can call my assistant, and she can get the message to me sooner. Love.*

> *Baby! Please. I need you to return the call. You don't know what this silence is doing to me. I am going to get dressed and head to your office, okay? Okay. Call me back. Okay.*

I splashed water on my face, gargled, and shot over to Capitol. There was no way she wasn't there on a Tuesday at 9:00 a.m.

> *Hello, can I help you?*

Siobhan Rei, please.

> *Do you have an appointment?*

No.

Let me see if Ms. Rei is available.
May I have your name?

Sentury Alysé.

Please have a seat.

I sat there and watched the woman get on the phone with someone and talk. I don't know to whom, I don't know if it was Siobhan Rei or not, but she spoke with someone.

Ms. Alysé?

Yes.

Ms. Rei isn't in. Would you like to leave a number where she can reach you?

I walked out. The air got so tight in there I couldn't breathe. Was I tripping? Did I make a mistake in my weakness, thinking the person who was supposed to have my back would be there for me? What was I thinking, showing up unannounced? What was I thinking about any of it? I was weakening by the moment.

What do you want?

I called LaTrice. It had been a long time since we'd spoke, and she knew me better than anybody else on the planet. She could hate me, but I needed her. The tone of my voice knocked every piece of attitude out of hers.

What happened, Sentury?

I sat in my car in the parking lot of Capitol Records, and I cried gut-wrenchingly as I told my best friend of twenty-nine years about the roller coaster my life had been since she walked out of my life.

Sentury, I'm so sorry.

I couldn't get myself together. I cried, and Trice listened, and then I cried some more.

Where are you now?

In front of her job.

What? You're in LA?

Yes.

My God, Sentury, what are you doing there? Go home.

Wait...

As I am listening to her and putting my car in gear, Siobhan Rei walked out of the building, holding hands with a woman. A beautiful woman.

She's here.

Go talk to her.

She's with another woman.

Run that bitch over!

So many things ran through my mind as LaTrice was in the background, cursing Siobhan Rei to the pits of hell. I watched as Siobhan Rei playfully moved a piece of hair from this beautiful woman's face after the wind just so happened to blow it out of place. She was perfect. I started to get out of the car without a second thought.

LaTrice was still on the phone, which was in my hand, at my side, not over my ear. I walked slowly. I think I was hoping the slower I walked, the greater the chance I never got to them. Siobhan Rei looked up, noticed me, and didn't bat an eye. She leaned in and kissed the perfect woman as a car picked the woman up and whisked her off. Then, Siobhan looked me in my eyes as I approached.

What are you doing here?

Didn't you see my calls?

Yeah.

Why didn't you answer?

I was busy!

With her? You were busy with her!

That's not your business.

What?

Did that bitch just say it's not your business? Fuck that, Sentury, smack that bitch and go home!

You got somebody on the phone? Oh, you call yourself getting ready to check me?

Trice, let me call you back.

Hell nah!

(Disconnect)

You get back in your car, you go back to Las Vegas, and you wait to hear from me.

But...

I won't tell you again.

The way she looked at me with such disgust and disappointment was something my heart couldn't take. Maybe I had made a mistake. Maybe I should have gotten in contact with her before I left Vegas. You don't just show up on people. You don't just show up at someone's job. You don't. I was so wrong. Oh my God, I was so wrong.

Siobhan Rei doesn't know this me. The reckless me. I tried to hide her, I tried to control her, but she got the best of me, and now I don't know what happened. I don't know if she cost me my relationship, my perfect relationship with my perfect woman. I've spent the time doing the work, making myself whole. I did what I needed to do, but I had a weak moment. I fucked up! I fucked up! I fucked up! I fucked up! I fucked up! I should have never gone to LA. I am stronger than that. I could have handled this better. Could have done better! Fuck! Fuck! Fuck!

September 26, 2012

She hasn't called me yet.

September 27, 2012

She hasn't called me yet.

September 28, 2012

She hasn't called me yet.

September 29, 2012

She hasn't called me yet.

September 30, 2012

I can't take this shit! I can't! I don't deserve this! She hasn't called me yet! It's been almost a week! Why wouldn't she call me? I won't. I can't!

October 10, 2012

My heart aches. My spirit aches. My soul aches. My head aches. My face aches. Everything aches. I'm drunk. I've been drunk. It's all I can do. Drink and cry. Cry and drink. I fucking stink! It fucking stinks in here! I just want the pain to stop. I am aching in a place I can't get to. I want to rub it, but I can't find the place to rub, so I can't rub it. I feel my soul reaching out, but there is no one there to greet her. Honey is there. She's always there. She came today and found me in this mess of a life.

Oh no.

I was on the floor crying. I'm drunk, and I stink. The person whom I gave up my life for is MIA, and I have no parents. My life is fucked up, and Honey walked in on me.

Come on, baby, get up.

She called me baby. I miss her calling me baby. She's loved me since we were twenty years old, and she still looks at me as she did when she first met me in the mall all those years ago. She looks at me as if I'm beautiful, even in my mess. Honey. (Name Omitted). The most beautiful woman in the world.

Let's clean you up, okay?

Don't leave me, Honey, okay?

I'll never leave you, but tell me how much you drank.

Everything.

You drank everything?

Since last week.

Okay, okay, we are going to get you together.

Me and you?

Me and you.

Honey picked me up. I'm bigger than she is, but she picked me up. She took me to my shower, and she undressed me. She was so delicate in everything she did. She took care of me as she did when I was sick, but I'm not sick this time. I just want the pain to stop. It will because Honey will fix it. She always fixes it.

You're so beautiful to me.

Thank you.

Is your girlfriend going to be mad at you?
Tell her I'm sorry you love me.

Don't worry about that right now.

I want you happy, okay? Just say okay.

Okay.

Okay.

Can you tell me what happened?

Mm-hmm.

What happened, Sentury?

(Sleep)

When I dream, I dream of Honey. That's when I'm safe. You know the Selena song "Dreaming of You"? Of course, you do. I am you. You know what I know. Selena said there's nowhere in the world she would rather be than in her room, dreaming of that man. For me, it's not a man, but it's a she. Honey. My dreams are so real it's as if she's here. In this dream, she put me in the shower, and she washed me. She hummed to herself as she washed my body and my hair. She took care of me as she always did.

When Honey was done, she dried me off, used my body butter all over my body, and put my panties on me. She kissed my thigh, but that's it, and it was only once. She put one of her tee shirts on my body, and she laid me in the bed. She brushed my hair and rubbed my face. She stood over me and just looked at me…the same look she always gives me. The look of adoration, of love. In my dreams, Honey loves me and only me. There is no one else.

When I woke up, I was in Honey's arms. I had on exactly what I had on in my dream. It felt good, but I was still drunk. I'm still drunk. I have to be drunk. I don't feel much when I'm drunk.

Hey, you.

Hi.

How you feeling?

Thirsty.

Let me get you some water.

Did she call?

Huh?

Siobhan Rei. Did she call?

No, Sentury, she didn't.

Why doesn't she want me?

I'll get you the water now.

Honey stayed with me. She always stays with me and makes sure I'm okay. I'm okay. I just need more vodka. My soul aches.

October 11, 2012

Being sober fucking sucks! Honey took my fucking debit card, fucking bitch! I hate her! No, I don't. I don't hate her! I hate my life! She's just trying to be helpful, and if I can't buy anything, then I can't be drunk. But I need to be drunk. I need to not feel what I'm feeling right now. I'm not in a good headspace. I'm not okay. I'm being backed into a corner I can't get out of. I don't need to be here.

Fragile people are fragile even when they're not. Those predisposed to depression, anxiety, or other mental health conditions always have that in them, no matter how hard they try. I'm trying. I really am, but I have triggers, and abandonment is one of them. Siobhan Rei was the last person I thought would ignite that trigger.

Where have you been?

Busy.

I hadn't spoken to Siobhan since I saw her with that other woman, and she never explained anything. She never called to check on me; she never even asked me why I was there. How could somebody be so cruel but claim to love me?

I never told you I loved you.

What?

I never said I loved you, Sentury. I don't.

How? Siobhan, don't do this.

My name is Siobhan Rei.

I'm sorry, I just…

I know what you were just doing, and as long as you just don't do it again, we will be fine.

What are we doing?

With what?

Us.

You have a place to live, right?

Yes.

Money?

Yes.

Social media clout?

That's not what…

Do you have it?

Yes.

Do I fuck you?

(Silence)

I fucked you, so I know the answer. You have everything you wanted. You are the face on my arm at industry events, and I'm fucking you. You're my girl.

Who was that woman you kissed at your job?

Had you not been there, that's a question you wouldn't be asking me, isn't it?

Technically.

Technically or not, you should have had your ass in Las Vegas until you heard from me.

Look how long it took to hear from you.

I was proving a point.

I could have been dying, Siobhan Rei! You didn't call or answer my calls because you were proving a point?

Are you dead?

What?

Are you?

No.

Then save the dramatics for someone who cares.

When will I see you again?

*Soon as you're back to being the woman
I met. Until then, we are on break.*

(Silence)

I need to process this. Now.

October 12, 2012

By the time anybody reads this, I will be gone…if anybody reads this. If anybody will miss me, they won't miss me for long, so my suggestion would be not to waste your time on such a temporary feeling. My life has been filled with several temporary moments, temporary feelings. Moments of bliss that were a mask for a tormented soul that was masked in the moments of bliss.

I appreciate those times in my life. Those are the times when I was most alive. When I felt seen, human, and present. My thirty-four years of life—some people would say it's a short time—was an eternity of pain, and I'm tired. I'm tired of the darkness, the cloud over my head, the overwhelming sense of the end. I knew it was coming, but I didn't know how.

You never know how, but when it's time, you begin to recognize the signs. I've lost everything; I have nothing. I don't have any family; I don't have anything. Everything in my life that I've touched or been a part of has failed, so what is my true purpose in this life? To teach a few lessons? To show people a few cool

B. Danielle Watkins

354

things? That's not fulfilling; it's not even enjoyable to always be someone's lesson. To always have to learn the lesson.

I must sound ungrateful for the things this life has provided me, but I'm not. If I hadn't had this life, I wouldn't be able to come to these realizations, and for that, I will express gratitude. I was an amazing athlete, a dedicated daughter, friend, and lover, and that's it. That's the mark I left on the world, so when you think of me, if you think of me, think of those things.

From the outside looking in, I'm sure my life looked amazing, grand, even attainable. You might ask what I have to complain about. My response is you never know what a person is going through under what you see as a great life. I've hurt for a long time, and I've realized nothing in this world will change the pain I feel.

Even in the moments when I thought I was happy, I wasn't. Nothing will make me happy. I am not meant to be happy, and now I've accepted that for what it is. Some people just will never be happy.

So many times in my life when I was pushed to my lowest—just reminders of where I was meant to be. So much heartache and pain, so many disappointments and lows. Life has a hell of a way to make sure you stay in your lane, and now that I've learned my lane, I will do life a favor and make my own way this last time.

Is this selfish of me? Maybe, but we are all selfish in some way. You've done selfish things too, things that will make you happy, despite those around you. So why can't I? I want the pain to end on my terms, no one else's. I want to never feel disappointment again, and the only way to control it is to take control of my life, whatever that may be. I've gone as far as I am going to go in this world.

There is a place of quiet and stillness that is waiting for me. If I know I'm there, then I achieved my goal. If I don't, I still achieved my goal because in death, just as in life, my spirit will be felt, even if it is just a whisper in the wind.

I tried. I failed. And I'm sorry.

Epilogue

On October 13, 2012, Sentury Alysé was found unresponsive in her Las Vegas apartment by (Name Omitted). After several failed attempts at resuscitation, (Name Omitted) called for paramedics.

When first responders arrived, they found (Name Omitted) inconsolable on the floor next to the deceased body of Ms. Alysé.

INTERVIEW TRANSCRIPT:

Investigator: What is your relationship to the deceased?

(Name Omitted): Ex-girlfriend and friend.

Investigator: How did you get into the apartment?

(Name Omitted): I have a key.

Investigator: Why were you there?

(Name Omitted): I'd been calling her all night, and she wasn't answering. I was concerned.

Investigator: Was there reason for concern?

(Name Omitted): Yes.

Investigator: Care to elaborate?

(Name Omitted): She's been going through a lot lately, and she wasn't as strong as she seemed to be.

Investigator: You're saying she did this to herself?

(Name Omitted): I'm saying I wish I would have come sooner.

After the initial sweep of the apartment, several empty prescription pill bottles were found with the labels ripped off and burned in the bathroom sink. Investigators are looking into whose pills these were and how Ms. Alysé may have gotten ahold of them.

The apartment was clean, and Ms. Alysé had clothes neatly laid out on the bed, as if she were planning to get dressed. Of the items retrieved from the apartment: her driver's license, car keys, diary, filing cabinet, laptop, and cell phone.

Ms. Alysé's autopsy report concluded she died from a toxic combination of pills; it was ruled a suicide, closing the case of Sentury Alysé.

Police Exhibit 34-881

10·13 12

I'm Sorry!
tell my mom I love her and
I didn't mean to hurt her!

tell Nancy to never forget me
I loved her most of all.

Sent. A.

LOCAL FILE NO.   STATE FILE NO.

1. DECEDENT'S LEGAL NAME (Include AKA's if any) (First, Middle, Last)	2. SEX	3. SOCIAL SECURITY NUMBER
Sentury Diane Alysé	F	987-65-4329

4a. AGE Last Birthday (Years)	4b. UNDER 1 YEAR Months / Days	4c. UNDER 1 DAY Hours / Minutes	5. DATE OF BIRTH (Mo/Day/Yr)	6. BIRTHPLACE (City and State or Foreign Country)
34			06/08/1978	Las Vegas, Nevada

7a. RESIDENCE-STATE	7b. COUNTY	7c. CITY OR TOWN
Nevada	Clark	Las Vegas

7d. STREET AND NUMBER	7e. APT. NO.	7f. ZIP CODE		7g. INSIDE CITY LIMITS? ☒ Yes ☐ No

8. EVER IN US ARMED FORCES? ☐ Yes ☒ No	9. MARITAL STATUS AT TIME OF DEATH ☐ Married ☐ Married, but separated ☐ Widowed ☐ Divorced ☒ Never Married ☐ Unknown	10. SURVIVING SPOUSE'S NAME (If wife, give name prior to first marriage)

11. FATHER'S NAME (First, Middle, Last)	12. MOTHER'S NAME PRIOR TO FIRST MARRIAGE (First, Middle, Last)
Carlos Alysé	Amelia Kindred

13a. INFORMANT'S NAME	13b. RELATIONSHIP TO DECEDENT	13c. MAILING ADDRESS (Street and Number, City, State, Zip Code)

14. PLACE OF DEATH (Check only one: see instructions)

IF DEATH OCCURRED IN A HOSPITAL: ☐ Inpatient ☐ Emergency Room/Outpatient ☐ Dead on Arrival	IF DEATH OCCURRED SOMEWHERE OTHER THAN A HOSPITAL: ☐ Hospice facility ☐ Nursing home/Long term care facility ☒ Decedent's home ☐ Other (Specify)

15. FACILITY NAME (If not institution, give street & number)	16. CITY OR TOWN, STATE, AND ZIP CODE	17. COUNTY OF DEATH
	Las Vegas, Nevada	Clark

18. METHOD OF DISPOSITION: ☐ Burial ☐ Cremation ☒ Donation ☒ Entombment ☐ Removal from State ☐ Other (Specify)	19. PLACE OF DISPOSITION (Name of cemetery, crematory, other place)

20. LOCATION-CITY, TOWN, AND STATE	21. NAME AND COMPLETE ADDRESS OF FUNERAL FACILITY

22. SIGNATURE OF FUNERAL SERVICE LICENSEE OR OTHER AGENT	23. LICENSE NUMBER (Of Licensee)
T.K.	8302300-kl

ITEMS 24-28 MUST BE COMPLETED BY PERSON WHO PRONOUNCES OR CERTIFIES DEATH	24. DATE PRONOUNCED DEAD (Mo/Day/Yr) October 13, 2012	25. TIME PRONOUNCED DEAD 15:32

26. SIGNATURE OF PERSON PRONOUNCING DEATH (Only when applicable)	27. LICENSE NUMBER	28. DATE SIGNED (Mo/Day/Yr)

29. ACTUAL OR PRESUMED DATE OF DEATH (Mo/Day/Yr) (Spell Month) October 13, 2012	30. ACTUAL OR PRESUMED TIME OF DEATH 0100	31. WAS MEDICAL EXAMINER OR CORONER CONTACTED? ☒ Yes ☐ No

CAUSE OF DEATH (See instructions and examples)

32. PART I. Enter the chain of events—diseases, injuries, or complications—that directly caused the death. DO NOT enter terminal events such as cardiac arrest, respiratory arrest, or ventricular fibrillation without showing the etiology. DO NOT ABBREVIATE. Enter only one cause on a line. Add additional lines if necessary.

		Approximate interval: Onset to death
IMMEDIATE CAUSE (Final disease or condition resulting in death) →	a. Probable Opiate and Benzodiazepine toxicity	>2 hours
	Due to (or as a consequence of):	
Sequentially list conditions, if any, leading to the cause listed on line a. Enter the UNDERLYING CAUSE (disease or injury that initiated the events resulting in death) LAST →	b. ___	
	Due to (or as a consequence of):	
	c. ___	
	Due to (or as a consequence of):	
	d. ___	

PART II. Enter other significant conditions contributing to death but not resulting in the underlying cause given in PART I

33. WAS AN AUTOPSY PERFORMED? ☒ Yes ☐ No
34. WERE AUTOPSY FINDINGS AVAILABLE TO COMPLETE THE CAUSE OF DEATH? ☒ Yes ☐ No

35. DID TOBACCO USE CONTRIBUTE TO DEATH? ☐ Yes ☐ Probably ☐ No ☒ Unknown	36. IF FEMALE: ☒ Not pregnant within past year ☐ Pregnant at time of death ☐ Not pregnant, but pregnant within 42 days of death ☐ Not pregnant, but pregnant 43 days to 1 year before death ☐ Unknown if pregnant within the past year	37. MANNER OF DEATH ☐ Natural ☐ Homicide ☐ Accident ☐ Pending Investigation ☒ Suicide ☐ Could not be determined

38. DATE OF INJURY (Mo/Day/Yr) (Spell Month) n/a	39. TIME OF INJURY n/a	40. PLACE OF INJURY (e.g. Decedent's home, construction site, restaurant, wooded area) n/a	41. INJURY AT WORK? ☐ Yes ☒ No

42. LOCATION OF INJURY: State:	City or Town:

Street & Number:	Apartment No.:	Zip Code:

43. DESCRIBE HOW INJURY OCCURRED: n/a	44. IF TRANSPORTATION INJURY, SPECIFY: ☐ Driver/Operator ☐ Passenger ☐ Pedestrian ☐ Other (Specify)

45. CERTIFIER (Check only one):
☒ Certifying physician-To the best of my knowledge, death occurred due to the cause(s) and manner stated.
☐ Pronouncing & Certifying physician-To the best of my knowledge, death occurred at the time, date, and place, and due to the cause(s) and manner stated.
☐ Medical Examiner/Coroner-On the basis of examination, and/or investigation, in my opinion, death occurred at the time, date, and place, and due to the cause(s) and manner stated.

Signature of certifier: ___

46. NAME, ADDRESS, AND ZIP CODE OF PERSON COMPLETING CAUSE OF DEATH (Item 32)

47. TITLE OF CERTIFIER	48. LICENSE NUMBER	49. DATE CERTIFIED (Mo/Day/Yr)	50. FOR REGISTRAR ONLY- DATE FILED (Mo/Day/Yr)

51. DECEDENT'S EDUCATION-Check the box that best describes the highest degree or level of school completed at the time of death.	52. DECEDENT OF HISPANIC ORIGIN? Check the box that best describes whether the decedent is Spanish/Hispanic/Latino. Check the "No" box if decedent is not Spanish/Hispanic/Latino.	53. DECEDENT'S RACE (Check one or more races to indicate what the decedent considered himself or herself to be)
☐ 8th grade or less	☒ No, not Spanish/Hispanic/Latino	☐ White
☐ 9th - 12th grade; no diploma	☐ Yes, Mexican, Mexican American, Chicano	☒ Black or African American
☐ High school graduate or GED completed	☐ Yes, Puerto Rican	☐ American Indian or Alaska Native (Name of the enrolled or principal tribe) ___
☐ Some college credit, but no degree	☐ Yes, Cuban	☐ Asian Indian ☐ Chinese
☐ Associate degree (e.g. AA, AS)	☐ Yes, other Spanish/Hispanic/Latino (Specify) ___	☐ Filipino ☐ Japanese ☐ Korean
☒ Bachelor's degree (e.g. BA, AB, BS)		☐ Vietnamese ☐ Other Asian (Specify) ___
☐ Master's degree (e.g. MA, MS, MEng, MEd, MSW, MBA)		☐ Native Hawaiian ☐ Guamanian or Chamorro ☐ Samoan
☐ Doctorate (e.g. PhD, EdD) or Professional degree (e.g. MD, DDS, DVM, LLB, JD)		☐ Other Pacific Islander (Specify) ___ ☐ Other (Specify) ___

54. DECEDENT'S USUAL OCCUPATION (Indicate type of work done during most of working life. DO NOT USE RETIRED).
unemployed

55. KIND OF BUSINESS/INDUSTRY
n/a

REV. 11/2003

B. Danielle Watkins

360